WAYNE STINNETT

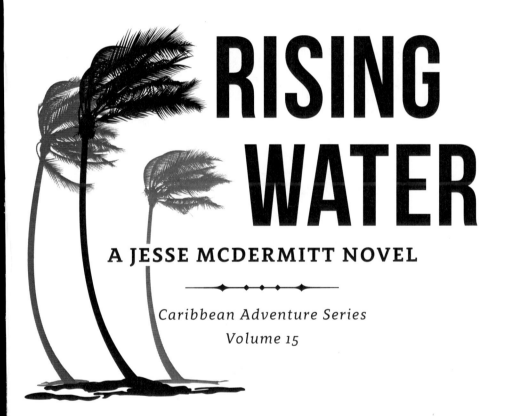

RISING WATER

A JESSE MCDERMITT NOVEL

◆ ▪ ▪ ▪ ◆

Caribbean Adventure Series

Volume 15

2019

Copyright © 2019
Published by DOWN ISLAND PRESS, LLC, 2019
Beaufort, SC
Copyright © 2019 by Wayne Stinnett

Library of Congress cataloging-in-publication Data
    Stinnett, Wayne
    Rising Water/Wayne Stinnett
    p. cm. - (A Jesse McDermitt novel)
    ISBN-13: 978-1-7339351-2-8 (Down Island Press)
    ISBN-10: 1-7339351-2-6

Cover photograph by B. Campbell
Graphics by Wicked Good Book Covers
Edited by The Write Touch
Final Proofreading by Donna Rich
Interior Design by Ampersand Book Designs

This is a work of fiction. Names, characters, and incidents are either the product of the author's imagination or are used fictitiously. Any resemblance to actual persons, living or dead, businesses, companies, events, or locales is entirely coincidental. Most of the locations herein are also fictional or are used fictitiously. However, the author takes great pains to depict the location and description of the many well-known islands, locales, beaches, reefs, bars, and restaurants throughout the Florida Keys and the Caribbean to the best of his ability.

FOREWORD

I've taken a few literary liberties in this story. For those who have been paying close attention, you will know there is a significant time jump over the last few novels. When I wrote my first one, I intentionally set it in 2005 at the time of Hurricane Wilma. My thought at the time was that by setting it eight years in the past, I could jump ahead in subsequent books and be caught up to current time at some point. Well, that didn't work out so well.

After five years of writing, and more than a dozen novels later, I'd gained only seven years in the overall story. Knowing that I would be in my hundreds before the stories became current, I moved ahead with big sweeps of time between stories, but with the same four to six months of writing and publishing time.

So, this story is set in late 2017 when Hurricane Irma ripped through the BVI and the Florida Keys. While some of the characters have changed a little in this work—you can't stop children from growing—Jesse seems to be the same guy he was in Fallen Out, which starts the series in 1999, when Jesse retired from the Marine Corps at the age of 37. That was nearly twenty years ago in Jesse's life.

Sure, Jesse now has some lines on his face, and there's some gray in his hair and beard, but keep in mind; this is a guy who trained hard for twenty years as a Marine, and has since lived off the grid, catching and growing his own food. He swims at least three times a week, which I agree is one of the best forms of exercise. So, at the age of 56, he hasn't slowed down very much.

So, now that we're almost current in time, I find myself doing something I've never done before; writing about the future. The next book leaps ahead two years to the fall of 2019. Now there's a scary prospect. I've always weaved real events into my stories. What if events in the next story come true?

In the early part of this book, Jesse encounters a couple of dive masters off the coast of Saba, Boone and Emily. These are characters from my friend and audiobook narrator, Nick Sullivan's first tropical adventure, *Deep Shadow*. The action and dialogue are identical in both the scene in his book and the one in mine. But with the change from third person narrative in his, to first person from Jesse's point of view in mind, the scene is different. It's fun doing these little mini-collaborations with friends.

You can buy Deep Shadow Here.
WWW.AMAZON.COM/DP/B07CP668GH/

Many thanks to our team of beta readers who tear apart what it took me months to create, in just a matter of hours. Then they help me put the pieces back together again. Thanks Dana Vilhen, Katy McKnight, Debbie Kocol, Thomas Crisp, Ron Ramey, Torrey Neill, Mike Ramsey, Alan Fader, Charles Höfbauer, John Trainor, David Parsons, Drew Mutch, Deg Priest, Glen Hibbert, and Debbie Cross, for helping to polish up the manuscript.

We'd also like to give our appreciation to those who followed in the process of turning a story into a book. Thank you Marsha Zinberg, of The Write Touch for another excellent and timely job of editing and fine tuning my story. Thanks also to my final proofreader, Donna Rich, who has been the last eyes on all of my books, I'm pretty sure. Narrator extraordinaire, Nick Sullivan, always has a few suggestions as he records the audiobook; they say reading aloud is the ultimate test of a story, and I agree. But, even after all these people, dozens of readings, it's still just a manuscript. That's when Colleen Sheehan of Ampersand Book Design molds it into a real book, along with my cover designer Shayne Rutherford of Wicked Good Book Covers.

Without all these people, experts in their fields, this story would be far less entertaining. Thank you.

One Human Family

This book is dedicated to the men,
women, and children of
the Florida Keys, both Conch and Newcomer. It takes a
special breed of person to live and
work on islands connected
by miles of bridges and a single ribbon of highway.
Even more so, when tragedies
happen like Hurricane Irma.
That's when you see the worst of nature
and the best of humanity.

"The world breaks everyone, and afterward,
some are strong at the broken places."

- Ernest Hemingway

If you'd like to receive my newsletter,
please sign up on my website:

WWW.WAYNESTINNETT.COM

Every two weeks, I'll bring you insights into my
private life and writing habits, with updates on
what I'm working on, special deals I hear about,
and new books by other authors that I'm reading.

The Charity Styles Caribbean Thriller Series

Merciless Charity
Ruthless Charity
Reckless Charity
Enduring Charity
Vigilant Charity

The Jesse McDermitt Caribbean Adventure Series

Fallen Out
Fallen Palm
Fallen Hunter
Fallen Pride
Fallen Mangrove
Fallen King
Fallen Honor
Fallen Tide

Fallen Angel
Fallen Hero
Rising Storm
Rising Fury
Rising Force
Rising Charity
Rising Water

THE GASPAR'S REVENGE SHIP'S STORE IS OPEN.

There, you can purchase all kinds of swag related to my books. You can find it at:

WWW.GASPARS-REVENGE.COM

MAPS

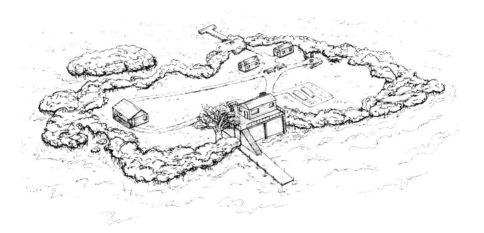

Jesse's Island in the Content Keys

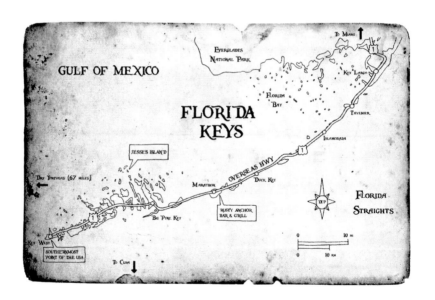

The Florida Keys

CHAPTER ONE

Smooth white sand glistened in the hot Caribbean sun. The pristine beach stretched the length of the island's southern shore, unmarred by civilization. Glittering sand gave way to clear water, which changed in color from gold in the shallows to turquoise and aqua as the water deepened.

A young couple walked along the shoreline, both wearing swimsuits, the man carrying a small cooler. He was tall and fit, with sandy hair and brown eyes. She was nearly as tall, with long hair the color of summer wheat and a blue bikini that matched her eyes.

They'd walked the length of the island's southern shore and had made love in a hammock on the eastern tip, just a quarter mile from the island of Tortola and the entrance to Soper's Hole. The couple had found the spot and the hammock the night before, christening it "their spot."

"I can't get over how beautiful this place is," Alicia said to her husband of just three days.

Jerry Snyder took his bride's hand. The two strolled through the shallow water along the unspoiled beach, simply relishing the sun, the beauty around them, and each other.

"Doesn't compare to you," Jerry replied, pulling her close and kissing her.

Little Thatch Island, one of the westernmost of the British Virgin Islands, was privately owned. Jerry's cousin had gone to college with the owner, and they'd gotten a great deal on their honeymoon stay.

The couple held each other close, their kisses becoming more passionate. The odds of anyone watching them were very slim so they were without inhibition.

There were only a handful of resort homes on the island, which measured half a mile long and a few hundred yards in width. Summer was the slow season, so Jerry and Alicia had it nearly to themselves.

There was only one other couple on the island, also newlyweds. They were staying on the north shore. Jerry and Alicia had met them on the ferry ride over from Tortola. Unlike themselves, the other newlyweds were fair-skinned and Jerry figured they'd spend the whole week indoors, screwing their brains out. That left the rest of the sixty-three-acre island to him and his new wife, both tanned Californians.

Jerry pulled his wife closer, cupping her bottom and pressing her against him. He could feel the heat rising in his groin once more. Alicia slid a hand into his board shorts, gently tugging at him.

Suddenly, she jumped away, pulling her hand free and sidestepping quickly. When she looked down, she screamed. Jerry stared at her; it wasn't the reaction he'd been hoping for.

He started to move toward her. "Are you—" Then something bumped his leg. "What the hell?" He lunged to the side, joining his wife.

When he looked down, Jerry saw what had startled them both and laughed. He first assumed it was a blue trash bag, with a pair of discolored boat fenders sticking out of it.

"What is it?" Alicia asked, backing away.

"Just a bag of garbage," he replied, smiling and reaching down to grasp the bag's far side and flip it over.

When it rolled, he recognized the unmistakable form of a woman's body, the right arm now draped across the torso, but no hand attached.

A mannequin. That was Jerry's second thought.

Then a crab crawled out of the place where a head would be and scurried across the breasts, dropping into the water.

Jerry involuntarily convulsed as the reality of what lay in the water at his feet finally hit him.

Jerry and Alicia sat on the sand in the shade of a grove of coconut palms. The Royal Virgin Islands Police had arrived an hour earlier and secured the area, surrounding the beach with yellow crime-scene tape.

Two police boats were beached not far from where the couple had found the decapitated and mutilated body. The police had moved it to the beach to prevent it floating away in the slow, northwesterly-moving current.

Another boat was patrolling The Narrows, a natural channel between Little Thatch and Saint John, less than a mile away to the south.

One of the police officers, who'd earlier identified himself as Detective Sergeant Bryce Lettsome, broke away from the group that had been examining the body. With notepad in hand, he started toward the couple sitting on the white, powdery sand.

Jerry stood and offered a hand to Alicia.

"Thank you for your patience," the detective said as he came nearer.

"Have you found—the rest of her?" Alicia asked, rising to stand next to Jerry.

"Not yet. Is dere anything you would like to add to your statement?"

"Like we said, there's not much we can tell you," Jerry offered. "We were standing in the water when something bumped against us. At first, I thought it was a trash bag with a couple of boat fenders in it. When I rolled it over, I thought maybe it was a store mannequin, or something."

"That's when we noticed the bloody stumps," Alicia added. "It was ghastly."

"You said you rolled di body over," Lettsome said to Jerry. "Why?"

"I thought it was a garbage bag," he replied. "I was going to drag it to shore and dispose of it."

"Do you think a boat propeller cut off her head, hands, and feet?" Alicia asked.

"It is too soon to tell," Lettsome replied. "You heard no commotion last night?"

"We were walking right here," Alicia said, her voice cracking slightly. "On this beach. We could hear music coming from over on Tortola, and a couple of boats passed by."

"But nothing unusual," Jerry added.

"You will be staying here until di end of di week?"

"Two weeks," Jerry replied, now beginning to worry about having gotten involved. He had to be back at work a week from Monday. He'd been hired by the Newport Beach Police Department just over a year ago. He pointed to his right. "The first house. The one with the red roof. We're here for two weeks."

"Thank you," Lettsome said. "If I have more questions, I will call before I stop by. We have your cell number from when you called dis in."

The detective turned and ducked under the yellow ribbon, which fluttered in the breeze.

Jerry took his wife's hand and they turned to walk back to the rental house.

"There's no way that was done by a boat prop," Jerry said, his voice low.

Alicia looked over at him. "No?" she asked.

"Think about it, babe. The head, or an arm or a leg, maybe. But the head, both hands, and both feet?"

Alicia stopped dead in her tracks. "You mean—"

Jerry pulled her along. "Without teeth, fingerprints, or footprints, the body isn't identifiable. That woman was murdered."

CHAPTER TWO

The air felt sticky against my skin; it was dense, almost constricting in its closeness. While it wasn't terribly hot, the humidity was well above ninety percent making the air feel so thick that it seemed as if I'd need a sharp machete to hack my way through it.

The sun was only a few degrees above the eastern horizon, but it already felt intense, searing exposed flesh. That heat combined with the high humidity meant it was going to be another oppressive day. In other words, a typical late-summer day in South Florida. It wasn't a matter of *if* it was going to rain, but where and how soon.

From the trees on shore, a staccato of cicada calls rose and fell, the sound moving around the island's fringing mangroves like an undulating wave. They'd come just about the same day every year, so we were ready and had erected screens over the garden area to keep them out.

A light breeze carried the scent of rain to my nostrils and I turned to face it. The familiar, yet difficult-to-describe odor was there all right; that earthy, musky smell you sense just as the first fat raindrops splatter onto the ground, kicking up dust.

I'd always assumed the smell was steam, from the instantaneous sizzle of hundreds of individual water droplets on sunbaked concrete, asphalt, or sand. But I've experienced the odor many times out on the water. The smell was being transported on the wind. I'd since learned that this "rain scent" had nothing to do with the hot ground. At least not directly. It was caused by plants. When it starts to rain after a long dry spell, many plants will secrete tiny bacterial microorganisms.

The breeze was out of the southeast. I couldn't see any clouds in that direction, but most of my view was blocked. There were only a few puffy white clouds far to the south, down over Big Pine Key, which wasn't visible from my low dock.

The view of the horizon from my island was quite limited all around. The island itself blocked any view to the north. Half a mile to the west and southwest, two small, unnamed mangrove keys obscured most of the water view that way. Cutoe Key, a mile away across Harbor Channel, stretched out to the south, with Big Spanish Key beyond it. Together, they blocked most of the southern horizon where the clouds had formed. The only clear view from my south dock was to the east across skinny water, and straight up Harbor Channel to the northeast. In that direction, the horizon was three miles away. Up on the deck that surrounded three sides of my house, you could see almost twice as far, even over the tops of some of the smaller keys.

Summer storms had a way of sneaking up on a person in the backcountry of the Middle Florida Keys. It was always a good idea to keep a sharp weather eye.

Finn raised his big yellow head, his black nose twitching. He'd been asleep, soaking up the warm mid-August sun, while I washed down one of my boats. He looked up at me, his head cocked a little off-center. It was his typical curious expression, one he used quite a bit. His bright eyes were asking a question.

"You smell it too?" I asked.

Finn crossed his forelegs and laid his head on them, his big amber eyes closely watching me. He was in the prime of his life and knew that the rain smell didn't always mean rain was coming. Finn loved a good summer rain. But during the hot summer months, he spent a lot of time napping; Finn's *high* speed was very laid back. When it was this hot, I'd learned to take a page from his book, to work slower and pace myself. His idea of pacing himself was to be comatose. We could learn a lot from our four-legged friends. A dog's life wasn't without its appeal.

Hearing footfalls on the steps going up to the deck, I turned and saw Jimmy heading down.

"Hey, Jesse. I heard the engines. You taking her out, man?"

"Thought about it," I replied. "Maybe after I go down and clean the bottom."

He looked down at the green slime along the boat's waterline. "Dunno how that stuff grows so fast when she's inside all the time."

"Reflected light," I said. "There isn't much on the inboard side. One day, I'll put some steel caisson sections around the bottom of the boathouse."

Jimmy sat cross-legged next to Finn, scratching the thick fur around the dog's neck and ears. "She hasn't been out on the blue in a while, man."

He was right. *Gaspar's Revenge* had been my primary fishing vessel for many years. She was a forty-five-foot convertible, built by Rampage Yachts and the perfect offshore fishing machine for me. But my new job had kept me away a lot lately. After submersible training, I'd worked aboard *Ambrosia* as chief mate to get the required sea service time to qualify for my Master Unlimited papers, which would allow me to command just about any commercial vessel. I still had another six months to go there. During that time, we'd crossed oceans and hemispheres. Ostensibly, we gathered research data, mostly for ocean engineering projects. On occasion it'd been a little more than that.

Jimmy was the caretaker on my little island and had been for a long time. He was also first mate aboard the *Revenge*, whenever we chartered, which hadn't been often in the last year. He had his own place on the west side of the island and kept busy working on the garden and aquaculture system. We raised vegetables for our own consumption, as well as catfish and freshwater

Louisiana crayfish, which Jimmy sold to a few restaurants up and down the Keys that had Cajun-style food on their menus, turning a very healthy profit. It was nearly impossible to get fresh crayfish and bayou flathead catfish in the Keys. Jimmy, and Carl before him, had cornered the market.

Carl Trent and I had built the house Jimmy now lives in. He and his wife, Charlie, had been the caretakers for many years, until they moved back to Alabama.

Turning, I gazed back at the clouds building to the south. "Probably raining down on Big Pine. Maybe over in Marathon, too."

"Could smell it from over on the porch, man. It won't last long. Want some help down there with the scrubbing?"

"Thanks. Come on down when you're ready."

Sitting on the edge of the dock, I strapped a bulky twenty-pound weight belt around my waist, situatied the heavy weight at my back, and then pulled my mask on. I slipped into the warm water behind the *Revenge*. It was only six feet deep, so all I needed was a mask, snorkel, and scrub brush. The brush had very soft bristles and a short handle; perfect for cleaning the algal growth off the underside of the boat.

Standing on the sandy bottom, only the top of my head and snorkel were visible above water. I took a deep breath and submerged, positioning myself under the hull. With the weight on my back, I could lie on the bottom with the boat's keel only about two feet above me. The weight gave me the much-needed negative buoyancy, to allow me to move the scrub brush, instead of the scrub brush moving me.

Underwater, you could really see what a boat was. Everything built above the waterline stripe was for looks and convenience. Everything below that was hydro-mechanical. It was the shape of the hull that determined how the boat worked with the water.

The *Revenge* was a semi-displacement hull vessel, with prop tunnels for the massive twin propellers. With her powerful engines, she could nearly climb up on top of the water, slicing across the surface with her deep V hull, displacing far less than half her weight. My sailboat, on the other hand, had a full displacement hull. *Salty Dog's* hull cut through the water, so her top speed was limited, and based completely on her length at the waterline. While moving, she displaced just as much water as she did at anchor. A true planing hull, like my Maverick flats skiff, had a nearly flat bottom. On plane, it skimmed across the surface, displacing only a few gallons of water to keep its 1500 pounds afloat.

I moved methodically, pushing the brush against the hull in long strokes. Small fish darted out from under the pier, catching little pieces that fell away from the hull. Jimmy dropped under the boat off the port side, just after I'd surfaced to take my third breath. We worked quickly and soon had all the growth removed. Bottom cleaning was a necessary part of the maintenance on a boat, and I had a few of them to keep clean. Jimmy and I had had lots of practice.

"That didn't take long to grow back," Jimmy said, as we levered ourselves up onto the dock and climbed up. "I just cleaned it a month ago."

I looked off to the south. The clouds were darkening, looking more menacing. "Days are already getting shorter. Soon, we won't have to do this for a few months."

Looking past me, Jimmy saw the approaching storm. "No boat ride today," he said, obviously disappointed.

"Yeah, we'll be moving her back inside."

"No hurry, *hermano*. That squall won't get here for twenty minutes, if at all."

He helped me to back *Gaspar's Revenge* under the house again and get her tied up. Then we went up to the deck to watch the approaching weather.

"We haven't had a charter in a while," Jimmy remarked. "Don't get me wrong. I don't need the extra money just now, but it's fun sometimes."

"Some of them are," I agreed.

"Those Miami guys keep emailing. The photographers."

"Peter Simpson?" I asked. "He's wanting a night dive?"

"No, man, noon. A shallow reef with pretty models again."

How many years had it been since the grenade attack against me and the *Revenge*? It had resulted in one of Peter's models, a young woman named Annette, getting killed. It'd happened out on G Marker, south of Big Pine. The attackers had been trying to lure me into the open by dropping grenades on sensitive reefs. When that didn't work, they'd tried a more direct approach, attacking my divers. The small, gold ring in my left ear commemorated that loss.

Early mariners were less afraid of drowning than of not being properly buried, so they wore gold rings in their ears to pay for a funeral if their bodies washed ashore. My first mate on that dive, Travis Stockwell, also wore a gold earring like mine—they'd been given to us by the dead girl's father. At one time, Travis had worked for Homeland Security and had been Deuce Livingston's immediate boss. Now he was head of security for Armstrong Research. I called both men my friends and had worked with Deuce's team of highly trained snake-eaters a few times.

For quite a while now, we hadn't chartered more than once a month or so. That was about all I could handle. Owning a charter boat that didn't charter was a waste. And a boat like *Gaspar's Revenge*, which could take you far offshore, needed a regular workout.

"Ask Peter if he and Tom would be interested in diving the Tortugas next week. You can pick the day."

"For real?" he asked, suddenly excited. "That's way the hell out there."

"They can meet us at the fuel dock in Key West Bight before sunrise and we'll get them back in time for a late supper at Turtle Kraals."

"You're on, dude! I know they'll go for that. How much?"

"The regular full day rate plus fifty percent," I replied. "It'll take more than half a tank to get out there and back. You and I can hang out in the city when we get back, if you want. Haven't done that in a while, either."

"*Tres amigos* loose on *Cayo Hueso*, Finn!" Jimmy reached down and held his hand out. Finn obligingly slapped it with his paw—his own version of a high-five.

"But right now, I think I'm gonna steal a page from Finn's book, and relax a while," I told him.

When I stepped inside, though my house wasn't air-conditioned, it felt noticeably cooler. Finn went straight to his big, shaggy rug in the middle of the room. It was four feet round and made of a heavy cotton fiber at least an inch thick. He made almost three complete revolutions around his bed before dropping his hind-quarters and then his chest onto the center with a heavy thud.

My home only had two rooms; three if you counted the head. The front room included a small galley set up in the corner with propane appliances and a small table for two. A large workbench was mounted beneath a window on the north-facing wall, which overlooked the island's interior. The guts of an outboard's carbu-retor were scattered across the workbench's surface, waiting on a part. Against the wall that separated the front room from my bedroom was a smaller workbench. It had a dozen small drawers and a large, lighted mag-nifier for working on fishing reels or lures. Next to it was a ladderwell and deck hatch that led down to the boathouse below.

I sat down in one of two recliners next to the south-facing window and picked up a book I'd been reading on the natural history of the Florida Keys and South Florida.

The rain started as soon as I opened the book—just a few heavy drops at first. The scent returned, stronger than before. The plants on my island were reacting to the rain, rejoicing in it. Although we *saw* at least one rainstorm a day during this time of year, this was the first rain to reach my island in a couple of weeks. In the next few days, I would've had to pump water up to the cistern from the *Revenge's* onboard water tank.

My 1000-square-foot metal roof drained into gutters, which fed into a single small holding tank below the large cistern. From there, rainwater was pumped up to the cistern. Its open top added another thirty-four square feet of rain-catching surface area. The cistern could hold over 1500 gallons of water to supply the whole island, including the aquaculture garden. We used fresh water sparingly.

It was rare that I had to pump water during the rainy season. But after December, it was a monthly occurrence, taking two whole days. *Gaspar's Revenge* only had a 100-gallon water tank and it took the reverse-osmosis wa-ter-maker an hour to fill it. Working on nothing else, Jimmy and I could fill the cistern in two eight-hour days. But we rarely had eight uninterrupted hours. Living off the grid on an island was hard work. But it only took two inches of rain, running off the roof and into the holding tank, to nearly fill the cistern. A spill gate allowed excess rainwater to drain down to the boat-house, where it flowed back into the sea.

The smell of the rain reminded me of when I was a kid, growing up in Fort Myers. It was a simpler time then. When it rained, I'd join my friends racing Popsicle stick rafts along the curbs on our street. The kid with the fastest raft had to be careful, though. Many a stick raft had disappeared down the storm drain on the corner. The same rain scent also reminded me of a later time during high school, walking with my girl-friend at a lake near where I lived, when a sudden storm drenched us as we ran back to my car. I soon fell asleep and dreamed of being a kid again.

CHAPTER THREE

A low, rolling thunder woke me. It was dark, and a muted hum told me the pump under the cistern was running; a welcome sound. The rain smell was gone, but it was still raining. Half-awake, with the book I'd been reading lying open on my chest, I heard the pump stop and wondered how much rain had fallen. The cistern had a float switch that would keep the pump from running when the tank was full and the excess rainwater would just drain off. As lightly as the rain was coming down, the float switch in the holding tank had turned the pump off. I recognized the dark as temporary—not night.

My roof had open rafters—no ceiling. The bare metal was a wonderful conduit for rain sounds, making even the lightest rain audible, and the soft rhythm on the metal roof continued as a fine mist of rain still fell outside.

A vent ran the length of the roof's ridge and there were vents in the floor, as well. The air up near the metal roof would get hot and rise toward the ridge vent, drawing in cool air from the boathouse below, so that on a hot day, my house was still comfortable.

Looking at my watch, I realized I'd been asleep for only an hour; it wasn't even noon yet. An hour is a long time in the life cycle of a rain event in the Keys. I rose, and Finn lifted his head. Looking out the window between the recliners, I could see that the sky was clearing; the back edge of the storm was approaching.

Thunder rolled and echoed across the water. It was somewhere off to the northeast now—out over the Gulf of Mexico, beyond where Mac Travis lived. At just shy of two miles away, Mac was my nearest, and really my *only* neighbor. At least until you got down to the north end of Big Pine Key, nearly six miles to the south. Mac lived on Upper Harbor Key, the last island before Harbor Channel flowed into the Gulf at Harbor Key. His island was one of the few in the area that even had a name.

A noise from my bedroom caused both me and Finn to jerk our heads around. It was similar to the sound that a pump shotgun would make, but it was only my Armstrong satellite phone, trying to connect.

I went into the other room and picked it up, then hurried outside for better reception. On the *Revenge*, the phone would automatically connect to the onboard comm center, via Wi-Fi. Without that, it needed a clear line of sight to the southern sky. Since the caller ID never showed anything when another Armstrong phone was calling, I didn't bother to look at it. Armstrong personnel were the only people who had my number.

I stabbed the *Accept* button. "McDermitt."

"It's John."

"Hey, John. Good to hear from you. How are you getting along?"

"About as good as a one-eyed senior citizen can, I reckon," John Wilson replied. "Chasing young girls used to be pretty easy. Now they just have to turn right, and I run into a tree."

I laughed, hearing voices and what sounded like music and glasses clinking in the background. "Where are you, John? I hear music."

After John had lost an eye in a submersible accident, he and Jack Armstrong had insisted that I take the old man's place within the organization. I'd agreed, even though I'd known that I could never fill his shoes. John and his daughter, Sara Patrick, had been my instructors during submersible training, and later she'd been my immediate superior and mentor for six months aboard *Ambrosia*, as I worked to fulfill the required sea time for a master's unlimited license.

"Beach bar," he replied. "Hey look, where are you deployed right now?"

Though missing an eye, he'd fully recovered, but as far as I knew, John Wilson no longer worked for Armstrong Research. Since the accident he'd pretty much led the life of a retiree. But there was only one reason he'd ask that question.

"I'm in the Keys with the *Revenge*," I told him. "The *Dog's* at a friend's place in Belize, and *Floridablanca* is in Antigua."

"Perfect. How soon can you be in the BVI?"

"Tomorrow, by air."

"With *Floridablanca*?"

"Three days," I replied. "What's going on, John?"

"I'll tell you about it when you get here. Come to *Pirate's Bight* on Norman Island. I'll meet you there on Saturday at oh-six-hundred hours."

"You gotta give me more to go on than that, John." There was silence. "John?" I looked at the screen. The call had ended.

Norman Island in four days? What the heck was going on?

Armstrong would know, so I pulled up the number for the bridge phone on the *Ambrosia*. After several clicks, Captain Nils Hansen answered.

"Nils, this is Jesse. Is Jack aboard?"

"No, he left three days ago for New Jersey to check on a new build."

"Sara?"

I didn't like calling her on the ship's phone, but if she were on duty, she wouldn't have her personal sat phone with her. And if she weren't on duty, Nils would have the switchboard behind him in the control center patch me through.

"One moment," Hansen said.

Those six months working with Sara on *Ambrosia* had felt like an eternity. Being that close to her and not being able to touch her had pushed the sexual tension between us off the chart. We'd gotten to know each other a little after carving out some time in our schedules. We'd both lost our spouses to violence. I'd had a succession of relationships and had screwed most of them up. Sara, on the other hand, hadn't been involved with anyone since her husband had been killed a few years earlier in Afghanistan. She'd admitted to a few one-night stands, purely to satisfy her physical desire, but no serious dating.

Neither of our lifestyle choices was conducive to a relationship, and we both knew that—probably she even better than I did. I'd nearly forgotten how to talk to a woman close to my age, but the times we'd met after our first encounter—the first being Rusty's wedding—were fun. Sara and I were friends, but we'd both known that we wanted more. She'd arrived at the *Rusty Anchor* to help me celebrate. That night we'd finally succumbed to our mutual needs and she'd confessed that it was the real reason she'd come.

Since then we'd made time for dozens of discreet escapes. Usually we only had a day together and we'd spend it staring breathlessly at ceiling fans in beach bungalows all over the Caribbean, exhausted and tangled in sweaty sheets. But during those six months of sea time, she'd been 100% business, and a real hardass of a boss.

When Sara answered, I asked her if she knew where her father was.

"Yes," she replied. "Did he call you?"

"He did."

"Do what he says, Jesse."

"That's all I needed," I replied. John was back in the game, it seemed.

"Are you sure?" she asked.

"Well, *that* need is always there."

"That's good to know," she said, using her professional voice. Hansen was standing right next to her.

I knew that *Ambrosia* was in the Leewards; had been for a couple of months. "Can you get away? I'll be in Antigua tomorrow evening."

"Yes," she replied. "Tomorrow afternoon will be perfect. Goodbye, Captain."

Afternoon? She must have to get back aboard the ship early. I hated flying commercial, but my plane had limited range and would require too many stops to get there by afternoon.

Slipping the phone into my pocket, I went back to the living room and looked around. I spotted my personal cellphone on the workbench beside the scattered carb guts, picked it up and dialed.

Chyrel Koshinski answered on the first ring. "Hey, Jesse. How goes it?"

"Good," I replied. "How're the new digs?"

Because of traffic during certain times of year, Deuce had moved our office from a small strip mall on Islamorada into a brand-new four-story office building on Atlantic Boulevard in Key Largo. We had the whole fourth floor.

"I love it!" Chyrel replied. "The internet and power here are so much more reliable. What can I do for you today?"

"Hey, look, I need to fly to Antigua, earliest arrival I can make from Marathon."

"Hang on."

While I waited, I grabbed my go-bag from the closet in my room. In it were two changes of clothes and necessary toiletries to get me through three days; nothing more. I opened the top chest drawer, retrieved my passport, and stuffed it into the bag. Anything else I'd need would be on *Floridablanca*.

"Okay," Chyrel said, "if you can get going right now, you might be able to catch the Marathon shuttle flight to Miami. It takes off in less than two hours. You'll have to just hang out there in Miami for about three and a half hours to catch the last flight to Antigua, arriving just after 10 pm local time. Otherwise, the next available flight arrives there tomorrow afternoon."

"Book tonight's flight for me," I said. "I'm heading out the door. Thanks."

"You got it."

Ending the call, I shoved the cell into my pocket along with the Armstrong sat phone. That much technology in my pocket used to be a rare thing. A couple of years ago, the most high-tech thing you'd catch me with was my dive computer. The weight in my pocket reminded me to grab the chargers for both phones. I had dozens, because I was always forgetting to take them.

Jimmy was approaching the door when I stepped out into the light rain.

Crap! The charter.

He saw the bag in my hand. "Aw, man."

"Sorry, Jimmy. I gotta be in Antigua tomorrow morning. Something just came up."

"Dude, I just got a confirmation from Peter for a week from Monday. He said Tuesday, too, and he'd pay more if we anchored off Fort Jefferson for the night."

"I'm afraid we'll have to cancel," I said, then had another thought. "No wait. Tuesday and Wednesday? I might be back by then. If I'm not, you can take them out."

"Me?"

"Why not? You've got a six-pack license. Hire someone to do the monkey work—slinging and filling the tanks— and you move the boat around to the good spots and help with the image editing."

"You sure, man?"

"Sounds like a laid-back charter. You know how Peter is. And you said yourself, the *Revenge* needs to get out and run. Just one thing..."

"I know, I know. The same rules even if you're not there. Dude, I thought we were beyond that."

"Drive down the road sometime. There's a reminder of how fast you're allowed to go, posted about every two or three miles."

"Yeah, but you smoked—"

I fixed him with a stern look. "*No mas, mi amigo.*"

He nodded. Jimmy smoked a lot of weed. I never cared what he did on his own time, but the rule had always been clear: *not on the boat.* When he came to work for me on the island, the rule expanded to include that. Then I'd broken my own rule.

Finn looked anxious to go. If I were flying *Island Hopper*, my old amphibian, I'd take him with me. But not on a commercial hop.

"Sorry, Finn, you gotta stay here and keep an eye on Jimmy."

"That's harsh, man," Jimmy said, but he smiled anyway. "Don't worry, I'll take good care of him. Not gonna say where you're going?"

"Antigua," I replied. "To see Sara."

"Kim and Marty will be home this weekend."

"Dammit, I forgot. Thanks. I'll call her."

My youngest daughter and her husband worked for Florida Fish and Wildlife's Division of Law Enforcement. They also lived on the island. I'd built two identical bunkhouses years ago; identical, but mirror image to each other. The west bunkhouse was later divided, creating a small office with two bunk beds for when Chyrel was on the island, which wasn't that often anymore.

Kim had taken over the other half of Chyrel's bunkhouse, and I'd built a small kitchen and bedroom area for her, removing the bunks. Later, when she and Marty married, we converted it back into a bunk house, and moved her and all her stuff into the eastern bunkhouse, giving them a little more room. It now had two small bedrooms and a bathroom. They'd been on assignment up in the Everglades for the last couple of weeks, staying at a camp in Flamingo.

I patted Finn's flank and he looked up at me, his tail wagging him. "Be good," I told him. "I'll be back soon."

Then I went down to the boathouse. The sun was shining again when I opened the big spring-loaded door and idled my little Grady-White out into Harbor Channel. Turning east, I brought her up on plane and headed for the narrow cut through the shallows. As I turned into it, I glanced over to the left and saw that Mac's boat was tied off to its piling. He must have called it an early day on account of the rain. Maybe Jimmy could hire Mac for a couple of days.

Mac Travis was probably more of a recluse than I was. He'd once worked for a guy named Woodson, who'd built or repaired many of the bridges that connect the numerous islands of the Keys. Wood owned the island, but since he'd died, it went to his daughter, Mel, Mac's girlfriend. These days, Mac was a fisherman, diver, lobsterman, or pretty much anything else that required a boat or a strong back. It wasn't common knowledge, but I knew that Mac had found and lost fortunes beneath the waves.

Once in deeper water, I turned south and fished my cell phone from my pocket, then ducked behind the small, tinted windscreen when Rusty answered. "I need a ride to the airport," I said, trying to stay out of the wind. "Gotta catch the 1330 flight to Miami."

"What the hell you wanna go there for?" my old friend asked.

"I don't. I'm changing planes there for Antigua and I'll be gone a few days."

"I can't get away," Rusty said, "but hang on a sec."

I heard him calling to his wife, then he muffled the phone.

"You on your way here now?" he finally asked.

"Yeah, be there in fifteen minutes."

"Sid's picking up her niece at the airport, arriving in less than an hour. Hammer down, bro."

"Thanks," I shouted.

I ended the call and pushed the throttle down a bit more.

Sidney was waiting at the dock when I idled up to the *Anchor*. "Thanks for waiting," I said, as she helped me tie off the Grady.

"We gotta hurry," she said. "Naomi's plane arrives in thirty minutes. Wave to Rusty, now. No time for chit-chat."

Grabbing my go-bag, I hurried after her, waving at Rusty out on the back deck. In minutes, Sidney was pulling out of the shell driveway and onto Overseas Highway, headed north. She glanced over at me, eyeing my small go-bag, as she shifted quickly and smoothly up through the gears in her BMW two-seater. "So, where are you heading this time?"

"Meeting Sara in Antigua," I replied, as she wove through north-bound traffic.

It was always such a shock when I left my island and en-countered the full press of civilization. Out on the island, we sometimes saw a boat going by out on the Gulf, and occasionally a flats guide or Mac would stop by, but visitors to my island were rare. Encountering heavy traffic put me on edge, and Sidney's driving scared even Rusty.

She glanced over again and flashed her million-watt smile. "Booty call, huh?"

"I like the term 'rendezvous,'" I said. "Less suggestive."

"Oooh—how Bogey and Bacall-ish."

Laughing as she whipped the Bimmer into the airport, I mustered my best Bogart impression. "We'll always have Paris."

Sidney was one of those women who refused to grow old, physically and emotionally. She was the same age as Rusty and I and had once graced the pages of Playboy magazine. She was every bit as pretty today. Her figure had filled out over the years, and she likely outweighed me by five or ten pounds, but at six feet in her bare feet, her curves were in all the right places. She was six inches taller than Rusty, but then most people were taller than him. He never let it bother him.

Sidney had told me one time about the day she'd met Rusty. The first thing he'd asked her was how tall she was, and when she'd told him, he'd grinned at her lecherously and said, "I like to climb."

They had the same zest for life, comparable moral character, and were equally passionate about a lot of the same things. The "peas and carrots" line from the *Forest Gump* movie played in my head.

Sidney parked the car and we hurried inside. She was wearing heels, putting her right at my height, but they didn't slow her down any. I followed her toward the ticket counter, looking around the small terminal. "There's Naomi now," she said, hurrying toward a bunch of people waiting for baggage.

At the counter, I presented my driver's license and told the agent I had a reservation. "You just made it, Mister McDermitt," she said, handing me a boarding pass. "Go ahead through the security gate. Your flight is departing in thirty minutes."

As I turned around, I almost ran into Sidney.

"Jesse, this is Naomi. She's staying with us for a week. Naomi, this is Rusty's friend, Jesse." The woman at Sidney's side was younger, probably in her twenties or early thirties. She had Sidney's, height, hair color and smile. "Naomi is my niece," Sidney added, as I shook the younger woman's hand. "My sister's girl."

"Pleased to meet you," I said, picking up my bag. Then to Sidney, I said, "Tell Rusty I'll see him when I get back. I gotta run. My flight takes off in half an hour."

"Go," Sidney said, shooing me with her hands. "We'll see you when you get back. Naomi's here on a modeling assignment."

As I went through the security check, placing my little bag on the conveyor, I glanced back at the two of them. They were pulling Naomi's luggage from the carousel. Sidney's niece lifted a dive bag and placed it on a small cart.

"Have a wonderful flight, sir," a young man wearing a TSA uniform said, as he pushed my bag toward the end of the counter.

I lifted it and looked back again, just before going through the door to the waiting plane. Sidney and Naomi were pushing the little cart toward the exit.

A model carrying dive gear? I thought.

CHAPTER FOUR

The second leg of my flight landed on the island of Antigua at 2215, only a few minutes late. I used my real passport on entering, since my boat was docked under that name. I had other passports on my boat and not all had the same name or country of origin. Having just my carry-on bag, I was out of the terminal building in minutes, approached the cab at the front of the line outside, and hopped in.

The ride from the airport on the north side of Antigua to Nelson's Dockyard in English Harbour, on the south side, took forty minutes. The marina and docks were modern, but still had the feel of the centuries-old waterfront that was Admiral Horatio Nelson's base of operations in the late 1700s. Though still a young man at twenty-eight, Nelson was basically unemployed after the British surrendered America's dependence at Versailles. Nelson was posted to the Caribbean as the senior captain of the outpost. Two decades later, after commanding a decisive victory over the combined French and Spanish fleets off Cape Trafalgar, Spain, Lord Admiral Nelson was killed in action. It was rumored that his body was preserved in a rum barrel, to be returned to England for a state funeral. It was also rumored that sailors aboard the ship had unknowingly tapped Nelson's rum keg. I didn't know if any of that was true, but Pusser's still bottled a fifteen-year-old dark rum called Nelson's Blood.

Once I'd boarded the plane out of Marathon, I'd sent a text message to Sara, letting her know that I'd be on the boat by midnight. I didn't want to seem too eager, but I got a feeling that our rendezvous wasn't going to be just pleasure.

After paying the driver, I grabbed my bag and walked out onto the long, dog-leg dock jutting out into Freeman's Bay. *Floridablanca* was tied up in a premium spot at the end of the pier on the protected side. It was an eighty-foot slip and *Floridablanca* was only fifty feet long, but the location allowed me a fast departure, without maneuvering around the pilings or other boats. The ease of departure offset the extra cost of the premium slip.

My vessel appeared to be secure, and thanks to the technology aboard, I knew that to be true. The lights were on in the lower stateroom, filtering through the curtains that covered the three round portholes. I glanced at my watch. They'd be turning off within an hour. The stateroom lights were on a different timer than the salon lights, which came on at local sunset and went off ten minutes after the stateroom lights came on. This made it appear as if someone were aboard.

I swung a leg over the port rail and stepped over into the cockpit. The keypad next to the hatch lit and a light above the hatch came on, bathing the cockpit in a warm orange glow. I turned off the security system and glanced up to the aft corner of the overhead on the port side. A tiny red light was just visible on the face of an infrared camera mounted high in the darkened corner.

I already had my satellite phone out of my pocket when it vibrated. I touched the screen and saw that I had an incoming video message. When I touched the screen again, I was looking at myself, looking at my phone. I closed the security app and unlocked the hatch.

The air inside *Floridablanca* was a little musty, since I hadn't been aboard in a few months. After dropping my bag on a lounge chair to starboard, I went about sliding the large salon portholes open.

It was a warm night, but a cool ocean breeze out of the east began to move the air around inside the salon. The musty odor would be replaced with the smell of the sea in just a few minutes.

I went forward and up to the bridge deck. A red over-head light came on automatically, illuminating the whole bridge with a subdued light. I glanced to my right, where a second camera mounted on the starboard side came on. There were motion sensors on the bridge as well as the cockpit. At the control panel, I switched on the boat's systems.

The low hum of the air-conditioner told me that it would soon be more comfortable. I checked over the electrical system. Shore power was connected, and the batteries were all fully charged. There were no red lights on the panel to indicate a problem, water tanks and fuel tanks were all reading full, and the bilge pumps were online. Though built nearly half a century ago, *Floridablanca* was an antique on the outside only. Her systems were all brand-new and quite sophisticated.

I powered up the computer under the starboard desk and activated the closed-circuit security cameras located in several strategic places around the boat. The monitor filled with six images showing live video from the command bridge where I stood, from the aft cockpit, both side decks, the engine room, and the flybridge. I could again see myself, looking at the monitor.

Back down in the salon, I grabbed my bag and carried it to the lower stateroom, where I dropped it, still packed, on the deck in the hanging locker. The purpose of a go-bag was to always have something ready. I rarely opened it but did now. From inside a concealed panel in the boat's bulkhead, I retrieved a Colt 1911 pistol and put it in the bag, then took my passport out and zipped the bag closed. I put the passport in the top drawer of the chest.

Everything I'd need for a month at sea was already aboard, with the exception of fresh food. So, the clothes and toiletries in my go-bag would remain there. There was enough canned food in the lazarette and pantry to last a month, but I'd emptied the fridge and freezer before I'd left *Floridablanca*, giving several fillets and some fresh vegetables to a young couple loading a tiny dinghy with groceries.

After a quick shower, I returned to the salon and closed the portholes before going up to the bridge again. I sat in the helm seat and put my feet up on the starboard desk to send Kim a text message that I wouldn't be home this weekend. Then I set my phone on the helm and got a beer from the small refrigerator.

Movement on the monitor caught my eye. The port camera showed someone carrying a small bag walking along the dock toward my boat. When the figure stepped into the small cone of light from one of the dock lamps, I smiled and put the beer back. It was Sara.

"Ahoy, *Floridablanca*," she called from outside, as I hurried down to the salon.

I opened the hatch and stepped out into the cockpit. "I'm glad you could come early."

Sara handed me her bag, and I helped her over the railing, vowing for the hundredth time to cut out a section and install a chain. She took her bag from my hand, dropped it on the deck and stepped into my arms. We kissed and held each other close for a few moments before Sara began to push me backward toward the hatch, her kisses becoming more passionate. I willingly obliged, and we stumbled into the salon, pawing at one another's clothes.

"My bag," she softly murmured, as I started to close the hatch.

I broke away from her, but not before she pulled my shirt off over my head. After retrieving her bag, I closed and locked the hatch. Within seconds, we were back at it, urgently pushing and pulling one another toward the lower stateroom like anxious teenagers, while trying to remove the rest of our clothes.

The air-conditioner continued to hum as we fell apart exhausted, with the sheets tangled around our legs. Sara blew at a strand of hair that lay across her face. "I've really missed you," she said, her chest rising and falling heavily.

A soft glow from the lights in the marina filtered through the covered portholes, dimly lighting the stateroom. I looked over at Sara and couldn't help but smile. "You're like a wild animal. You know that, right?"

"You're complaining?"

How many times had we done this? I wondered. Fallen into bed after little more than a hello. That's how it had happened the first time.

Sara and I had an agreement. Neither of us was looking for a relationship, at least not one with all the usual emotional baggage. So, we made ourselves available to one another physically, and without strings. Monogamous, but with no promise of a future. So far, it had been a good understanding and we'd found time for each other at least once a month. If I had to guess, we'd probably had our little rendezvous close to forty times.

"You'll never hear me complain, lady."

"Good." She sat up, then swung her long legs off the bunk and grabbed one of my light-weight work shirts from my hanging locker. "Do you have any food on board? I'm famished."

I glanced at my watch. "It's like 0200. You want breakfast or dinner?"

"Depends on the menu," she said, climbing up the steps to the galley. Sara knew her way around my boat at least as well as I did. I'd bought *Floridablanca* from her father, John Wilson, after his accident.

"Nothing perishable up there," I called after her. "My plane only landed an hour before you got here. I didn't even have time to shave."

"I like the scruffy look on you." A light came on up in the galley and I heard the pantry open and close. "You flew commercial?"

"Yeah, I did, or I'd have never made it in time. Wasn't too bad. *Island Hopper* is a great little plane, but she doesn't have much range. I'd have had to make too many fuel stops; hence the name. Island hopping isn't something you do in a hurry."

A moment later, Sara stood in the hatchway, the light behind her silhouetting her body through the light-weight fabric of my shirt, leaving very little to my imagination. She hadn't buttoned it. She tossed something toward me, which I caught in my left hand as she came down the ladder and leapt onto the bunk beside me. It was a zippered bag of jerked beef slices.

I laughed. "You sure know the way to a man's heart."

"It's still good, right? I mean, it's dried and sealed."

"Yeah, this'll last a hundred years," I said, handing her the bag.

She opened it and took two slices out, handing me one. The scent of exotic Caribbean spices filled the air. "It'll have to do until morning. We need to keep your strength up."

CHAPTER FIVE

It was well past sunrise when Sara and I finally locked up the boat and went ashore for breakfast and shopping. Any excursion ashore meant multitasking. It usually involved walking, so even if I was just going to the marina store for a six-pack, I loaded up. It was always best to be prepared for anything, so I kept my boats well-provisioned and the tanks topped off. My grandfather had taught me that.

My parents had died when I was just a kid and I went to live with my dad's parents. Pap always drove a four-wheel-drive vehicle; pickups when I was young, then later big SUVs. He rarely hauled anything or went off-roading, but I remember after a hurricane, he and I put his old Dodge to work, going around the neighborhood and clearing the roads by dragging trees and other debris out of the way. His four-wheel drive came in very handy that day, as did the truck bed, when we started cutting up fallen trees.

"What are you grinning about?" Sara asked, as we walked back toward the harbor after breakfast at Pillars.

"Just remembering back to when I was a kid and spent the entire summer after my sophomore year splitting firewood."

"Firewood? You grew up in south Florida."

"Better to have it and not need it, than need it and not have it."

She looked up at me as we walked the brick path back to the marina. "You're an odd sort, Jesse McDermitt. How much time do we have?"

I glanced at my watch, knowing what she wanted to do, but wishing it was what I had in mind instead.

"I told him 0930, so less than an hour."

"This way," she said, tugging on my hand.

We spent the next half hour buying clothes at Cotton Club. Sara insisted on keeping my wardrobe fresh. Once we deposited the bags aboard *Floridablanca*, we went out to the road to wait for the cab ride to the grocery store. It was only two miles away; an easy walk. But the walk back with bags of meat, fish, and vegetables would be grueling. It was already in the mid-80s.

"So, are you going to tell me?" I asked, as we sat on a bench.

"Tell you what?"

"What your dad's up to in the BVI."

Sara looked around casually. But I knew she was checking to make sure nobody was within earshot. "Dad should be the one to tell you. And you really do need to be up there within three days."

"What is it?"

"Nothing's been substantiated," she replied. "There was a huge gun battle down in Venezuela yesterday. Several cartel members were killed, and a narco sub was stolen."

"So? Those cartel people are always killing each other."

"There was an increase in chatter on a few known terrorist websites. An Islamic State cell seems to have been responsible for the attack and the theft of the sub."

Terrorists with a submarine? That was a scary thought.

"Not that I don't want to spend the rest of the day with you," I said, as a cab approached, "because I do. But why the slow boat to China?"

"It happened two days ago. We think the target is going to be in the Virgin Islands, most likely Charlotte Amalie. If it can run day and night without stopping, it would take them four days. But intelligence tells us they're following the island chain, possibly to arrange fuel delivery. They can't possibly be there for at least five days."

I stood and waved to the driver. "Targeted? Using what?"

"Ten tons of Semtex."

I stopped at the door of the cab. "Ten tons? Do we really have time for a grocery run?"

"All I know is that Dad wants you on Norman Island in three days, but not before. My guess is that he and Uncle—er, Mister Armstrong want you out on the water. Others, including the U.S. Navy, are moving into various positions along the expected route."

I was tense during the whole trip to the store and back. If what Sara had said was true—that terrorists were out there somewhere in a sub with ten tons of explosives—I wanted to be moving to intercept.

But experience had taught me that Armstrong's reach and abilities were many-faceted. I was another spoke in a great big wheel.

An hour later, we were back aboard *Floridablanca*, putting the supplies away for my journey. I was anxious to get underway and put *Floridablanca* to work on her mission. The sophisticated passive sonar on *Floridablanca* could pick up nearly any sound in the water. Narco subs were usually just subs in name only. Most were little more than partially submerged covered hulls with a noisy engine and a snorkel to provide air.

"When do you have to get back?" I asked, after everything was put away.

"Tonight. And you should get plenty of rest. From here to the Virgin Islands, you can stop over in the Netherlands Antilles, or just push straight on and trust the autopilot."

"Can't you come with me?"

"You still don't trust technology, do you?"

"It's not that," I said. "I just don't get to see you very often."

"And that's the way that is, Jesse." She smiled and started for the lower stateroom. "You just want me to take the night watch, right?"

Our relationship wasn't like that of most couples. I'd been divorced twice and widowed once, with a string of unsuccessful relationships between and after. But Sara had lost her husband in Afghanistan just four years ago and I knew she was still in love with his memory. I didn't fault her. Losing a spouse was like losing a part of yourself. At least with divorce or a breakup, the love died first.

"Oh, you're good," I said, slowly following after her. "Of that there isn't any doubt."

"A good night pilot?" she asked, as she slowly went down one more step.

"Yeah, there's that, too."

CHAPTER SIX

The time we had together was too short, as always. But we'd agreed a long time ago that we wouldn't interrupt our work for personal pleasure. It was one of the rules that kept our relationship from blossoming into something else—something with deeper emotional connections. Not that we weren't connected. We were also very good friends and colleagues, and we worked and got along very well together.

"I know you're going to push straight through," Sara said, standing on the dock by my boat. "And you're going to be tempted to run fast."

"You think you know me that well?"

"Don't push it. It would only attract attention we don't need." She leaned over the rail and kissed me. "Get some rest, Jesse."

And with that, she was gone. I watched her walk down the dock for a moment and then forced myself to turn away. If she did look back, I didn't want her to see me longing after her like some kind of love-starved pup.

I went down to the galley, put away the dinner dishes, then climbed up to the command bridge to prepare for the morning's departure. Looking out through the open starboard hatch, I could see the sun was just going down behind the hillside. It was still more than an hour until sunset, though. At the nav desk, I brought up the chart plotter and laid in a course for Norman Island in the British Virgin Islands. It was almost exactly 200 miles.

"Huh," I said aloud. Sara had been dead on. The volcanic islands of the Netherlands Antilles lay just a few miles west of the precise midway point on the chart. A rhumb line from Antigua to Norman Island passed just to the east of Saint Kitts, Nevis, Sint Eustatius, and Saba, so anchoring on the west side of one of those islands wouldn't add too many miles to the trip. I made a small adjustment on the chart plotter, adding a waypoint. I'd anchor in Gallows Bay on the lee side of the island of Sint Eustatius, or Statia, as the locals called it.

Exhausted from my encounter with Sara, and looking forward to tomorrow, I went to bed early and was asleep before my head hit the pillow.

It was still dark when I woke. Sara's scent lingered on the pillow beside me, bringing back the recent memory of our lovemaking. I pushed aside those thoughts and rose from my bunk, padding barefoot up to the galley. The odor there was also enticing, but in a different way.

I poured a mug of coffee from my pre-set machine and carried it up to the command bridge, where I started the single main engine.

Sitting at the helm, I looked over the engine gauges. The old GMC two-stroke diesel was running perfectly. That engine had been manufactured at the outset of the Second World War and put on a shelf in a warehouse for nearly three decades, but it just never failed to do exactly what it was built to do—run for long periods of time. Its simplicity and rugged dependability always comforted me.

The sky across the bay began to lighten, and after a moment, I went down to the galley and filled a Thermos, then got dressed for the day.

Ten minutes later, I threw off the dock lines and slowly idled away from Nelson's Dockyard Marina, pointing *Floridablanca's* bow toward the mouth of the bay.

It was a short distance to open water and once clear of the bay, I engaged the autopilot and pushed the throttle up to *Floridablanca's* cruising speed of nine knots.

With nothing showing ahead of me on radar, I scanned the sea surface with binoculars, looking for anything too small for the radar to pick up. In deep water, that could be anything from a cargo container to a submarine's snorkel. Seeing nothing, I went aft and opened the hatch to the large lazarette.

The storage on *Floridablanca* was incredible. Below the covered cockpit, which measured fifteen feet across and ten from the aft rail to the house, was 150 square feet of storage. It was only five feet down to the hull, but a lot of gear could be stored there. It could even be another cabin.

After getting what I needed, I climbed back up and closed the hatch. A few minutes later, I had the towed sonar array in the water and trailing 500 feet behind *Floridablanca*, running ten feet below the surface.

Passive sonar isn't directional. It's simply a way of listening to the sounds in the water. But with "the fish" far behind the boat and connected to the sonar system on the bridge, any sounds it and the transponder in the keel picked up could be compared by the computer. The difference in time it takes the same sound to reach the two transponders would give the direction from which the sound came. Actually, two possible directions at opposing ends of the compass. The human brain does the same thing, using the ears on either side of the head.

Owning not two, but three large boats, I always had to adjust my expectations. Both *Floridablanca* and *Salty Dog* were long-range boats, one power and one sail. The *Dog* could cross oceans without stopping; a true passage-maker. *Floridablanca*, on the other hand, needed to stop for fuel, but only every 3000 or so miles. *Gaspar's Revenge* was a big offshore fishing boat capable of fifty knots. Her range was considerably less, maybe 400 miles with an extra fuel bladder in the fish box, but she could get there in a hurry. So, planning a trip was different for each boat.

I spent the morning on the flybridge. Once far enough
away from Antigua that I wouldn't pick up the noise
from the busy harbor, I turned on the passive sonar,
adjusting it to squelch out my own engine noise. I was
listening for anything rhythmic. Normal ocean sounds
are sporadic and random, but an engine—even a very
quiet engine—made noise. And narcotics-smuggling
submarines typically weren't very quiet.

By 1100 the heat became oppressive and I went down
to the air-conditioned comfort of the command bridge.
With the engine running, I could operate the A/C and it
was very comfortable below deck. Anchoring out at the
end of the day would be a different story. I'd be strictly
on battery power.

The hours and the sea rolled by monotonously. I had
the stereo playing and my old Silvertone guitar on my
lap. I was trying to keep up with a Kenny Chesney song
I liked about a bar at the end of the world when I heard
a different rhythm that was throwing me off. I suddenly
realized it was coming from the sonar speaker.

I put the guitar on the watch bunk, grabbed the head-
phones hanging under the computer desk, and plugged
them in. It was a low hum, far off. But it wasn't steady.
It sounded like what a warped record would emit if it
played a steady hum, the pitch rising and falling in a
regular pattern every half second or so. I only heard the
sound for a moment before it stopped. The radar screen
was empty; there wasn't another boat around for twelve
miles. But the sound I'd heard wasn't naturally occur-

ring, of that I was certain. The sonar screen had indicated that the sound had emanated from the southwest, and very far away.

While I was fiddling with the sonar controls, my satellite phone rang. I removed the headset, grabbed up the phone, and hit the green *Talk* button. "McDermitt."

"Jesse, it's Jack. Where are you?"

Jack Armstrong was a billionaire a few times over, as were many of his associates. Together, they funded some of the side operations Armstrong Research did. I worked for the company's Expeditionary Division. It was my job to look for trouble.

"Hey, Jack. I'm about eighteen nautical miles due east of the southern tip of Saint Kitts. I just heard something on passive sonar, and there's not a boat within twelve miles on the radar."

"Keep your eyes open. There was a sighting earlier today just off Montserrat."

"Is that why you called?"

"Yes," he replied. "DJ is in the Turks and Caicos, about to get underway, but you're the only eyes and ears we have in the area. He's at least two days away."

Jack was speaking of DJ Martin, on the charter fishing vessel *Reel Fun*, normally out of Key Largo. DJ had been a paratrooper with the 101st Airborne before losing his right leg below the knee in Iraq.

"He's a little far from home."

"He got underway the same time you did. The Barkleys are up in Chesapeake Bay, too far away to be of any help."

"Anyone else?"

"*Ambrosia* is conducting research in the Windwards and can't be moved, and several others are working a project in Guatemala. What did it sound like?"

"Kind of a rhythmic buzz, pulsing a little, but not a diesel engine."

"This isn't your run-of-the-mill sub, Jesse. We're still gathering intel, but we think it was designed by Russian submarine engineers."

The narco subs I'd seen on the news and online were usually little more than regular boats, gutted of everything, with flat, water-tight decks. They were loaded with enough drugs or other contraband to nearly submerge their hulls relying on snorkels for air intake and exhaust. They rode so low in the water that they often had no radar signature. But they weren't true submarines.

"So, what's this thing look like?"

"Like a real sub," Jack replied. "We think it's very high-tech, with a reinforced hull, built in the traditional cigar shape with twin screws. Were you able to get a location on the contact?"

"Didn't hear it long enough," I told him. "Somewhere south and west of me, and far off."

"Just before I called?"

"Yeah."

"Sara just handed me a printout. A Venezuelan cutter just reported that it had picked up a similar sound just minutes ago. They'd reported yesterday that they'd engaged and sunk the sub, but we had our doubts. They were far to the south of you, close to the mainland when they heard it just now. They determined the sound was moving north-northeast and estimated its position about a hundred miles due west of Saint Lucia."

"That's a good two hundred miles from where I am."

"That would be about right, given the time since the theft of the sub and the reported sinking. Where are you stopping?"

"Gallows Bay on Statia."

"Good choice. Anchor deep, far from shore. This thing's high-tech, but it's slow. You might hear it on sonar again."

"Any update on what their target might be?"

"Originally, we thought it was the cruise ship pier in Charlotte Amalie," Jack replied. "But somehow someone leaked information. Probably the Venezuelan cartel who built the sub. They have people in the Venezuelan navy. The terrorists may know that we know. We have no idea what a secondary target might be."

"Anything else?"

"John's the best sonar man around," he said. "Pick him up Saturday morning and keep your ears on. He'll tell you where to take up position. You and DJ will be filling in acoustic gaps for other organizations."

I ended the call and looked out over the water on the port side. The idea that a sub loaded with terrorists and ten tons of high explosives could be out there somewhere, just under the waves, was a bit disconcerting. But if they could see me, I would look like an ancient trawler, no threat to anyone. No wonder Sara had insisted on cruising at slow speed. I had to assume that they had sophisticated sonar, as well.

With only three hours of daylight left, I checked the chart plotter. I was more than halfway up the east side of Saint Kitts. If the sub was southwest of my location, the island would block any sounds the passive sonar might pick up. I bumped the throttle up to ten knots, anxious to get past the island. It would be nearly dark when I dropped anchor.

Saint Kitts slipped slowly past; the three peaks of its highest mountains just visible on the horizon. The mountains were volcanic, as were most of the islands in this part of *El Caribe*, though the only eruption in recent times had been down on Montserrat, just southwest of Antigua, where a 1995 eruption had buried the capital city of Plymouth.

Soon, as I got nearer, the volcanic peak of The Quill on Statia began to slowly rise up out of the water. With the sun barely above the western horizon, I motored around to the lee side and headed toward Gallows Bay. It was really a bay in name only, having a shoreline that barely cut into the mainland and a rocky jetty extending out a couple of hundred yards.

Still far from shore, I dropped the hook in forty feet of water and backed down, releasing 250 feet of rode. When I was sure the anchor was set, I shut down the engine. I was about a quarter of a mile off Interlopers Point, with no other boats around. More importantly, the radar showed no surface activity to the west. That meant no noise.

The fish hung in the water ten feet below the surface, drifting off to the west. I hauled the tether in a little, to allow it enough slack to hang below the surface. I didn't want anyone running over it.

Returning to the command bridge, I turned the sonar volume up and tied it into the boat's intercom system. There were a multitude of sounds—chirps, clicks, whirs, croaks—all naturally occurring in the ocean. The sonar display on the computer plotted many of them on a rectangular green display, with each sound represented by a curving line and showing its distance from the boat. I didn't hear anything rhythmic, which would indicate a man-made source.

I ate a microwave dinner on the flybridge as the sun slipped slowly into the sea's embrace. One by one, the stars began to appear. When I got a beer from the mini-fridge and popped the top, the sound seemed unusually loud in the near darkness. The only illumination came from the aft masthead light and a faint glow to the west, which quickly disappeared.

Once I'd finished my beer, I went below to shut off all non-essential systems. In the pilothouse, lit only by low-level red lights from the overhead and sonar and radar screens, I opened the hatches to allow the cool sea breeze to filter in before stretching out on the watch bunk. It was my favorite place to sleep on *Floridablanca*. I was soon fast asleep, hearing nothing but the underwater sounds of the sea.

CHAPTER SEVEN

I slept hard and there were no unusual noises from the sonar to wake me. Spending a day with Sara, then motoring for nearly ten hours had physically drained me, and the idea of a terrorist attack by submarine had taken a toll mentally. After taking a shower and eating a banana for breakfast, I carried a Thermos of coffee up to the command bridge and started the engine. It was daylight, but the sun hadn't yet risen over the island.

Half an hour later, I had the anchor up and began a wide turn around the bay, the sonar array still trailing behind me. When the depth finder showed 100 feet under the keel, I turned north to resume my course to Norman Island, about 120 nautical miles away. I slowly brought the speed up to eight knots. It would be close to midnight when I arrived, six hours ahead of my appointed meeting with John. My course would take me within a few miles of Saba in about two hours. It was the last island in the Netherlands Antilles, with nothing but a hundred miles of open ocean after that before I reached the British Virgin Islands.

The seas were calm, just a light chop, which had no effect at all on the big steel-hulled trawler. Saba came into view, just a few degrees off the port bow, Mount Scenery rising up nearly 3000 feet above the ocean. The volcano was considered dormant, having last erupted about the time of the Mayflower. But then, the Montserrat volcano hadn't erupted since about that same time either. Until it blew in 1995.

There was a muffled poof from the sonar speaker, followed by a pulsing echo that diminished quickly. I'd never heard anything like it. The closest I could describe to it would be the time a blue whale breached, as John Wilson and I were listening to ocean sounds off Puerto Rico.

I heard nothing more on the sonar, as Saba slowly drifted past just a mile off the port side. John had told me once that most of the sounds you heard in the ocean traveled a long distance and were unrecognizable to humans. The sound I'd just heard was obviously man-made, but I had no idea what it was.

After several minutes, the VHF crackled to life. "Mayday, Mayday!"

The desperate call, nearly covered by static, was barely readable, meaning the caller was probably many miles away. I turned up the volume.

"To any vessel northeast of Saba, this is the *Wavy Davey*. We are in distress. We have sustained major damage and are sinking fast."

As I reached for the microphone to ask the boat's position, the radio crackled again. "GPS is down but we are midway between Saba and Sint Maarten. Mayday, Mayday..."

The rule of the sea was to help any vessel in distress. But I didn't want to give away too much information about who I was or where I was going.

I keyed the mic. "Vessel in distress, this is the *Floridablanca*. I am just north of Saba bound for Saint Kitts. I believe I have you on radar, but I don't have visual. I wanna make sure this blip is you—do you have a flare gun on board?"

"Wait one," the voice said, steadier now.

A moment later, I saw the flare rising and arcing to the northeast, trailing white smoke. "I see it. You're about ten miles off my port bow. How many are you?"

"Three."

"Hang tight, I'll be there as soon as I can. If I had my old Rampage I'd be there in a jiffy, but this long-haul trawler can only hit fifteen knots."

"Roger, *Floridablanca*," the voice replied. "We'll be here. We might be in the water, but we'll be here. Thank you."

"My pleasure. Voyage was a bit dull, anyway. See ya in a few."

Pushing the single throttle to the stop, I turned the wheel as the antique diesel revved to its limiter, pushing my old boat to its top speed of fifteen knots. At least that was the top speed on the single original engine. The twin Mercedes powerplants would push the old, steel-hulled, raised pilothouse trawler across the water at thirty-five knots. But that attracted too much attention. Besides, the amount of time it would take to go down to the engine room to shift the main engine offline and bring the modern engines online would take longer than just pressing on.

The minutes ticked by as I raced toward the stricken vessel. I raised a powerful pair of binoculars to my eyes, looking for it. It wasn't there, and the radar no longer showed the echo. But I could see what looked like an orange, inflatable lifeboat resting on the horizon, probably four miles ahead.

I set the autopilot and quickly went down to the cockpit. It took a great deal of strength to pull the fish in, pulling hand over hand. But I finally returned it to the lazarette, along with the tether. When I went up to the flybridge, I could see debris floating in the water. It didn't look anything like what you'd expect from a boat sinking. Still several hundred yards away, I dropped the throttle to an idle, letting the boat's momentum slowly bleed off the speed.

"Ahoy the raft!" I called down from the flybridge.

"Ahoy our savior!" A young woman called back. The way she pronounced savior like *save-yuh* made me think she was English. She was with two men, one wearing a uniform of some kind.

Twenty feet from the raft, I shifted to neutral and hurried down to the foredeck. I threw a line and one of the men caught it and tied it off to the raft. I walked aft along the starboard side, pulling the raft to the only boarding opening in the rail, where I hauled it in close and tied the line off to a deck cleat.

Reaching down, I took the woman's hand and hauled her up through the opening. She couldn't have been more than five feet tall and weighed very little.

The uniformed man—really no more than a teenager—was hurt. Blood streaked down his face from a scalp wound. The other man helped him to the side of the boat, then the woman and I pulled him on board. The other man tried to lift himself up to climb aboard but slipped back a little. I grabbed the shoulder of his shirt, steadying him.

"Welcome aboard," I said, hoisting him up. "I lost your boat on my radar. Glad to see you got off safe."

"Yeah, the *Wavy Davey* is no more," the man said, his accent identifying him as American.

"Sorry to hear about that. You had her long?"

"About an hour," he replied.

The woman suppressed a snicker as I led them aft to the shade of the cockpit. "Before I ask for an explanation of that cryptic reply," I began, "lemme ask about something else. I just passed a lot of debris and none of it looked like it came from a pleasure craft."

"That would be the submarine that blew up," the American said.

"Sir," the woman began, obviously finding some comic relief in their situation, "we're not loonies, I promise... Sid here is a cop, and—"

I raised my hand to interrupt her. "You're talking about the smug-druggler submarine some terrorists stole? Got everyone going crazy up near the Virgin Islands?"

The American man looked surprised. "How do you know about that?"

I just shrugged, motioning toward the flybridge. "I overheard some chatter. Let's just say I know what bands to listen in on." I turned toward the police officer. "You Saba Police?"

"Yes, sir," the young man replied. "Aspirant... er... Cadet Sidney Every."

"And you two?"

"Emily Durand," the woman said, dipping a curtsy. "And this beanpole is Boone Fischer."

"We're divemasters from Bonaire," Boone said. "Just got here."

"And who may we thank for rescuing us?" Emily asked, a disarming smile on her face.

"Where are my manners?" I said. "You can call me Stretch. Stretch Buchannan." I used the alias I always gave when I didn't want anyone to know who I was. Opening the hatch to the salon, I nodded inside. "Hey, Sid, head into the wheelhouse and call this location in to the Dutch Caribbean Coast Guard. There's a GPS in there to the left of the wheel. Then sit your ass down and I'll take a look at that cut."

"I've got some first aid training," Emily said.

"Okay, good. There's a kit on the wall in there—you can't miss it. Patch him up."

"Aye-aye, Cap'n Stretch!"

As Emily and Sid headed to the wheelhouse, I turned and looked at Boone. "You carry yourself well, but you're not military, are you?"

"No, sir," he replied. "My father was Dutch navy but that's the closest I got." He pointed at my arm. "That tattoo. You were a combat diver?"

"Among other things," I replied. "Force Recon. Very retired. Come up to the flybridge with me, will you?"

Boone followed behind me. "Beautiful boat," he said. "What is she?"

"She's a 1969 Seaton RPH. Incredible range. I've always enjoyed speed in my boats, but at some point in your life you just wanna drift and take it all in."

At the helm, I picked up the binos and glassed the debris field. "I thought that looked like a conning tower." I lowered the glasses and studied Boone's face. "The sub blowing up. You have something to do with that?"

"Indirectly."

"Have a seat. Start from the beginning."

"Wait... do you have a satellite phone?"

I studied him a moment longer. "I might. Who do you need to call?"

"Rick Claassen. He's Navy Reserve and said he works with... the Joint Inter-something-or-other."

"Joint Interagency Task Force," I asked. "I know someone who works with them from time to time. Claassen... that name's familiar. Big Southern boy? Got a brother?"

"That's him. He's been passing along my info on the submarine."

I nodded and opened the drawer to the left of the helm, took out my sat phone and powered it up. "I'll need to make the call for you. Get the number ready."

Scrolling through my short contact list, I touched the one I wanted and held the phone to my ear until Chyrel answered. "It's me. Odd request. I need you to place a call and patch me in."

Boone retrieved a soggy receipt from his pocket and handed it to me. The number was still legible. I read it to Chyrel and she said to hang on. Then there were a few clicks and a buzzing sound. I handed the phone over to Boone.

"Rick, it's Boone," he said into the phone. I could hear an excited voice, talking fast, but couldn't make out what was being said. Boone listened for a moment, then interrupted whoever was talking. "The sub is destroyed. We managed to ram her and the crew blew her up."

That would explain what I'd heard on the sonar earlier. I made a mental note to ask John why it seemed to pulse.

Boone laughed. "My ears are still ringing. Yeah, I'm certain. Debris everywhere. She's gone, Rick." He listened a moment longer, then nodded. "Will do."

He listened for another moment, then handed the phone to me. I heard the click of the ended call but knew the connection to Deuce's office was still open. "Thanks, Chyrel."

"Any time, Jesse. I'm not even going to ask what that was about." I grinned and ended the call.

Boone held my eyes. "Your name's not really 'Stretch Buchannan,' is it?"

I studied his face for a moment, as Emily climbed up the steps from the Portuguese bridge forward of the pilothouse. I kept my eyes on Boone's, and the corner of my mouth came up at the advantageous interruption. "Well, hey there, Miss, come join the party."

Emily carried a pair of water bottles. "Hope you don't mind, but I swiped a couple bottles of water."

"No worries... *mi agua es tu agua*," I said, still looking at Boone.

"Sid's resting now, and I..." She trailed off, looking at the two of us. "What are you guys talking about?"

"Oh nuthin' much," I replied, relaxing a little. "Boone here was about to tell me how you found yourselves chasing a submarine full of terrorists. Why don't you join us—pull up some bench and contribute to story time?"

"Okey dokey," she said. "Let me just squeeze through the testosterone here and..." She mimicked a struggle through thick air, then plopped down beside Boone and handed him a water bottle.

I burst into laughter and Boone grinned. The tension broken; he began. "It all started with a shore dive..."

An hour later, as I came out of the pilothouse and started up the aft steps to the flybridge, I saw the *USS Tornado* approaching from the west. A Cyclone class patrol ship, the *Tornado* had spent time in both the U.S. Coast Guard and Navy, the speedy little ship primarily being used for interdiction and anti-piracy missions. She slowed and maneuvered closer, as the crew prepared a fast boat for launch. I could hear my sat phone ring as I went up the ladderwell. Boone was reaching for it.

"Hold up, Boone. I'll take it."

I looked at the screen. It was Armstrong, so I pushed the *Talk* button. "It's me," I said, not giving a name. "Just FYI, I've got some company. I'm between Saba and Sint Maarten."

"I already know the sub's been destroyed and who your guests are," he said. "The cell's handler has been discovered. We have someone watching him. How fast can you make Norman Island?"

I looked at my watch. "They're sure it's him?"

"Yes," Armstrong replied.

"Okay. Tell your man to stay on him." Boone was pretending not to listen, so once again, I needed to provide misinformation. I hoped Jack would get it. "I'm not far from Kitts—pull some strings and get me some fuel lined up. I'll contact you when I get there. Oh, and the *USS Tornado* just pulled up. Could you...?"

"Saint Kitts? You just passed there. Oh, yeah, company. At any rate, the navy will only want to talk to you long enough to get a statement. You didn't see it go down. I'll make sure they know that you need to be on your way quickly."

"Yeah, that'll work. Gotta go." I ended the call.

Boone watched as the *Tornado's* fast boat was lowered into the water. "Didn't mean to eavesdrop..." he began.

"Hard to avoid on a little flybridge." I said. "No worries."

"You're taking the boat to Saint Kitts? I think the navy's going to want to talk to us. I doubt they'll just let you drive away."

I smiled. "Oh, I think they might."

"Hey, fellas, here comes the cavalry!" Emily called up from below. "Boone, you wanna give me a hand?"

"You heard your girlfriend. Snap to it!"

"She's not..." I raised my eyebrows and Boone chuckled. "Whatever you say, *Stretch*. On my way, Em!" He headed down to join her at the starboard side.

The navy fast boat bounced across the waves and swiftly came alongside *Floridablanca*. Boone and Emily helped them tie up.

An officer who looked to be in his mid-thirties peered up. "Boone Fischer and Emily Durand?" The two nodded. "And is the Saban police officer on board?"

"Sidney Every. Right here," Sid said, from somewhere in the cockpit out of my sight.

"I'm Lieutenant Harper. I'm here to take you all aboard my ship for a debriefing. I don't normally join the boarding party, but... where's your captain?"

"Up here, Lieutenant," I called down. "Permission to come aboard. Join me up top, if you would."

As he came up, I saw Emily start to follow. Boone stopped her and whispered something in her ear.

"You're Captain Buchannan?" Lieutenant Harper asked, as he came up to the flybridge.

I motioned toward a chair behind the helm and he sat down. "No," I replied quietly. "My name is Jesse McDermitt. You should be getting a call—"

The microphone on Harper's belt squawked. "Lieutenant Harper, bridge."

"Excuse me," he said, reaching for the radio. "Harper."

"Yes, sir," the voice said over the small radio. "We just received a high-priority message from Fleet Com, sir. We are not to detain one Jesse McDermitt any longer than necessary."

"Roger that," Harper responded, as he looked over at me, and clipped the radio back to his belt. "You seem to have friends in high places, Captain McDermitt. Just who the hell are you?"

"That's classified," I replied. "Suffice it to say that I need to be on my way. For the record, the captain of the first boat to respond to the sinking of the terrorist's sub was Stretch Buchannan, no first name given. Captain Buchannan was fifteen miles away when the incident occurred and said that when he arrived on the scene, he saw nothing except debris in the water and the people who called the mayday."

"That's it?"

"I'll file an official report later and it will be forwarded to the commanding officer at Second Fleet Headquarters. His eyes only."

"Is there anything else we can do?"

"No, thanks," I replied, standing. I extended my hand and he took it. "Thanks for your service, Lieutenant Harper."

Glancing down, he noted the Force Recon tattoo on my forearm. "Yours, too, sir."

He descended to the deck and joined the others. "So, Captain Buchannan has been cleared."

Emily nudged Boone and he just shrugged. Harper continued, "You three will be joining us. The Dutch navy has been made aware and is letting us handle the debrief. Afterwards, we'll return you to Saba."

After Boone, Emily, and Sid stepped over onto the tender, Boone turned and looked up to where I stood on the flybridge. "Stretch! Thanks for the assist. And good luck with the rest of your cruise."

I grinned. "Here's hoping it'll be smooth sailing for all of us. You kids try not to sink any more boats, ya hear?"

My sat phone rang again. When I picked it up, I saw that it was John. I stabbed the *Talk* button as the launch pulled away and headed back toward the *Tornado*. "I'm on my way, John. Got delayed a couple of hours by a mayday call."

"Yeah, I heard. Did *you* blow it up?"

"No," I replied, sitting down and putting the boat in gear. "Believe it or not, a couple of divemasters and a Saban police cadet rammed it. The terrorists blew the explosives."

I could hear John laughing. Finally, he said, "You can stand down on Norman Island."

"Stand down?"

"Now, son, I might be old and have zero depth perception," John said, "but I ain't dead yet."

"What'd you do, John?"

"Just helped a young man on his quest to find seventy virgins. Guess that makes me a pimp."

CHAPTER EIGHT

The image of John Wilson taking out the handler of a terrorist cell brought a smile to my face. "So, what the hell am I supposed to do?"

"Mission accomplished, son. You're free to move about the ocean, but I'd keep a weather eye to the east."

"Why? What's up?"

"Might not be anything," he replied. "But the NHC is watching a tropical wave building over western Africa this afternoon."

The National Hurricane Center doesn't waste time and money. But that far away, even if it did become a hurricane, it would be a good ten days before it could reach the Caribbean.

"It'll be after dark before I can make it," I said, as I watched the *Tornado* retrieving the fast boat. "But if you buy me a beer, I'll tell you all about it, then you can bring me up to date on the storm that's brewing."

"You're on."

I ended the call and went down to the command bridge. The *Tornado* was three miles away and was soon making fifteen knots. I slowed and shifted the main engine to neutral. There was a metallic click as I pressed on a section of the dash and a panel popped up slightly. I raised it fully open, exposing the gauges and ignition switches for the compact Mercedes engines. After starting them, I shut down the main engine, then went down to the salon and opened the engine room hatch.

Switching the transmission from one engine to two had to be done manually, by first disengaging the main engine's output shaft through a manually operated clutch, then engaging the two engines mounted on either side of it. The main engine was a direct drive, with no gear reduction. If the engine turned at 1000 rpm, so did the propeller. The specially built transmission geared the auxiliary engines down by half, so if they were running at 1000 rpm, the prop was turning at 1500.

Back on the bridge, I put the transmission in gear and slowly moved the single throttle to quarter speed. The twin Mercedes engines were linked through a computer controller to maintain equal engine speed using a single throttle control. *Floridablanca's* speed quickly climbed to ten knots, and I again turned toward the northwest.

Once the *Tornado* was out of sight, I slowly pushed the throttle up a little higher, until *Floridablanca* began to climb up on her own bow wave. Soon she was crashing through the light chop at twenty-five knots. That would allow me to make up a little time without looking too conspicuous.

I arrived in Bight Bay at 2130, after stopping a few miles offshore and switching back to the main engine.

I motored toward the little restaurant and bar on the easternmost shore. *Pirate's Bight* was lit up, and I could hear music. It was Saturday night, and the bar was in full swing.

Pirate's Bight is an upscale place right on the beach, with dozens of lounge chairs laid out in rows on the sand, each with its own blue umbrella for the sun-sensitive tourists. Not exactly my cup of tea, but I wasn't planning to stay long. In fact, I hadn't even cleared through customs. If I stayed through the next day, I would go up to one of the ports of entry on the northern islands.

Norman Island is most noted for being the inspiration for Robert Louis Stevenson's novel, *Treasure Island*. Outside of fiction, the island really did have a reputation for buried pirate treasure. After a mutiny, the crew of the *Nuestra Señora de Guadalupe* buried dozens of chests of silver coins there. Some had been found over the years and people often came to the island to search for treasure. Like me, they didn't always arrive legally.

I anchored in twelve feet of water instead of grabbing a mooring ball. That seemed the logical thing to do when entering a country illegally. No sense giving my name and boat name to the harbormaster. There were at least ten other boats moored or anchored nearby. I backed down with seventy-five feet of rode, most of it being half-inch chain. There was no current in the bay, so all the boats were pointing to windward. Satisfied, I shut down the engine and within minutes had the dinghy in the water.

Puttering up to the sandy shoreline, I pulled the dinghy up alongside a couple of others, then trudged up toward the blue-roofed bar at the far end. John was just coming down the steps to the sand.

"Saw you when you entered the bay." John stared wistfully out at *Floridablanca*.

I shook his hand. "Having second thoughts?"

"About you?" he said, turning toward me with a wry grin. "Not a one. Come on in. Let's have that beer."

The room was raucous—the music loud and people shouting to be heard over it. More than a dozen couples were on the dance floor. Colored lights swept over them and flashing lights seemed to freeze them in wild gyrations.

John had a table in the corner overlooking the beach, far from the stage and dance floor. Once seated, I could look over the whole bay.

"So, a local cop and a coupla divers got it?" he asked, his voice raised enough to do battle with the music, but not so much anyone but me could hear.

"Not yet a cop," I replied, raising my voice slightly. "He was a trainee. The two divers were divemasters who just arrived from Bonaire. Apparently, they were the first to spot the sub during a shore dive off Bonaire a few days ago."

John raised his bottle. "Well, here's to sharp-eyed divemasters."

A second beer was already sitting on the table, full, with condensation dripping down the sides. I picked it up and touched the neck of his bottle with it.

"I thought you were retired."

John drank down the last of his beer and waved the empty toward a passing waiter. "Yeah, well, Jack thought a second pair of ears on *Floridablanca* wouldn't hurt in the search."

During my submersible training, I'd learned John's ear was so sharp he could tell the difference between different outboards.

"And the handler?" I asked.

"A bonus for being in the right place at the right time." He sat back in his chair and fixed me with his one eye. "Jack has a person here, not really on the payroll, just someone he trusts who keeps their eyes and ears open. This person identified the guy, name of Omar Sarif Salib, from a list of known terrorists abroad. We had a man on his way to take care of it, but Salib just sort of fell into my lap, so to speak. He needed a boat to take him to Saint Thomas, and I had one."

"He might have killed you before you got him there."

"I was counting on him trying, son. Halfway over, Salib made his move against me, thinking I was a help-less, one-eyed old man. Came at me with a jambiya."

"What happened?"

"Never bring a knife to a gunfight," John replied, with a wry grin. "I put a 9mm round right between two of the most surprised eyes I've ever seen."

I appraised the old man under a new light. I knew that he'd once been an Air Force special operator, but that had been years ago. I knew little else about his service.

The waiter placed another bottle on the table, and I waited until he turned away. "And the body?"

"You ain't squeamish, are you?"

I raised an eyebrow in mock indignation.

"I have a house here," he said, jerking a thumb over his shoulder. "Right up there on the hill. Keep a little thirty-foot center-console here in the bay, for whenever someone wants to go out fishing. Sometimes they'll want to display their catch for a picture at the docks. So, I have a special hook, a foot long, to hoist up the big ones. Sunk it into old Salib's shoulder, just behind the collar bone, and worked it down under his rib cage until it came out below the sternum. Then I shackled it to a thirty-pound mushroom anchor. He's at the bottom in 2000 feet of water, feeding those six-gill sharks and searching for his virgins."

"Sounds messy," I said.

"It's a fishing boat, son. I probably pumped enough fish blood out of the bilge to fill a couple of barrels. What's a little more? Nothing to worry about, though. The boat's on its way to a marina in Puerto Rico to be hauled out and steam-cleaned inside and out."

From where we sat, I could also see along the side of the open-air bar to the front, where I knew there was a road of sorts. There were loud voices out there, but I couldn't see anyone.

John heard the racket too and leaned over the rail. "Something's going on out there."

There was a high-pitched scream, and John and I both rose and leaped over the low railing.

For his age, John moved surprisingly fast. We both sprinted along the side of the building, dodging several people who'd come out to see what the commotion was about.

When I reached the front, I saw three men and a woman, all dressed in pale blue, pulling away in one of those off-road electric golf carts. The cart went up the road to my right, and I sprinted after them, while John fell back.

The vehicle was moving uphill, so I leaned into it, my legs carrying me slightly faster than the cart. Catching them would be the easy part; stopping them would be a little trickier. I angled into the right-hand rut of the trail, my feet kicking stones loose as I ran. My intention was to stop the cart by yanking the driver out of the seat.

The taillights illuminated the two in the back, both facing aft. A man held the woman tightly against him. He reached under his shirt and pulled a gun out. I immediately dove to the left, landing behind a large rock.

No shot rang out.

"Where's this road go?" I asked John as he reached me. The lights of the cart had disappeared over a rise.

"It loops back around to the beach," he said, breathing heavily. "But other trails branch off to go down to the caves on the south side and out to the cliffs on the windward side."

"Recognize them?"

"Not exactly," John replied, as we trotted up to the rise. The cart was gone.

"What do you mean?" I asked, standing there in near total darkness.

"There's a group out on the east end, sort of a commune. They all wear light blue clothes, sometimes just a T-shirt, but usually a toga-like thing."

"A commune? Like in the '60s?"

"They have a small one here, but the main camp is up on Tortola."

There was nothing we could do, so we started down the hill.

"I don't think that girl was with them of her own accord," I said, as we neared the main entrance to the restaurant.

"She was wearing the shirt," John said. "They're a weird bunch up there. Talking love and peace all the time, drug-addled smiles on their faces, but sometimes at night it sounds like a crazy orgy. There's a fence and sentries around the property, so you can't get close, not that you need to, with all the noise they make. Harmless hippies, mostly."

"The guy on the back of that thing pointed a gun at me."

"You sure?" he asked, as we reached *Pirate's Bight*.

There were a number of people milling around outside. Some were obvious locals, but most were visitors—all of them were young.

"I've had a gun pointed at me before, John. It was a Glock, either a 9mm or .40 caliber."

"Got that good a look, huh?"

"John," a young black woman called out, moving toward us. "What is going on out dere?"

"Nothing, Mitzi," John said. "Just that group from up on the cliffs."

Mitzi wore a black apron around her narrow waist, and a crisp white linen shirt over a black skirt, both amply filled. I assumed she was one of the bar or restaurant staff. Her skin was nearly as dark as her apron, smooth as polished obsidian. But her eyes were what caught my attention. Big, light-brown eyes, almost orange, with sort of a cat-like quality.

"What was di scream about?" she asked. "It sound like a child."

"You know how they get sometimes," John said, holding the door and motioning the others inside. "Screams, moans, laughs, all kinda noise."

"If you ask me," she said, following the others in and talking over her shoulder, "those people are possessed by di devil hisself."

Back at our table, I leaned over and asked John, "What about the gun?" The band hadn't started back up yet.

"There aren't any cops on Norman Island to call," he replied. "And just a handful up on Tortola. Guns aren't permitted anywhere in the BVI."

"Not permitted is a lot different than not found. I know of two people on this island who have guns."

Mitzi came over from the bar with two more beers. "Try dis, gentlemen." She pulled out a chair and joined us.

I looked at the bottle. It had a colorful label proclaiming it to be *Island Hoppin' IPA*, from St. John Brewers. The label showed a deHavilland Beaver similar to my own *Island Hopper* flying over the bay.

"I don't like those Onayan people up dere, John," she said. Then she turned and smiled at me. "I am Mitzi Lettsome, di manager."

"Where are my manners?" John said. "Mitzi, this is my friend Jesse McDermitt, out of the Florida Keys. We work together sometimes."

Her smile diminished slightly but was still bright. "You are a fisherman, too?"

"Only when I have to," I replied, taking a tentative sip of the cold beer. "Very pleased to meet you."

"Likewise."

"Why don't you like those people?"

"Gilbert Mashonay came here about three years ago," John said. "Bought a defunct tree farm. A self-proclaimed spiritual teacher."

"At first, he liked to throw money around," Mitzi added. "Handsome man, but he know it. It is not good for a good-looking man to know dat he is pretty. He bought a tract of land up on di bluff right away, and within a month dey start buildin'. One big house at first, den many small ones."

"Is that why you don't like them? Over-developing?"

"Dey just weird, I tell you," she said. "Strange people start to arrive soon after dat. Mostly young people, but a few older ones, too. Dey all have dat same far-away gaze as di *Myoo*."

"*Myoo*?" I asked.

"That's what they call him," John said. "I've heard some call him Onay; the last four letters of his name. I guess those are the ones closest to him."

Mitzi shrugged. "I looked on di internet. A *myoo* is a teacher. It means *enlightened one* in Zen Buddhism cultures. I think dey growing ganja up dere."

I chuckled. "Wouldn't be the first time somebody on one of these islands turned to that."

"True," Mitzi replied, with a knowing grin. Then her features changed. "But some of di people coming here to go to di Onayan commune almost need to be carried. Like dey was possessed by *jumbee*. I have a cousin in Road Town; a policeman. Dey found a woman's body last week up on Little Thatch. A woman with a blue shirt."

"Drowning?" I asked.

"He don't think so," Mitzi said. "Di woman was missin' her head, both hands, and both feet."

My new job was to look for situations where people were exploiting others or the environment. And this was sure starting to smell like one of those.

CHAPTER NINE

At a light tapping on the door, a slight man sitting at a desk looked up from the book he'd been reading. He removed his glasses and turned the book face down, placing his glasses on top. With dark brown hair, gentle green eyes, a lithe build, and slightly Asian features, he was a strikingly handsome man.

"Please enter." His voice was soft and serene, much like his features.

The door quietly opened and a woman entered. The pale blue sarong she wore was simple. It hung loosely, wrapped around her body just below her arms, and tied behind her neck. She walked quietly on bare feet to where the man sat at his desk.

"They have returned, Onay."

"And the new couple?"

"Resting quietly now with the others."

The man rose from his chair and came around the desk to where the diminutive, fair-skinned woman stood. He put his hands on her bare shoulders, and held her at arm's length, gazing into her ice-blue eyes.

"Very good, Sunna. You will see that they are kept sedated tomorrow. We can't have people just leaving because they think they want to."

Sunna Johannsdottir had been the man's personal assistant, secretary, and confidante for four years. Her responsibilities were many and varied. She oversaw the seven leaders of the multi-national sect, who in turn kept the people busy, happy, and productive.

"And the other new arrivals?" he asked the Icelandic blond beauty.

"They are acclimating well," Sunna replied, holding the man's gaze. "Six men and eight women will be ready to go to the farm in a week."

"Bring this new girl to me," he said, turning back to his desk. "I will meditate with her, and perhaps she can convey to the boy why they should stay."

"Yes, *Myoo*." Sunna turned and with a wicked grin, left the office.

Onay went back to his leather chair and picked up the book, replacing the reading glasses to balance on the end of his nose.

After a few moments, Sunna returned with the girl who had tried to leave with her boyfriend. The Reverend looked up as the two women approached. The younger one wore the traditional long, blue garment that all newcomers wore. It was lightweight, with short sleeves, a modest V-neck and three buttons. It ended just above the knees. She couldn't have possibly reached her twentieth birthday yet. A flower, still blooming.

"Please have a seat." He motioned toward the chair opposite him, then looked up at the tiny blond woman. "That will be all, Sunna."

"Yes, *Myoo*," Sunna replied. She moved the girl in front of the chair and helped her to sit.

The Reverend watched. The girl's eyes were heavy and stared down at his desk. No, not really at it, but through it to the floor, or perhaps the bare sand below the house. Sunna left and quietly closed the door as Onay continued reading.

After several minutes, he placed a small strip of blue linen in the book and closed it, placing it on his desk along with his reading glasses.

"What is your name?" he asked the young woman. His voice had a tranquil quality that immediately put most people at ease.

The girl blinked and she looked up, as if seeing him for the first time. Her eyes were soft and brown, what some would call doe eyes, but dull and unfocused. She was otherwise very pretty, with long hair the color of spun gold hanging across her shoulders in front and back. Her high cheekbones and erect posture spoke of a strong European lineage and good upbringing. Her hands were folded primly in her lap.

"What is your name?" he asked again, his voice still gentle and reassuring.

"Phoebe," she mumbled softly.

"Phoebe," Onay repeated softly, as if savoring the feel of her name on his tongue. He smiled, showing perfect white teeth. "That is a very pretty name. I think it suits you very well, Phoebe. Do you know who I am?"

Phoebe's eyes tried to focus but didn't quite get there. "No," she whispered.

"I am *Myoo*."

Again, the girl's eyes tried to focus, a vague recognition appearing there for just a moment. Then it was gone. Her hands moved to her knees, palms up, the tips of her thumbs touching the last two fingers in the *prana mudra* of ancient India. This *mudra* helped to activate dormant energy in the body and aided the awakening and enlivenment of the personal *prana,* putting one more in tune with the *prana* around them. *Prana* was the vital life force within all living things. Onay smiled.

The girl's eyes finally met his and her visage became noticeably calmer. "You are *the Myoo*," she breathed.

Onay stood and went around the desk. He took Phoebe by both hands, and delicately helped her to stand. "Come with me."

Leading her across the room, he stopped at a large, round mat on the floor. It was pale blue like the sky, soft, and thick. The mat was located in an alcove of the room, surrounded by a low, moon-shaped sofa, which was made of the same soft, blue material. Above the sofa's short backrest, clear glass rose, curved into the same crescent, from the sofa to the ceiling.

Beyond the glass were the rugged cliffs. More than fifty feet below the precipice was the dark, immutable sea, waves crashing against the jagged shoreline. The sea stretched out to the horizon, where it met the stars.

Releasing the girl's hand, *Myoo* stepped out onto the center of the mat. He turned so that he was looking along the edge of the cliff and extended a hand to the young woman. She stepped out onto the mat and faced him. Her features had calmed.

Myoo unfastened the loop on the shoulder of his simple blue *dhoti* and pulled the end of it down off his shoulder. With a gentle sweep of his arm, the floor length robe was folded, and he placed it on the couch behind him. He wore nothing under it.

Gently, Onay unbuttoned the girl's tunic and pushed it back off her tanned shoulders, letting it fall to the mat. "We will meditate now."

CHAPTER TEN

The sound of the anchor rode clanking across the rollers seemed loud in the predawn light. I'd decided to stay in the BVI for a day or two, which necessitated a visit to one of the ports of entry to the north. John still doubted that what I'd seen had been a gun. But I was certain of it, and something about the woman on the cart bothered me. Though her features seemed nearly catatonic, I sensed fear. I wanted to get to the bottom of this cult group, or whatever it was.

The nearest customs office was six miles north in Road Town, on the island of Tortola. I was leaving early so I could arrive there when the office opened at 0830, and hopefully be back by early afternoon. While there, I wanted to see the larger compound John had mentioned.

Mitzi had told me that the people within the compounds called it the Onayan Commune. They even called *themselves* Onayan, taking the last part of the name of their leader, Gilbert Mashonay. I guess it was better than Mashers. Everything she told me brought to mind the

Rajneeshee cult that had sprung up in Oregon back in the '80s.

The ride across the still waters of Sir Francis Drake Channel took less than an hour. Clearing into the BVI took longer. I used my real name and passport, as I'd done in Antigua. I finally found my way outside to hire a taxi for a tour.

"Do you know where the Onayan Commune is?" I asked the driver, as I climbed into the front seat of the van.

He looked over at me, about to put the van in gear. "You know someone dere?"

"Would I have to?" I asked, arranging my small backpack on the floor between my feet.

"You just don't look like di type who wants to go dere."

"I just want to see what all the hype is about."

"I know where it is," the driver said, dropping the van into gear, and pulling away from the curb. "But I tink dey won't let you past di gate."

The ride took nearly as long as the crossing, the roads getting progressively poorer as we went. After passing through Parham Town, the road turned north and became so rough I thought the van might lose a wheel. Or the nut behind the wheel.

Occasionally, I could see glimpses of the sea off to the right, as the road climbed and wound along the rocky eastern coastline.

"Di turn off is jus' around di next bend," the driver said. "Di gate will have people dere, and dey will not let you in."

I took a $100 bill out of my pocket and handed it to him. "Slow down once we're out of site of the gate and I'll jump out. Come back to the same place in exactly three hours and there's another hundred in it for you."

The driver took the bill and looked over at me, almost running off the road. "I tink dat you are a crazy mon. But I will do it."

As we passed the turnoff for the commune, I glanced over. The fence was set back off the road, but visible in places. Beyond the gate stood a small building. A man in a blue shirt leaned out of a window hinged at the top and propped open, watching us pass.

A few seconds later, I spotted a grassy shoulder on the left side of the road and pointed to it. The van slowed and I opened the passenger side door. Hitting the ground, I rolled across the grass and came up into a kneeling position. The van continued over a rise and disappeared. Hearing and seeing nothing, I scrambled into the jungle on the same side of the road as the compound.

I knelt in the damp earth and studied the fence before me. The barbed wire was supported by a post and I noticed that the top wire was wound around ceramic insulators—an electric fence. The three lower strands of barbed wire had no insulators, and I assumed only the top one carried a charge.

As I pushed down on the second strand, it gave just enough that I could carefully put one leg over the wire. I cautiously slipped my body between it and the electrified strand above, then pulled my left leg through.

Squatting on the other side of the fence, I opened my small backpack. I'd come prepared. In minutes, I pulled on a pair of dark woodland camouflage pants over my shorts and then a camo shirt over my T-shirt. I pulled off my worn Topsiders, stuck them in the pack and laced up my black jungle boots. Using water-soluble camo paint, I quickly streaked my tanned face with black lines to break up the outline, then pulled on my boonie cover.

Before leaving, I took a handheld GPS from my back-pack and marked my position. Then, moving off toward the south, I made my way slowly and deliberately toward the gate, so as not to make a sound, while always remaining out of sight. Having instructed Marine snipers and scouts in the art of cover and concealment during my last years of service, it came naturally.

The guard shack came into view, and I slowed my pace. I wanted to see if I could garner anything there before proceeding. If there was more than one sentry, they might talk amongst themselves.

I watched for a moment at a discreet distance. I heard no voices. Through the window, it appeared as if there was only one guard, a lanky man with long, blond hair and a scruffy beard. Cautiously, I moved closer. Regardless of what John said, I knew at least one of the Onayans was armed. It was highly likely that a sentry would also be armed.

Getting low, I moved closer still. A sound from across the main road froze me and I dropped to a prone position on the loamy ground, all senses fully alert.

The guard stuck his head out of the window opening again. The window was propped up by a stick wedged in the frame. That gave me an idea. Whatever the sound was across the road, the sentry dismissed it and pulled himself back inside.

Slowly, I crawled along the access road until I was twenty yards from the shack. I hefted a rock about the size of a baseball and watched the shack. The guard was looking toward the road where the van had disappeared fifteen minutes ago.

I threw the rock high over the shack, and it crashed through the bushes on the far side of the approach road then rolled through some brush for a moment.

The guard leaned out and looked in the direction of the sound. I quickly sprinted across the access road and dropped to the ground on the other side. Methodically, like a shark moving toward an injured fish, I crept toward the shack. When I reached the back of it, I moved around under the side window opposite the door, which faced the main road.

Hidden from view at the corner beside the propped-up window, I stood with another rock in my hand. After launching it across the road, I stepped out, poised and ready. When the guard stuck his head out, looking away from me, my right fist came down hard on the side of his head. He never saw what hit him and collapsed over the windowsill.

Quietly, I removed the stick propping the window open, dropped it on the ground below the unconscious man, and lowered the window on squeaky hinges, until the frame rested on the man's shoulders.

I proceeded around to the door and stepped inside. The sentry wasn't going to wake up any time soon, and if someone found him before he woke, they'd assume he'd dislodged the stick and the heavy window frame had struck him on the head.

A clipboard hung on a wall by the door. There were entries on the top several sheets; dates, times, names, and an occasional note. Most were logged at regular six-hour intervals—the changing of the guards. There were a few other entries at odd times, some with more than one name. Many of the names were foreign, but some seemed American. None were familiar to me. The latest was at 0557, with the name Ronald Olafson, who, I assumed, was the sleeping sentry. He was due to be relieved at noon. That gave me an hour. More, if my subterfuge worked.

Against the back wall was a small desk with two drawers. The top one held an old instamatic camera, along with dozens of pictures of different people, all dressed in the same blue clothes. I flipped through them.

No, they weren't *all* dressed the same. Each was wearing the same blue, but most were just wearing T-shirts. A handful included men and women wearing clothes with a little more style, eastern-looking garb.

A beautiful blonde with striking blue eyes caught my attention. In the margin at the bottom someone had written Sunna Johannsdottir, which I assumed was her name. Her features were straight up Northern European and the camera angle suggested she was shorter than the photographer. In fact, she looked no bigger than Boone's girlfriend, Emily Durand, from the sunk *Wavy Davey*.

Another picture was of a man with dark brown hair, wearing some sort of blue robe or toga. The word Onay appeared at the bottom. Gilbert Mashonay was a handsome man, with gentle features, green eyes, and an easy smile.

The pictures must be how a new sentry might recognize someone wishing to gain entry.

The bottom drawer contained a holstered Glock 34. So much for there not being guns on the island.

I unholstered it and checked the action. There wasn't a round in the chamber, though the magazine was loaded. It wasn't in the greatest shape either; probably hadn't been cleaned and oiled in over a week. Removing the slide quickly confirmed that. So much for readiness.

Underneath the gun were a number of black cloth bags with drawstrings, each big enough to hold a gallon of milk. There was little else in the shack.

Leaving the outpost, I moved along the side of the road, staying just inside the tree line but keeping the double ruts of the road in sight. It wound its way up a hill and soon, I could hear sounds. I crossed the road and continued up the hillside until I reached it again, switching back as it rose up to the top of the hill. I trotted across the road once more and disappeared into the lush foliage.

The sounds grew louder. I crossed the road one more time, where it began to level off near the summit. Finally, I could see a clearing ahead. It was a terraced farm.

Low to the ground, I crept from tree to tree, staying in the shadows. The crops directly in front of me were row after row of various vegetables. Then I noticed that every third row was a long line of dark green, leafy bushes. The wind shifted and I could smell it. Mitzi was right. They were farming marijuana. I knew the smell.

Further along, I noticed that there were several rows of small trees, trimmed to about thirty or forty feet in height. There were people working there, all of them wearing the same blue T-shirts the sentry and the girl on the cart had worn, as well as most of the people in the pictures. I moved steadily closer.

The workers, an equal mix of men and women, weren't busy in the branches, trimming or harvesting fruit. They seemed to be concentrating more on the trunks of the trees and the bases around them. A few of them were digging in the ground beneath the branches.

They looked like ordinary trees, similar to syca-mores, but with rounder, more pronounced three-bladed leaves. They grew like Japanese maples, with many thin branches reaching straight up for the sky, giving the tree the shape of a champagne flute.

Curious, I removed a small camera from my pack and took a few wide-angle pictures, then zoomed in close on the workers, to get photos of each one's face. I took pictures of the trees themselves, focusing for a tight shot of the leaves. The workers seemed to be carefully stripping small bits of bark from the trunks. My angle was a little uphill, so I couldn't really see what the others were digging for, but they all had wicker baskets.

Checking my watch, I saw that I only had about an hour to get back to the pickup point. I turned and started making my way down the hill. When I reached the road, I waited. The guard was probably awake by now, or his relief had arrived. I listened carefully but didn't hear anything, so I sprinted across the road and disappeared into the dense woods again. I continued down slope until I reached the road once more.

Hearing something coming down the hill, I made myself invisible, camera at the ready. Soon a golf cart came into view, being driven by a man who might have been the brother of Ronald Olafson. After it disappeared, I crossed the road and moved quickly down the hill again. Once more I had to wait until the cart passed.

Finally, I reached a point where the hill leveled off. Checking the GPS, I angled away from the road toward the pickup point. I could hear the cart arrive at the guard shack as I once more slipped through the barbed wire fence and hunkered down to wait for my ride. If he was punctual, he'd arrive in ten minutes. While I waited, I quickly shed my boots and camo clothes, dampened a rag with water and wiped the grease from my face.

The sound of conversation and laughter reached my ears. Apparently, the two guards were talking, though I couldn't hear what was being said. From their tone, it seemed the guy I'd cold-cocked sounded defensive and the other guy was doing most of the laughing. If they'd inspected their surroundings and weapons, they might have noticed that the firing pin was missing from the Glock. So much for situational awareness.

After just a few minutes, I heard the whine of a gasoline engine coming up the road from the north—the direction my van had disappeared. I was just about ready to stand and flag him down when I saw there was more than just one person in the van, and the driver was white.

It slowly rolled toward my position and I got a good look at the driver and the people in the back. There was another man in the passenger seat, but everyone in back had black hoods over their heads. Just like the ones I'd found in the guard's desk. I got several pictures as the van passed.

CHAPTER ELEVEN

"Sassafras?" I asked over my secure video connection. "You mean like tea or root beer?"

I'd waited until I was halfway across Drake Channel before contacting Chyrel, after first calling John and telling him what I'd found. Chyrel was our research genius, having formerly been a computer analyst with the CIA.

"Not anymore," Chyrel replied. "The FDA outlawed it after scientists found that it caused cancer in lab rats. Food and Drug was happy to do it, because of the trees' illegal use."

"What's illegal about a sassafras tree?"

"Safrole is an oil produced from the tree's bark and roots. It's used to make MDMA, a hallucinogen commonly called ecstasy."

I'd heard of the synthetic drug. It was common in the club scene, particularly in techno-music dance clubs. It caused a person to become more extroverted, even those who were typically shy or reserved, giving them an elevated sense of well-being, emotional warmth, empathy toward others, and enhanced sensory perception. In other words, a huge physical turn-on. But it was a dangerous drug; one of the possible side effects for the casual user was a trip to the morgue.

"Didn't know it came from a tree," I admitted. "I was under the impression that it was synthetic."

"It is," Chyrel agreed. "Safrole is just one of the ingredients. Need anything else?"

"Let me know if you find out anything on the people in the pictures I sent you," I said.

"I will. Facial recognition software can take a long time. Any idea on nationality or anything that could narrow the search?"

"A few of the names in the ledger seemed Northern European or Scandinavian."

"That'll help," Chyrel said. "There are cameras everywhere in Europe. I'll narrow the search."

"Thanks, that's it for now."

Reaching over, I closed the computer's video app, and returned the screen to the navigation chart. I was twenty minutes from Norman Island.

Marijuana and ecstasy? I wondered.

I had had my own personal dealings with pot and knew there were many different kinds—a far cry from the Panama Red and Colombian Gold that was prevalent when I was a kid. In my lifetime, grass had morphed into pot, which changed to weed, and was now called tree. I'd tried it once in high school and didn't like it. I'd tried it again three decades later and had gotten hooked. But I hadn't touched it in a few years now.

Today's pot farmers were a different breed. They wore lab coats, protective goggles, and gloves. They grew high-grade marijuana in temperature-, light-, and humidity-controlled labs with sophisticated irrigation systems. Much like my garden on the island. Under those ideal conditions, they grew various strains that had different effects on people. That made me think that the Onayans weren't growing it to compete with the high-end stuff, that was cultivated and sold in states where it was legal.

Maybe they had a lab for pot growing. If they did, and had the know-how, they could also make ecstasy right there on Tortola.

But to do what with it? I wondered, as *Floridablanca* continued to eat up the miles.

The BVI were a long way from the primary MDMA market—the streets and clubs in the inner cities of the United States and Europe.

This *was* just the sort of thing I'd signed on with Armstrong Research to do. But I didn't think it would be necessary to bring the vast corporate assets to bear. At least not yet. With any luck, I could make a difference all by myself. Or with a few friends.

Thirty minutes later, I piloted *Floridablanca* back into Bight Bay and approached the mooring field. I'd paid for a ball before I departed and had left my dinghy tied to it.

I tied off to the mooring ball and moved the dinghy aft, securing the painter to the stainless-steel rail next to the transom door. Then I went inside and retrieved my satellite phone. Minutes later, I pulled the little tender up onto the sand at *Pirate's Bight*.

The sun was hot on my back as I trudged up the beach toward the open-air tiki-style bar. There weren't many people around; Sundays were turnover days in the Caribbean. Flights loaded with sunburned tourists took off and returned later with excited people ready for a week of fun in the sun.

"Hello, Captain," Mitzi said from behind the bar as I walked in. She gave some instructions to one of the bar staff, then came around and joined me, carrying a cold bottle of water.

I thanked her for it and then asked if she'd seen John Wilson yet.

"Not since dis morning," she said, taking my elbow and leading me to a table in the corner. We sat at the same spot John and I had the previous night, overlooking the beach.

I took a long pull from the water bottle. "He was here this morning?"

"No," she replied. "I live in John's house."

"Oh, I'm sorry," I stammered. "I didn't mean to pry."

"Nothin' like dat," she said, smiling brightly. "At least not anymore. We just friends now."

I looked at her more appraisingly. She was probably twenty or twenty-five, but I've never been good at guessing a woman's age. John was in his late sixties.

Was she the source John had said found the terrorist cell's handler?

"You were right," I said. "The Onayans are growing marijuana at the compound on Tortola. Probably manufacturing MDMA, too. That's a synthetic drug commonly called—"

"Ecstasy," she finished, bobbing her head. "I know of it. It has become a big problem here in di islands." Her eyes looked suspicious. "How do you know dis?"

I took a shot in the dark. "When John said we sometimes worked together, he didn't mean that we fished together."

Her features melted into an amused smile. "You're armed?"

The question was a surprise, and I looked around quickly, expecting trouble. "Not at the moment."

Mitzi laughed. "I meant Mister Armstrong's Mobile Expeditionary Division. A.R.M.E.D."

That was the first time I'd heard it referred to in that way, but it confirmed my suspicion that she was part of the organization. "No, I contract with the operational readiness side of things."

"Same, same," she said.

"And you?"

She smiled and nodded. "Not directly employed. I just see tings and tell John or Mister Armstrong. For dat, I get a small monthly stipend. So, you went dere and saw what dey are doing?"

"Yeah. Rows and rows of marijuana plants and sassafras trees."

"And you know di ganja bush when you see one?"

I arched an eyebrow. "I'm no saint, Mitzi."

"Nor I," she said, with a knowing smile. "What is a sassafras tree?"

"It normally grows in the northeastern U.S. and southeastern Canada, west to Iowa and as far south as central Florida and Texas. Also, in some parts of China. It's not native to the Caribbean."

"What is it used for?"

"In earlier times, it was used to make tea and root beer," I replied. "But these days, the oil from the bark and roots is used in the manufacturing of ecstasy."

"Ah, dat would explain how it suddenly became easy to get here."

"Really?"

"I don't remember it ever being a thing in dese islands until about a year ago."

John mounted the steps and came toward us. I rose and shook his hand as Mitzi went back to the bar and brought another bottle of water.

John sat down and nodded toward Mitzi. "She's okay, ya know. Her and her cousin both have been on Jack's payroll for a few years now. You can speak freely around her."

I nodded. "Already figured that out."

Mitzi returned and sat across from us.

"So, whaddya have planned?" John asked after I'd explained things more fully and shown him the pictures.

"I don't know yet," I replied honestly. "In my past life, I was a door kicker. Any ideas?"

John leaned forward, elbows on the table, hands clasped together, and lowered his head. After a moment, he looked up and fixed me with his one eye.

"The woman's body makes things a little different," John said. "Normally, we'd put someone on the inside, gather evidence, pick up some intel, and learn their scheduling. Then get out and turn it over to the authorities."

"I hear a but," Mitzi said.

He nodded. "The taking of a life changes things. What if we got enough actionable intel to get the right person on a murder charge?"

Mitzi shrugged. "What do you mean?"

"There's no death penalty in the BVI or the UK," I said. "The trial would take years, and the killer would get three hots and a cot for the rest of his life."

Mitzi frowned. "Dat's a very cynical way of looking at it."

"Jesse's a cynic when it comes to the legal process," John said. "True, the killer's future would be considered luxurious compared to the future that dead woman has."

John sat back and took a deep breath. He let it out slowly. "But 'call it in' is what we're supposed to do in a situation like this."

"Call what in?" I asked. "The police up on Tortola have a body, not us. We have proof of ongoing criminal activity that might or might not be linked to the murder investigation."

"Always the maverick, aren't you?" He said it more as a statement.

Mitzi took his hand, and he looked over at her. "John, you know di Ministry of Natural Resources and Labour have been pushing for not just legalizing ganja but growing and harvesting it demselves."

"Yeah," John said, letting out another defeated breath. "Growing pot in the islands is almost a rite of passage and they're not gonna get more than a slap on the wrist for that. Their culture condones it, so that angle is out. I can see he's not gonna call it in anyway." He shrugged. "Try to expose them for making X?"

I grinned. "I'm thinking the smiling Buddha would frown on that."

"Ha ha," he said, in a mocking tone. Then he rubbed the stubble on his chin. "I wonder what Mashonay's immigration status is here in the BVI. He's American, right?"

"He has an American accent," Mitzi offered. "I met him once."

"If he did kill someone or was a part of it, you want to just throw him out of the country?" I was sure there was more to it than that.

"No, that's not where I was going." John placed both palms on the table, leaned back, and looked alternately at each of us. "It makes a big difference on how we approach things if he and his people are here as tourists or as religious workers."

CHAPTER TWELVE

Later that night, I sat on the flybridge to watch the sun go down. *Floridablanca's* stern swung lazily from northwest to west, depending on how the wind came over the island. The sun seemed to be heading toward the horizon right between the two extremes, so my view was perfect. It looked like it would probably disappear over Privateer Point on St. John, just three miles away.

There was a buzzing noise forward; a dinghy starting up and heading away from the beach. After a moment, it slowed, coming close to my boat. I turned in my chair and looked out over the side.

What was she doing here?

"Hello, Captain," Mitzi called up. "Do you plan to keep dat view all for yuhself?"

I went down to the cockpit and opened the transom door. When Mitzi neared the swim platform, I grabbed the line off the bow of her little jet-drive tender and tied it off on the rail opposite my own dinghy. She took my extended hand and stepped over.

"Is John okay?" I asked, wondering what she'd come out here for.

"John is always fine," she said, smiling up at me. "Dis is my one night off, and I saw you out here alone." She lifted a canvas bag that obviously had a bottle in it. "So, I came out to drink and watch di sun go down wit yuh. If yuh have glasses, we have a party."

"Uh, yeah," I said. "Head on up to the flybridge and I'll grab another glass."

A moment later, I returned to the bridge and found Mitzi relaxing with her feet up on the aft settee. I handed her a rocks glass, then opened the cooler. "Ice?"

"Just one, thank you." She opened the drawstrings on the bag and took a bottle out. "You strike me as a rum man. Am I right?"

"When I drink, yeah," I replied, dropping an ice cube into her glass, then sitting in the helm seat. "What is that?"

"Another Tortola cousin blends dis," she replied, turning the bottle toward me in the gathering darkness.

"Tortola Spiced Rum?"

"He starts with Cruzan dark," she explained. "Den he adds his own choice of spices, and ages it for two years. Try it."

After I poured two fingers into Mitzi's glass, she put her hand to the bottom of the bottle and continued the pour, filling the glass halfway.

I poured two fingers into my glass, neat, and took a sip. "That's pretty good."

"He makes his own recipe, too. But I tink his blend is better."

Looking over at her, I studied her profile as the sun shone full on her ebony face. Her eyes showed a mix of ancestry, as did her facial features. She had the high forehead and cheekbones of Europeans, both of which were more pronounced in the low-angled sunlight. Though not tall, her dark legs, bare except for her tight, white shorts, looked long, stretched out on the white sofa cushions.

"I like to watch di sun go down," she said. "In di winter, it is always over water from di bar."

"How long have you worked there?"

"Since I was twenty," she replied.

"That tells me nothing." I took another sip of the spiced rum. "Could have been two weeks ago or ten years."

She turned her head and smiled broadly, showing perfect white teeth. "Let's say dat I have been working dere for less dan fifteen years."

Early thirties, I thought. *A bit older than I'd guessed.*

The sun moved closer to the horizon. It was clear now that it would set beyond Privateer Point, but not by much. A slight swing to the north on the anchor rode would give us a water view, between Tortola and Saint John.

We watched the sun retreat from the sky, each of us lost in our own thoughts. It quietly slipped below the point and was gone. A moment later, there was a flash of light just a few degrees to the north of where the sun had disappeared.

"Was dat lightning?" Mitzi asked. "Just a little to di right?"

"I thought I saw a flash," I replied, still counting in my head.

Light travels so fast that it's almost instantaneous. There just wasn't a distance far enough on Earth that it wouldn't seem so. A flash of light 186,000 miles away would be seen one second after it was emitted. The Earth is only 25,000 miles around and standing at sea level, the horizon was only three miles away. So, a visible flash on Earth takes only a nano-second to reach the eyes. Sound, on the other hand, is much slower, taking nearly five full seconds to travel a single mile.

When I reached forty in my head, I heard a low rumble coming from the west-northwest, the same direction we'd seen the flash.

"Eight miles away," I said. "Might be a storm brewing."

"What is dat in kilometers?"

I ran the calculation in my head, almost before she finished the question. I'd worked with snipers and scouts from all over the world, so these conversions came naturally to me. "Almost thirteen kilometers."

"Di western end of Tortola is about dat far."

My sat phone rang on the console, and I picked it up. "It's John."

"Don't tell him I am here," Mitzi said.

I touched the *Talk* button and held the phone to my ear. "Hey, John. What's up?"

"Just a few minutes ago, there was an explosion on Little Thatch Island."

My feet came off the seat cushion and hit the deck with a thud as I sat up straight. "What kind of an explosion?"

"Not sure yet, what or exactly where. I'm listening in on the Royal Virgin Islands Police band. They have boats on the way to the west end of Little Thatch. That's where the call came in from. Isn't that where the woman's body was found last week?"

"Yeah," I said. "Keep me posted on anything you hear, okay?"

"Will do."

I ended the call and turned the helm seat around, switching on the chart plotter. Then I laid in a course for the west end of Little Thatch. It was exactly eight miles away, the line on the plotter pointing directly to where we'd seen the flash.

Mitzi put a hand on my shoulder. "An explosion?"

"Cops are heading there now," I said, not turning around. "Not far from where your cousin found the body last week."

"He didn't find it," Mitzi said. "Bryce went out on di call, but a young couple on dere honeymoon found di body."

"Call your cousin," I said. "See if you can find out anything about an explosion in that same area."

She took a cell phone from her pocket and looked at the screen. "Just one bar," she said, scrolling through her contact list.

Mitzi touched the screen and held the phone to her ear. "Bryce, dis is Mitzi. What is going on out on Little Thatch?"

She listened a moment, then said, "Yes, we know dat. Will you call me when you get dere?" She looked down at the phone and shook her head, looking at me. "Di signal is gone. But he promised to call. Bryce knows what we do."

"I assume he has a satellite phone?"

"Yes."

I opened the cabinet below the console and handed her my sat phone. "Call him back and tell him to call you on this number."

She quickly punched in the number and waited. "It is Mitzi again. When you find out anything, call me on dis number."

She listened a moment then said, "Yes, John and one other. It is his phone I'm talking on." Another moment passed as she listened. "Okay," she said and ended the call.

"What'd he say?" I asked.

"Dey already arrived. Di explosion destroyed di house di couple who found di body were staying in. Dey were outside on di beach and are okay."

"That's a relief. Why'd he ask about John?"

"Like I said, he knows what Armstrong Research is involved in, and he knows John."

"I don't suppose he said anything about what caused the explosion, did he?"

"He did," Mitzi said, a grave look on her face. "Di couple said dat a boat came close to shore and fired some kind of rocket at di house."

"Wait here," I said, rising from the helm seat. Without waiting for an answer, I scurried down to the engine room and took the main engine offline, then pulled the lever that engaged the dogs for the two Mercedes powerplants.

Mitzi was waiting in the cockpit when I climbed up through the hatch and into the salon. Seeing me, she came inside. "What are you doing?"

"We're going to Little Thatch," I said. "You have to come with me."

"What for?"

"We're going to take that young couple aboard, so whoever tried to kill them won't get another chance. Can you move the dinghies to the mooring ball and cast off?"

"Right away, Captain. I was born on a boat."

Going up to the command bridge, I raised the hidden panel, revealing the controls for the twin engines, and started them. It only took a few minutes for Mitzi to release us from the mooring ball, and then I quickly turned *Floridablanca* toward the bay opening.

A waxing crescent moon hung about thirty degrees above the horizon off to port. When Mitzi returned to the bridge, I brought the engines up to speed. We were soon traveling at twenty-five knots, across a sea that was nearly as tranquil as a pond. Not that it mattered. *Floridablanca* was all steel, including the cabin and pilothouse. She could bull her way through very rough sea conditions.

I checked the radar; there were few boats out on the water, none close. Most were stationary, already anchored for the night. Two boats were underway, one heading southeast, three miles directly ahead of us, and another heading away from us to the east, six miles off our starboard beam.

Switching on the AIS, I saw that the boat heading east was a sailboat called *Write of Passage*. The boat ahead of us wasn't showing an automatic identifier.

Floridablanca rode high when going fast. So, she wasn't very maneuverable at speed. Unlike *Gaspar's Revenge*, the old Seaton could roll if turned too quickly at high speed. That was the downside of her all-steel construction.

The boat ahead was bearing away to our starboard side, so I angled a bit more to the west, to allow plenty of room, but not so much that I couldn't see them.

"Open that top drawer to the right of the computer monitor," I told Mitzi. "There's a small black case in there; open it, and hand me the scope."

She did, and I powered the 3x night-vision scope on, raising it to my right eye. The boat was easy to spot, as it was moving at about twenty-five knots, creating a white wake and bow wave that stood out in the light of the moon.

"Take the helm," I said, stepping aside, but not releasing the wheel. "Keep us on the course the chart plotter is showing. I want to get a better look at that boat."

When Mitzi had control, I stepped out of the pilot-house and went forward, steadying myself against the low bulkhead of the Portuguese bridge.

Finding the boat again, I zoomed to full magnification and watched it. It wasn't a collision danger, but it was heading away from where we were going.

When it passed far enough and I could see the stern, there was no name there. It was a center-console about thirty feet in length, with twin outboards. Two men were standing at the helm.

Through the night optics, I could tell by the shade of their shirts that they were both wearing either light blue or pink T-shirts. I assumed the former.

CHAPTER THIRTEEN

I went back inside and took the helm again. As Mitzi stepped aside, the boat rolled slightly to port, throwing her off balance. I caught her easily around the waist and pulled her close until she regained her footing.

Mitzi put an arm around my shoulders and her other hand on my belly, stepping up on her toes, her mouth just inches from my ear. "I was hoping you'd grab me like dis up on di roof."

I was thankful for the low-level red lights in the pilothouse, as I felt my face flush.

"Yeah, um—"

On the nav-desk, my sat phone rang.

"You are a bull, Captain Jesse," she said, patting my belly and smiling up at me. "But dis have to wait. Dat's probly Bryce."

She picked up the phone and answered it without looking at the screen. Pulling it suddenly away from her ear, she held it against her breast for a moment.

Finally, she extended it to me. "It's John."

I held the phone to my ear. "Glad you called, John. Mitzi's cousin said someone fired an RPG at the house the couple who found the body was staying in. We're headed there now."

"Why is she with you?"

"Because her cousin's in charge of the investigation." I replied. "He's not likely to turn material witnesses over to a complete stranger. We're going to bring them to your house."

We arrived off the western tip of Little Thatch Island twenty minutes later. Three police boats were there, two on the beach and one just offshore, its engine bubbling quietly as it pointed into the slow-moving current. As we approached, the boat started moving toward us.

The house was smoldering; small fires still burned all around where it had once stood. There was little left to indicate a building had once been there.

"Call your cousin and let him know we're here," I told Mitzi, then pointed toward the demolished house with my chin. "I'd like to talk to him and the couple that was staying there."

She made the call, and a moment later, the police boat came alongside. "Drop your anchor here, Captain," a uniformed officer called over. "I will take you and Miss Lettsome ashore."

We were only in fifteen feet of water, so I dropped the hook. *Floridablanca* drifted back until I'd paid out ninety feet of rode. I locked the windlass brake and backed down on the anchor until I was sure it was secure on the sandy bottom.

A few minutes later, I stepped off the police boat into waist-deep water near the beach. Then I turned and helped Mitzi down, and we waded ashore together. There were three cops running a bucket brigade from the pool behind the house, dousing dozens of small blazes.

I knew from experience that the RPG warhead had been an HE round—high explosive. If it had been white phosphorous, there would be a lot more fire.

The concrete block and stone house had simply been blasted apart. There was little left but the foundation.

We approached two black men in shorts and button-down shirts—casual attire that signaled the island equivalent of plain-clothes cops. They were talking to a sandy-haired man and a woman, both tall and athletic-looking, dressed in shorts and T-shirts.

"Bryce," Mitzi said, as one of the men broke away and came toward us. "Dis is—"

"McDermitt," I said, extending my left hand, and handing him a card I'd taken from my shirt pocket. "Jesse McDermitt. I work for Armstrong Research as sort of a scout, you might say."

"He sometimes works with John," Mitzi added, glancing up at me for a moment.

Detective Lettsome turned my card toward the light from the flames, then put it in his pocket. "I could have guessed dat, seeing you come here in John's boat. I am Detective Sergeant Bryce Lettsome."

I shook his offered hand. "*Floridablanca* is mine now. John sold her to me."

"Ah, I see. You do di job for Armstrong dat old John Wilson used to."

"That's pretty much it. I understand this was caused by a rocket-propelled grenade. Lucky it wasn't WP."

The detective studied my face, then looked me over in the flickering firelight, pausing at the tattoo on my forearm. "Yes, I am certain dat is what we will find. What can The Royal Virgin Islands Police do to help Armstrong Research?"

"Actually, I think it's the other way around." He looked at me, puzzled. "The lives of your witnesses are in danger. Likely your life as well. Where do you plan to keep them?"

"Dey canceling di rest of dere stay and flyin' out tomorrow. If we need dem later, we bring dem back."

"Yeah," I said, nodding. "That's about what I figured. Think the people who did this might also come to that conclusion? Maybe have someone watching the airport? If an RPG did this, imagine what one would do to an airliner."

Lettsome looked quickly over toward where the house had once stood, then turned slowly to look at me. "A very good point, Captain McDermitt. I hadn't considered it. What do you propose?"

"Just call me Jesse," I replied, nodding my head toward the southwest. "John's house, up on the hill over *Pirate's Bight.*"

The detective looked out to sea. I knew what was going through his mind. No cop wanted an outsider taking over an investigation, or even contributing. Particularly civilian outsiders.

"We have another asset who will be here in the morning," I added. "They'll be safer there than on a plane or even in your jail."

"You seem to have a lot of knowledge about my case," Bryce said.

"Not really. Just looking at events and guessing what the next step might be. On the way over, I saw a boat heading away from here. Two men aboard."

"We saw dem on radar but had to get here first. Did you get di boat's name?"

"No name on the stern," I replied.

"Dat's too bad," Bryce said, motioning the other cop and the couple over.

"They were both wearing blue shirts."

His head snapped around. He knew what that meant. "How could you see di color?"

"I couldn't really," I said. "I saw them through a night-vision spotting scope. Everything's gray-green."

"Den how do you know dey were blue?"

"I've used the equipment a few times before; twenty years as a Marine sniper. You learn to recognize what colors the different shades of gray-green represent. They were either blue or pink. I'm guessing blue."

"It will be up to di Snyders, but I must first make a phone call."

"What's up to us?" the sandy-haired man asked, as Lettsome fished a phone from his pocket.

He was my height, with hair shorter than the trend—neatly trimmed. His eyes seemed to take in everything. The wife was only a few inches shorter, a tall six-foot, and very pretty. She had long straight hair, dark blond. They looked like typical, well-educated, intelligent professionals. But the man had a military or police bearing that was unmistakable.

"My name's Jesse," I said. "This is Mitzi."

We shook one another's hands. Both of them had firm, sure grips.

"Jerry Snyder," he said. "And my wife Alicia. Are you with the police?"

Lettsome turned away and began talking on the phone, his voice low.

"No," I said. "But we're here to help."

Lettsome returned, stuffing his phone back into his pocket after the short call. "You are to contact *Ambrosia* when you leave, Captain McDermitt." Then he turned to the Snyders. "I doubt dere will be anyting here you can recover. We have arranged a place for you to stay on a nearby island. Dis man will take you dere."

"I thought you said you were going to fly us home," Jerry said. "Our passports were in the house."

"I understand," the detective said. "It may be dangerous for you to fly. We think dese people targeted you."

"Why?" Alicia asked, clutching her husband's arm.

He turned toward her. "Because we found the body. We're material witnesses in a murder investigation."

"You're a police officer?" I asked.

"Newport Beach PD," he replied. "California."

"Then you understand Detective Lettsome's abundance of caution," I said, nodding toward the demolished structure, "about putting you on an airplane."

He looked toward what was left of their honeymoon getaway and I could see the realization in his eyes.

"Yes, I understand." Jerry looked back at me. "But you're not a cop?"

"Captain McDermitt works for a private research company," Lettsome said. "Oceanographic research. Dey do a lot of work in dese islands and are very well-known and respected by di Virgin Islands Police."

Jerry Snyder looked me over. "You don't look like an oceanographer."

"I'm not," I said. "An associate has a beautiful house built on the hillside above Bight Bay, down on Norman Island. You'll be very comfortable there."

"We were very comfortable here," Alicia said, seeming very distraught.

I gave her my most disarming grin. "Yeah, but it's not likely to be as comfortable a place now. You'll be safe where we take you."

"Okay," Jerry said. "But we don't have anything; just what's in our pockets. All our clothes were in the house—everything we brought with us."

I glanced down at Mitzi. "There are stores on Norman, right?"

She nodded and I turned back to the young police officer. "We can stake you."

"I don't take charity," Jerry said with fierce conviction

"It's not charity," I replied, liking the kid even more. "Let's just call it an investment in relationship-building between private enterprise and the Virgin Islands government."

Once we were back on Norman Island, John was waiting for us on the beach. It was almost midnight and everything had been closed for hours. Only the essential security lights were still on.

"Have you eaten?" Mitzi asked the Snyders when we landed.

"Not since lunch," Jerry replied.

"I'll open di restaurant." She moved toward the building as John approached the dinghy. He was carrying a large black box by a handle.

John glanced over at Mitzi's retreating form, then looked back at me curiously. "I got everything all set at the house." He turned to the young couple and extended his hand. "I'm John Wilson."

They introduced themselves and shook hands. "Y'all go on inside and have a drink on me. I bet you're still a bit shook up. We'll catch up to you in a minute."

When they left, John fixed me with a blinding stare. "What's going on between you and Mitzi?"

"Whoa, John. Back the boat up. She came out to share a drink, and that's when we saw the explosion. That's it."

I had no idea if this outburst was because of something between him and Mitzi or because he knew the extent of my relationship with his daughter, Sara.

"You see to it," he said, jabbing me in the chest with a thick finger. "You hurt Sara with your running around, and I'll make you cry, boy."

John was a senior citizen by any definition. *Except* physical. He was four inches shorter than my six-three, but we were about equal in weight, and he didn't carry any extra baggage. Definitely not a man I'd want to confront.

"John, I'm a one-woman man. Have been for quite a while now. My running around days are long gone. Sara and I don't talk about the future, but neither of us sleeps around."

"Be careful," he warned, cutting his gaze toward the bar. "That woman's a barracuda. No man can resist her for very long. And no one man can ever satisfy her."

I didn't quite know how to take that. So, I chose humor, recalling Mitzi's question about our employer. "Should I be armed?"

"And legged, too," he replied, grinning. "And always be ready to use 'em."

We went up the steps and I held the door for him. The Snyders were sitting at the end of the long bar and Mitzi was behind it, an apron around her narrow waist and her back to us.

"What's on the griddle?" John asked, placing the black case on the floor.

"You get picky in your old age?" Mitzi asked, without turning around. I couldn't be certain, but I sensed a bit of wicked humor in her words.

The two of us sat adjacent to the Snyders. "Only with the company I keep," John said, looking over at Jerry. "You were para-rescue before becoming a police officer, right, son?"

"How do you know that?" Alicia asked.

John ignored her question. "That's a very noble profession for a man who is worth what you are."

Jerry rose quickly from his stool. "Just who the hell are you people?"

"Relax, son. We're on the good side. I was Air Force spec-ops, too. Jesse here was a recon Marine."

There was no back-down in Jerry's eyes, his posture, or his words. "And that gives you access to my financial dealings?"

"No, it doesn't," I said, realizing where John was going. He was already trying to recruit the kid. "Like I told you, we work for a research company, but that's not all we do." I turned to John. "Were you able to track the boat?"

He nodded. "Had a friend out on the water fishing. The boat disappeared from radar around the eastern tip of Norman Island."

"What boat?" Jerry asked.

"The boat with the people who tried to kill you."

Jerry slowly sat back on his stool. "I don't get it. What kind of research company has this kind of ability and clout with the local police?"

John went on to explain a little about Armstrong Research, the valid research we did, and our reach. The Snyders listened intently for the most part and didn't ask many questions.

Mitzi turned and placed two plates in front of the Snyders, then went back to the grill and returned with two more, placing them in front of me and John.

"Sorry," she said. "It is di best I can do on short notice."

"Smells great," I said. "Thanks."

We all dug in. John swallowed a bite of his fish sandwich and asked, "What did Jack say when you called him?"

I shrugged, figuring that John had talked to Jack Armstrong since I'd called him to report what I'd found.

"He said to take a few days off and enjoy myself."

"And the new kid, DJ?"

"I asked for him to keep his appointment. He's cruising through the night and should arrive by mid-morning."

"Mitzi and I will take the Snyders up to my house. What're you going to do?"

"Mashonay would be on Tortola, right?"

"Yeah."

"Then I think I'm going to go see what the compound here looks like." I took my handheld GPS from my pocket and set it on the bar next to him. "Show me where to go."

"Technology will always be the downfall of lawbreakers," John said, taking the device and powering it up. "Same with terrorists, and any other ne'er-do-wells. No matter how smart they think they are, the good guys always have better toys." He handed the device back and lifted the case from the floor. "I got something else for you. It just arrived about an hour ago."

When he opened the box, I saw a large, black, full-face diver's helmet. Actually, it looked more like a mask than a helmet.

"What is it?" I asked.

"You've heard about those Google glasses, that you wear and they display information on the inside of the lens? This is the U.S. Navy's version."

I lifted the mask out. It was heavy, probably three or four pounds. Aside from the usual air hose attachment, there were a pair of water-tight electrical connections and a large mass covered with thick black latex above the face plate and on both sides.

"When you float your GPS antenna, or when you surface, this thing will connect via satellite to a whole suite of apps. You can even have a heads-up display of the underwater topography, based on latest NOAA charts and civilian data."

"Civilian?"

"GPS and sonar can be interactive. So many boats today are equipped with advanced technology. Charts are literally being rewritten every day based on readings from pleasure craft operators. When you have your sonar and GPS active on a single screen, the equipment is sharing topographical information."

I looked up at John. "You mean Big Brother knows everywhere I go, whenever my GPS is on?"

"Only when it's paired with sonar. And the sonar findings and location are the only information that's shared."

"What else can this high-tech mask do?"

"A built-in mic is able to transmit through the floating antenna to nearby encrypted receivers, or to an encrypted satellite. The signal can even be broadcast through the water for a distance of about 200 feet when the antenna is below the surface. It can be connected to an encrypted computer, and you can give voice commands, like, 'search *Floridablanca*.' Then the computer will read back the headline results. You can say 'expand' and it will read the whole page or whatever data you ask for, and it can show it to you on a heads-up display in front of your left eye."

I took the box and put the mask back in it. "Thanks. This might come in handy. Who else has these?"

"SEALs are testing them, as are Marine combat divers."

"Who the hell are you people?" Jerry asked.

John grinned at the younger man. "Just researchers," he replied. "We sometimes research illegal activity and report it to the authorities, too."

We finished eating, then Mitzi locked up. I walked with them around to the front, where John's four-wheel-drive electric cart was parked.

Jerry rode in front with John, and Mitzi and Alicia climbed onto the rear-facing seat.

"You get any sleep?" John asked.

"I dozed a little on the way back," I replied. "I'll be in and out in a few hours and can sleep after."

"You be careful," Mitzi said.

"I also put the location of my house on your hand-held," John said. "Come there after you scout out their compound. There's usually a lot of noisy activity there on Sunday nights. Keep your head down."

The electric motor whirred, and the rear tires lurched, breaking gravel loose.

A lot of noisy activity? I wondered.

CHAPTER FOURTEEN

The Onayan compound was a little over a mile away, as the gull flies. That meant nothing on a tropical island. The GPS showed a road of sorts, several of them, in fact. Each followed the natural contour of the island.

I threw my lightweight pack over my shoulders, pulled a pair of night-vision goggles over my head, and started off in the opposite direction from where John's cart had disappeared.

Once away from the ambient light of the restaurant and bar, the goggles settled down and I could see clearly, so I picked up the pace to a slow jog.

The terrain was rugged, much of it uphill or down; very little in the way of level ground. But the road was mostly clear of trip hazards. After twenty minutes, the goggles began to pick up a faint glow to the east.

Checking the GPS again, I saw that I was only about 300 yards from the compound and the road I was on looped around to the north when it reached the rocky eastern coast. I assumed the entrance would be guarded, just like the one on Tortola. The waypoint on the screen was on the road, near where the satellite image showed it ended. The road itself was only a couple hundred feet from the shore, so I made an educated guess on where the compound was and left the road, angling up a steep hillside. The other compound had a commanding view, so I figured this one would, as well.

When I reached a fence, I studied it carefully. It didn't appear to be electrified. It had four strands of razor wire, though. That was a little more dangerous than regular barbed wire if you got tangled in it. After putting my goggles back in the pack, I dropped it onto the ground on the other side of the fence, then easily climbed over the wire at one of the posts.

Donning the goggles again, I set out a little more slowly, working my way up the hill.

A woman's scream froze me in my tracks, and I squatted, looking all around.

The scream had come from the top of the hill, to my right. Seeing nothing moving or man-made anywhere around me, I started that way, crouched low.

There was another scream, a man this time. It sounded more like a primal yell. I could see light through the trees.

I unslung my pack and opened it. Pulling out a holstered Sig Sauer P226, I removed it and clipped the empty holster to my belt, behind my back. I flipped on the Sig's infrared laser sight and a bright dot appeared on the ground in front of me, invisible to the naked eye. Though I didn't have to, I pulled the slide back a little. There was a round in the chamber, ready to rock and roll.

Pulling the pack on again, I quietly rose and proceeded up the hill, staying among the foliage as much
as possible.

The light ahead began to dance and flicker, rising
and dimming in intensity.

A campfire?

I knew there was no electricity on this end of the
island, and I didn't hear a generator.

The shouting ceased and a man's voice resonated
down as I moved nearer. I couldn't yet hear what he
was saying, but his tone sounded instructional, as if he
were lecturing in a college classroom.

Finally, I had to get prone, as a clearing opened up
ahead of me. There was a small fire burning, with people
sitting around it in a semi-circle.

A man and a woman, both wearing what looked like
Roman togas, stood next to a table, their backs to me.
They were both fair-haired, but the woman's hair looked
totally white through the goggles. Probably a platinum
blonde.

Blondie's garment was a simple wrap that went under
both arms from the back, crossed in front, and was fastened at the back of her neck, like a halter. The man's
robe went under one arm and fastened at the opposite
shoulder.

On the table were an assortment of what looked
like plastic bottles and stacks of nested cups. "That's a
good start," the man said, turning toward the table and
picking up one of the cups. "But all of you must fully

purge your rage, not just one or two. We have something here that will help."

His accent was easy to recognize, though the Frenchman had obviously been speaking English as a primary language for some time; his accent was very slight.

The group all wore simple T-shirts, though longer than usual. They sat cross-legged, backs ramrod straight, and hands resting on their knees.

"The purging must be as a group," the blond woman said, addressing the people around the fire as if she were a loving mother. "Have no fear, this drink will do you no harm. To become Onayan, you must completely shed all your hostile thoughts and darkest secrets." She had an accent as well, but it was so subtle I couldn't place it. Eastern or northern European, maybe.

Frenchy took two cups from the table and handed them to the two people nearest him. "You must lay your hostilities and negative thoughts bare for all others to see. This drink will help you."

Blondie took two cups and handed them to two others in the group. "There are no chemicals or mind-altering drugs in this drink. That is not the Onayan way. It is made simply from the plants you have been so lovingly cultivating this past week."

I made a mental note to return during the day to find out what kind of plants they were growing here, as the man and woman continued to distribute the cups.

"Please wait until everyone has theirs," the woman cautioned, her voice soft and reassuring.

The area around the fire was covered in what looked like gym mats, for lack of a better description, only thicker. The group was sitting on the mats, which appeared to be the same shade of gray-green through the night-vision as the clothes they wore; a shade I recognized as blue.

Beyond the group were at least four small dwellings, smaller than my own house, each no more than forty feet long and half that in width.

Bunkhouses?

The group appeared to be about an equal mix of men and women, most of them young, but some my age. I counted twenty, plus the toga-wearing man and woman. None of them looked armed, and I couldn't see anyone beyond the group, due to the optics dimming the available light because of the brightness of the fire.

Very quietly, moving at glacial speed, I crept forward and to the left to a more concealed spot where I could see better. Finally, I was in a position where my head and upper body were concealed by the large leaves of a hand leaf plant. I disturbed an anole, which jumped to another leaf. The little lizard bobbed his head a couple of times and extended his red throat pouch.

Sorry to invade your bedroom, little fella, I thought, peering through the leaves, as Frenchy finished passing out the drinks.

I couldn't help but think of the Jonestown massacre, where nearly a thousand people, a third of them children, drank poisoned Kool-Aid or were injected with cyanide. That had been a cult also.

"Drink up, future Onayans," Blondie said, as she and the man also lifted cups to their lips.

Some of those in the group laughed nervously. Others took tentative sips, and still others eagerly tossed the drink down. Afterward, they sat looking around at one another, as if they all expected someone to do something.

The man and woman standing in front of the group reached up and undid the fasteners of their garments.

"You may now disrobe," Blondie said, letting hers fall to the ground.

She was silhouetted against the flickering firelight, which diminished the capacity of the optics whenever I looked that way. But not so much that I couldn't tell, even from behind, that she had a shapely body.

The man also dropped his one-piece garment on the mat. Several of the people sitting in the group pulled their shirts over their heads. A few seemed a bit shy, but soon they were all sitting naked on the mats.

"Within a few minutes, you will begin to feel the effect of what you just drank," the man said. "You will have an overwhelming feeling of liberation at first."

"At the same time," the woman added, "you will be completely lucid and in full control of your actions."

"The mats are there," the man said, spreading both arms. "Use them to release your hostility. Remember, you are in full control, so be careful not to hurt anyone around you."

A man on the far side of the group shrieked with rage as he leapt to the side and began screaming and pummeling the mat.

Soon, others joined in, shrieking and yelling at the tops of their lungs, all of them writhing around on the mats. Many struck it with their forearms. Some began to push and wrestle with one another, making no distinction between man or woman.

The two leaders walked around the group, looking every bit like wolves deciding on their prey. Frenchy moved in among the writhing and wrestling throng of people, grabbed a woman, and rolled with her onto the mat. Blondie did the same with a young, dark-haired man.

This insanity went on for over thirty minutes. Then, one by one, the participants settled down, lying prone or in a fetal position, some curled up with someone else, or with a small group of others. Several began to cry, their plaintive wails in sharp contrast to the anger and fury I'd witnessed earlier.

I did notice that the man and woman who seemed to be leading the group hadn't seemed to go through the same process of rage and anger. Perhaps they'd already purged themselves of "hostile thoughts and dark secrets," but in truth, they just seemed to enjoy wrestling with the naked group.

Frenchy rose and stepped away from the group, stopping now and then to kneel and speak softly with one of the people. He helped the female leader to her feet, and together they returned to the table.

"That was great," the woman said, somewhat out of breath. "Do you feel better now?"

There was a chorus of shouts in the affirmative as the group of people began to situate themselves back into attentive sitting positions. However, they were no longer spaced as they had been before. Some had paired up, others were clustered together in groups of three and four, sitting close and leaning on one another.

The man picked up a plastic bag I hadn't noticed and walked among the group, taking something from the bag and handing one to each individual, while the woman passed bottles of water out to everyone.

"You've earned this," I heard the man say to a group of four young people. The woman also stopped and knelt with some of the group, answering questions and offering her advice and congratulations. Those in the group treated her in a way that was somehow different from how they acted toward the man; an odd sort of reverence.

I watched as the people put what the man had given them into their mouths, washing it down with large gulps of water. I checked my watch; it was 0130.

I hoped the group would break up soon and leave the cleanup until morning. I wanted a sample of whatever they'd drunk and one of the pills they'd all taken.

Blondie and Frenchy also took one of the pills. After only a minute or two, a slow transformation came over the group. No longer alert and attentive, those on the mats began to touch one another, stroking and caressing hair and faces. They all seemed to be smiling—languid, flushed sort of smiles, almost lewd, but also empathetic.

The man and woman disappeared into the group, which soon devolved into what I could only describe as a writhing mass of humanity. The sex started out gently, couples and groups moving together and joining in a variety of ways. It soon escalated, as they threw themselves into it, often changing partners.

The little anole on the leaf by my head suddenly jumped off and onto a branch. As it scurried away, I heard the snapping sound of a dry twig behind me.

"Don't even think about moving, man," a male voice said, very close to my feet.

Then I heard the unmistakable sound of a gun's slide being cocked. Louder, the man behind me said, "Sunna! We have an intruder!"

The female leader lifted her head above the others, the young men she was coupled with, as well as the others seemed unfazed by the shouting. "Where are you?"

Realizing that I had only one chance, I took a calculated risk, hoping the sentry who'd discovered me had looked up at the woman's question. I rolled onto my back and kicked out with my right leg, using all my strength and focus. At the same time, my Sig came up and the little dot fell on the center of the man's chest.

There were two more snapping sounds; both sickening. One was the striker of his Glock as he pulled the trigger and the other was his knee. He dropped his disabled weapon and went down, writhing in pain from the severely dislocated knee. He was screaming like a wounded hyena.

Continuing my roll, I snatched up the gun the man had dropped, stuffed it into my waistband, scrambled to my feet, and made a mad dash toward the group around the fire. The blond woman called Sunna rose, three pairs of hands trying to pull her back down. I recognized her as one of the people whose pictures I'd seen in the guard's desk up on Tortola.

"Who are you?" she shouted again, though not very coherently.

Ignoring her, I sprinted to the table and grabbed the plastic bag from which Frenchy had been distributing the pills and stuffed it into my pocket. Then I picked up one of the unused drinks the people had drunk from.

Quickly, I ran toward the woods on the other side of the perimeter, trying not to slosh out too much of the contents of the cup.

Once in the cover of the forest again, I stopped behind a tree and looked back. The sentry who'd discovered me was still down, clutching his knee. He was out and would need a doctor. The group on the mats, including Sunna Johannsdottir, was now in a sexual frenzy, perhaps charged by the intrusion. Beyond what I'd read, I had no idea what the effects were of ecstasy, which is what I felt certain was in my pocket. But those people were now into a full-on orgy.

I quickly shed my pack and pulled a water bottle from one of the side pockets. Dumping the water, I poured the liquid from the cup into the bottle and put the lid on tight.

Spotting movement beyond the bunkhouses, I made out a man running toward the group, a rifle in his hand. A scoped rifle. It was time to get small.

I stuck the bottle back in the pocket and threw my pack over my shoulder. I didn't run headlong into the dense foliage, but I did pick my way quickly, and moved down the hill in the direction of the road, as fast as I could go while making minimal sound. The scope on the man's rifle was a worry, but it was long and slim, more of a hunting scope. It definitely wasn't equipped with night-vision optics, which had a much larger objective lens, and was overall shorter and bulkier.

The fence was no more than a five-second obstacle, and once I was on the road, I picked up my pace, knowing there were no trip hazards. They had an electric cart. Even on this rough terrain, it would be faster than my slow jog. So, I needed to increase the distance they'd have to search. No matter how powerful an enemy might be, if he spreads his assets too thin, he is vulnerable.

Night-vision goggles work great for what they're designed for, which is seeing in the dark. They gather and intensify existing light, through electronic means. But the wearer has tunnel vision; no peripheral vision at all. You have to move your head to look left or right.

Or down.

My right foot came down on a loose rock and my ankle turned outward, pitching me into a sideways dive.

I rolled with it, already knowing that the pain would reach my brain before I hit the ground, and it did.

Fortunately, I landed in a patch of sandy soil where no cacti was growing. I stifled a moan and rolled, protecting my right ankle as best as I could. The goggles flew off my head.

As if in slow motion, I rolled again, scurrying behind a gumbo limbo tree, where I sat down with my right leg out in front of me.

The pain in my ankle throbbed with every beat of my heart.

This wasn't good, and I knew it. I took a mental inventory and decided that, aside from a couple of scrapes, my ankle was my only injury. I reached down and felt it through my boot, gently moving it. The pain was intense, but I didn't think anything was broken, though the injury would definitely slow me down.

The moon had set hours ago, and the only light was from the stars. It was a clear night, but my eyes had yet to adjust from the night-vision goggles to total darkness.

Using a low-hanging branch for support, I stood and put some weight on my injured foot. The pain was sharp, but I could hobble on it.

My eyes were adjusting to the darkness, so I looked around for the NV goggles. I found them just a few feet away, but they weren't operating.

I felt the lens and didn't detect a crack or any other damage, but when I moved my hand to the switch to reboot the system, I found the small battery compartment open. The battery was about the size of a quarter and as thick as three of them, but it was gone. Without light to see by, I had no chance of finding it. I didn't dare use the flashlight in my pack. That would be worse than the tunnel vision of the goggles; it would let the enemy see me.

I was reminded of what an old friend and former platoon sergeant, had told me: "Tracers work both ways."

So does light.

Hearing noise coming from up the road, I scooted back behind the gumbo limbo again, stuffing the useless goggles into my pack. I looked up the hill and noticed light bouncing along the road. The cart.

The headlamps on the cart worked in my favor. Now whoever was in the cart could only see what the lights shone on directly, and they were still far enough away that they couldn't see me.

Moving as quickly as my bad ankle would allow, I stepped farther away from the road and found another— much larger—gumbo limbo. In seconds, I was twenty feet up in the tree, using mostly my arms.

When searching for something, most people have their heads down, expecting gravity to do its thing and what they're looking for to be on the ground. Duck hunters and anti-aircraft gunners look up. So do trained warriors. But I was certain these commune people lacked any kind of skill in that department.

Flattening myself against the tree's trunk on the side away from the road, I shielded my eyes, so as not to lose my natural night vision when the cart came by.

I heard it approaching, less than a hundred feet away, the electric motor whining as the tires crunched across the rocks and stones.

"Go faster," I heard a voice say. "He has to take this road—it's the only one."

"I'm going as fast as possible, brother," another voice replied. "Why weren't we told that Sunna was doing the initiation herself?"

"I don't know," the first man said. "But we gotta catch this guy. She'll be very upset if we don't."

The driver said something else, but they'd moved past my position and too far away for me to understand.

Sunna Johannsdottir was somebody of importance, that was for sure. The tone of their voices conveyed fear and concern, beyond simply anxiety to please a boss.

I had no way of knowing if they had other security people on foot behind the cart, so I waited a few more minutes.

Finally, I climbed down from the tree and looked around the base of it. I found a dead branch about five feet long and a couple of inches thick to use as a walking stick, so I wouldn't have to put all my weight on my right foot.

The darkness was still my ally. The Onayan security people needed artificial light to move about. They didn't really *need* it, but they didn't know that, and weren't trained how not to rely on it.

I was. Hundreds of Marines had gone through my night infiltration course in scout/sniper school during my last few years in the Corps. Maybe thousands. The kids in my neighborhood hated playing hide-and-seek with me. Except one. Billy Rainwater had taught me a thing or two about moving unseen.

The stars above provided enough light for me to limp and stumble my way down the hill, and the cart lights would alert me long before those security guys got close.

I moved down the road toward the bay. The guy in the cart was wrong, or at least I thought he was. He'd said this was the only road on this end of the island, but I remembered the GPS showing a cutoff road about halfway between the bay and the compound. But I didn't remember seeing it on the way up here.

I powered the device on, with the lighted screen off, and checked my position. The cutoff road was no more than a hundred feet ahead. It ran north, to the top of the ridge, then followed it west.

Hearing the cart returning, I moved off the road, uphill this time, and found cover behind a large rock. I chanced a quick look at the GPS again, zooming out. I was only half a mile from John's house.

Deciding to stay away from the road, I took a bearing on where his house was; almost due west. I looked up at the night sky and easily found Saturn, low on the western horizon. I brought the GPS up in front of me, aligning it with the ringed planet. John's house was right under it.

Hobbling along at the speed of mud, I chased Saturn west, safe in the belief that I was probably making less noise than any pursuer.

CHAPTER FIFTEEN

Gilbert Mashonay rose from his bed and went to his desk. The vibration of his cell phone had awakened him and the light on the phone's screen showed him where it was. He noted the time on the face before he answered it: after 3:00 am.

"We have a problem," Sunna said.

"What is it?"

Sunna was sometimes prone to dramatics, but usually not at this hour. She handled the day-to-day operation of things and was Mashonay's best pupil ever. She understood immediately the deeper meaning of what he was doing.

"Someone from the outside was at the Norman Island commune tonight. They saw the rage therapy and initiation."

"And?"

"Jason discovered him, but the man reacted violently. Jason has a broken knee. Whoever the man was kicked Jason when he found him watching us."

"Have you found this man?"

"He escaped on foot, Onay," Sunna said, "taking some of our product."

This piqued Mashonay's attention and he felt the beginnings of his own anger rising from the pit of his stomach.

"What exactly does that mean?" he asked, measuring each syllable as he looked back toward his bed. The girl from two nights ago still lay sprawled on it with another of the new girls.

"After he broke Jason's knee, he grabbed a plastic bag with several pills in it, and one of the cups with the rage potion."

"A local who needed a fix?"

"I don't think so," Sunna replied.

"Why not?"

"He was white; a tall man, wearing dark clothing with some sort of electronic device on his head to see."

Mashonay felt the hot rage building as he walked back over to the bed and gazed down at the two nude bodies tangled in the bedsheets.

"Find him," Mashonay said, and ended the call.

Both girls stirred. The one who had tried to escape two days ago had needed more intensive treatment and meditation, so she'd remained in his house the whole time.

What was her name? he wondered, as the anger over his operation possibly being discovered began to boil inside him.

This isn't a good time, he thought. They had product nearly ready to ship and he'd been told it was much better now.

Penelope? he thought, his mind running in circles. *No, it was Phoebe.*

The other girl, a very pretty Korean with long dark hair and almond-shaped eyes, had tried to leave earlier the previous afternoon. She'd been brought to him, as well. He couldn't recall her name at all. Or even if she'd given it. Not that it mattered. The two of them together made wonderful bookends.

The new girl moved her head slightly, her eyes opening. She gazed languidly up at him.

"*Myoo*," she said with a soft sigh.

Mashonay had his own way of exorcizing his hostility, and he didn't need any potion. He grabbed the new girl by the arm, jerking her toward him.

She whimpered in dazed confusion, as Mashonay reached into a small ornate box on the nightstand and stuck another pill in the girl's mouth, then forced her to swallow copious amounts of water.

CHAPTER SIXTEEN

They say the shortest distance between two points is a straight line. While that's true, it's not always the fastest way to get from point A to point B.

The terrain was just what you'd expect on a volcanic island; treacherous. And with a bum ankle and no light to speak of, I had to move very slowly. I was under no illusion of invincibility. A younger me would have plunged headlong, ignoring pain. But I'm not ten feet tall and bulletproof anymore.

I finally saw the glow from a window ahead and below me. The GPS indicated that it was John's house. I looked past it, where Bight Bay lay sprawled against the night sky. Though the sea and sky were both black as pitch, it was easy to tell where the horizon was—it was where the stars ended. And Saturn was about to disappear over it.

I thanked the Roman harvest god for his guidance and blessing, then started down the steep hill, picking my way carefully. I was glad to have had the forethought to wear long pants and boots.

Finally reaching the house, I crossed the small back-yard and approached the steps.

John's voice came out of the darkness. "It's about time you got back." He rose from a chair that was pushed back in the shadow of a cluster of banana trees. "You hurt?"

"Twisted ankle," I said, limping toward him. "What are you doing out here?"

"Heard the commotion," he said. "Came out and saw the Onayan golf cart drive out onto the beach down by *Pirate's Bight*. Figured you'd have to return a different way, and you being a Marine...well, I figured it'd be a straight line and you'd wind up in my backyard."

Shifting the walking stick to my left hand, I let John take my right arm and pull it across his shoulder. Together we made it up the steps to the door, without my having to put weight on the ankle.

The only light came from an oil lamp in the living room, where a large window looked out over the bay. Mitzi and the Snyders were sitting on an overstuffed couch and recliner.

"Mitzi," John said, "grab a bag of frozen peas from the fridge."

"What happened?" Mitzi asked, moving past us into the tiny kitchen.

"Twisted ankle," John replied.

"Bring him over here," Alicia said, moving toward the recliner Mitzi had vacated.

John and Jerry helped me into the chair and then John pulled the handle, sending it flopping back and ratcheting my legs up. The suddenness of the movement shot pain up my leg and I winced.

"Sorry about that."

Mitzi arrived, as Alicia carefully removed the laces from my right boot, and gently slid it off. Then she eased my sock off. Even in the subdued light of the single lamp, I could see that it was swollen.

Mitzi gently lifted my leg, placing a green and white bag on the footrest. "Slide up a little," she said, "and take di weight of your foot on di bag."

I did as I was told and she placed a second bag on top of my ankle, sandwiching it between two bags of frozen peas.

"Thanks," I muttered.

John produced a bottle from a cupboard and used it to point at my leg. "How long ago did that happen?"

"Three hours."

He uncorked the bottle and handed it to me. I knew it'd be rum and wasn't disappointed. I took a long pull on the bottle, letting its fire in my belly do combat with the fiery pain coursing up my leg.

"What happened up there?" John asked, pulling two wooden chairs from the kitchen.

Mitzi and Alicia sat on either side of me, attentive to anything I might need. Jerry moved over beside his wife on the couch, while John corked the bottle and placed it on the small wooden coffee table, then took the remaining chair.

"Well," I began, "you were right about the weirdness going on up there."

I went on to attempt to explain everything I'd seen, heard, and learned, even though I knew it sounded extremely far-fetched.

Pulling from my pocket the bag that I'd swiped from the Onayans, I tossed it on the table. "I'm almost certain that those are ecstasy tablets."

Jerry picked it up. "Yeah, looks a lot like the ones I've seen on the streets back home. Newport Beach doesn't have a lot of crime—very few murders. But there's plenty of night life and this is the drug of choice in the dance clubs these days."

He opened the green bag and took one of the pills out. It was bright pink. "A bunny," he said, turning it toward me. It had a cute little light-blue rabbit face with one floppy ear and one straight.

"Now that's just sick," I said. "A kid could find those." I motioned to where John had dropped my pack next to the chair Mitzi now sat in. "Pass me my pack, will you?"

Mitzi handed it over and I took the water bottle from the pocket. "This is what they drank before they all went nuts and started beating the mats, wrestling, and screwing each other. One of the leaders, a woman named Sunna Johannsdottir, said it would help them to release all their rage and hostility, and that it was made from plants they were growing there."

"Johannsdottir?" Alicia asked, pronouncing what I'd read the same way I did, like it rhymed with boater.

"Not sure if that's the correct pronunciation," I replied, then spelled it out for her.

"That's Johannsdottir," she replied, pronouncing it like daughter. "It's probably an Icelandic name. In their culture, children are given a first name only. They don't hand the last name down from parents to child. That woman's father was a man named Johann. Had she been a boy, the last name would have been Johannson."

"Learn something new every day."

"Any idea what's in that bottle?" John asked Jerry.

He picked it up and looked at the contents. "No idea," he said, tilting the bottle near the lamp, then unscrewing the cap and smelling it. The contents were milky white and somewhat oily, as it clung to the side of the bottle.

"Smells sweet and fruity," he said, putting the cap back on. "If I could get it to the lab, the tech guys could run it through the mass spectrometer and tell you exactly what's in it."

"A mass what?" I asked.

"Spectrometer," Jerry said, placing the bottle on the table. "It breaks down a substance to its basic ionic elements and provides a percentage-based report of what it's made of."

"Is that something all police departments have?" I asked. "Would Detective Lettsome have access to one?"

"I don't know," he replied. "I'm just a patrol cop, but I think those things are pretty expensive."

"You should get some rest," Mitzi suggested. "We can worry about dat in di morning."

I knew John's house only had two bedrooms. "I'm good right here," I said. "A blanket and another shot of that rum, and I'll be out like a light."

John went down the short hallway and returned with a blanket and a pill bottle in his hand. "Take one of these," he said, placing the pill bottle next to the rum. "It'll reduce the inflammation and the rum'll let you sleep."

I looked at the label: prescription ibuprofen. Then I opened it, shook one of the pills out, and washed it down with a big hit from the rum bottle.

Mitzi went down the hall and came back with another blanket, placing it on the armrest of the couch.

"You can have my room," she said to the Snyders. "I'll sleep right here."

I don't know why, but I'd assumed she and John shared a room. Mitzi pulled a blanket over me. I was very tired and in minutes, was fast asleep.

The smell of bacon and coffee woke me. From the angle of the light streaming through the back window and door, I knew it was late morning. Checking my watch, I saw it was 0930. I'd slept for over six hours and I don't think I moved an inch during that time.

Alicia was in the kitchen, her back to me. I removed the blanket that was covering me and discovered I didn't have a shirt on, and my other boot and sock had been removed.

The bags of frozen peas were gone, and my ankle had been tightly wrapped in a stretch bandage and taped up like a football lineman's. I didn't remember any of that happening.

I located my shirt, which had been neatly folded on the table by my chair, grabbed it, and then felt around on my right side to find the recliner's handle. I slowly returned the chair to an upright position, pulled my shirt on, and then, pushing with my hands, stood and put a little weight on my bad foot. There was pain, but it was tolerable. The tape seemed to completely restrain my ankle; I didn't think I could move it if I wanted to.

Alicia heard me and turned around. "You shouldn't be up. I think you might have a torn peroneal tendon."

"You're a doctor?" I asked, as I took a tentative step.

"Fitness trainer and physical therapist," she replied. "Sit back down. I'll have breakfast ready in a minute."

"Coffee?"

She poured a cup and brought it to me. "Sit down."

"Thanks," I said, taking a sip. I pointed to my bandaged right foot. "This your work?"

"Yes, I immobilized your ankle. It might only be a sprain, but we don't know. Replace that every couple of days for a few weeks to allow the tendon to heal. Now sit down."

"Where is everyone?"

"Mitzi had to go down and open up the restaurant," Alicia replied, turning back to the stove. "John and Jerry went with her to bring back your friend."

Friend? I thought. Then I remembered that DJ would be arriving this morning.

Taking one more step, I slowly turned and tested my ankle with more weight. She might be a therapist, but she was wrong. I'd once torn that tendon she'd mentioned and knew what it felt like. This was probably nothing more than a sprained ankle. It would heal, but I wasn't going to be running a marathon any time soon. I returned to my chair with my coffee. The smell of frying bacon was causing my stomach to rumble.

The coffee was good. Not as good as what Rusty served back home, but beggars can't be choosers.

"You're not eating?" I asked, when Alicia placed a single plate on the table in front of me.

She flopped onto the couch. "We ate earlier."

I reached for the plate, realizing that the bag of pills and whatever was in the water bottle were both gone from the table.

Alicia rose and went toward the kitchen. "This isn't how I wanted to spend my honeymoon," she mumbled, barely audible.

She was pissed—I could see that. "Getting upset over something you have no control over is a waste of time and energy."

"Excuse me?" she said, turning.

"You don't really think someone killed that woman and blew up the house you were staying in just because they wanted to ruin your honeymoon, do you?"

"That's really no business of—"

"You made it my business when you complained about it."

I'm not a big fan of complaining and couldn't tell yet if the woman was a spoiled princess or just misguided. Either way, there wasn't time for her to be crabby. That was my job.

"Look," I said, putting my fork down. "None of this is personal. I don't know you or your husband, and odds are after this is over, we won't ever see each other again. And I'm okay with that."

She started to say something else, but I raised a hand and stopped her. "You and Jerry might be in danger. Lettsome's murder investigation looks like it's tied to what we're investigating. Don't ask who Armstrong Research is, or what we do. Just consider us private investigators. Those who want to hurt you don't know us and don't know where we are. So, you're safe here."

"Unless one of those people sees us."

"Just don't go outside."

"Jerry's already down there. In public."

I'd wondered about that. Why did John need him along? Sure, he was a cop, and John was more than able to handle himself, but these people were using RPGs.

"Why did he go with John?"

"Chain of evidence," she huffed. "Now he's involved up to his armpits; lying to the local police."

"Lying? How?"

"Mister Wilson called the detective early this morning and asked about that mass spectrum thing. He and Jerry hatched a plan to tell him that Jerry had been the one who went and got the pills and whatever was in the bottle. The detective is on his way here."

"Wait," I said, putting the plate on the table and limping toward her. "That makes no sense. Even in the BVI, he would've needed a search warrant before that stuff could be used as evidence."

The front door opened and John entered, followed by Jerry Snyder, DJ Martin, and finally, Detective Lettsome.

"I see you're up," John said. "How's the ankle?"

I wheeled, ignoring the pain, and strode over to my friend and mentor. "What the hell is this chain of evidence crap?"

Lettsome dropped a bag just inside the door. "Calm down, Captain McDermitt. It was di only way to get di information about di pills and what was in di bottle."

"Relax, Jesse," John said. "We've done this before."

"Done what?"

"My father is di magistrate on Tortola," Lettsome said. "I called him right after John called me. He issued a surveillance warrant, based on di workings between di police department of Newport Beach, California and Her Majesty's police, here in di Virgin Islands. Dat was di only way we could get what you found into evidence."

"It's on its way to the lab on Tortola," John said. "We'll have the results in a few hours."

I glared at Lettsome. "You mean you know the evidence wasn't obtained legally?"

"It is di way we sometimes do things here."

I'd never really been averse to taking shortcuts, so long as all the players were on the same page.

I shrugged. "It's your country and your laws."

"How've you been?" DJ asked, stepping toward me and extending his hand.

I shook it and grinned. "Apparently knocked the hell out for the last six hours. How about you?"

"Doing well, brother," he replied.

While I finished my breakfast, John filled me in on his and Lettsome's late-night phone calls. Alicia still appeared upset, but Jerry didn't seem to notice. Maybe she was a drama queen and always upset about something. But I got the impression he was just inattentive.

"I agree with Officer Snyder," Lettsome said. "Di pills look identical to MDMA—molly or ecstasy—dat has been turning up around di BVI. But we have to wait for di lab results."

"Then what?"

"We raid di Onayan communes," he replied with a shrug. "If dey are manufacturing drugs, dey will be arrested."

"Just like that?" I asked. "Is your force capable of going up against armed aggressors who have rocket-propelled grenades?"

"Our police force is very capable," he said, but his voice belied his conviction.

"Okay, so we wait," I said.

DJ smiled. "Did I ever tell you I was an amateur botanist?"

I knew right away what he was getting at. John must have mentioned to him what I said about the drink being made from plants they'd grown. I'd planned to go back up there today to get pictures but that was before I was detected.

"They'll be on the alert," I said. "You'd never get close enough."

"Seriously?" DJ said, with a smirk.

Though he didn't look the part, with his long hair, very long goatee, and titanium lower left leg, DJ had once been with the Army's 82nd Aviation Brigade's long-range surveillance detachment, and had jumped into enemy territory more times than I'd jumped out of a perfectly good aircraft during my whole twenty years in the Corps.

"It's a hell of a hike," I said, glancing down at his leg. He was wearing long pants, so the prosthetic wasn't visible.

He looked down at my still slightly swollen and bandaged right ankle. "Yeah, well, I'm fifty percent less likely to do that."

CHAPTER SEVENTEEN

"Hold on, please," Detective Lettsome said, "I'm putting you on speaker, so I can write dis down." John and I both leaned forward as Lettsome put his phone down and got a pencil and notepad from his bag. "Go ahead."

"The pills are definitely MDMA," a woman with a British accent said. "A very high grade."

"And di drink?"

"The chemical breakdown is very high in sugar. Like an energy drink on steroids, yet the ingredients are mostly common juices or nectar from a wide variety of plants and fruits. Nothing illegal there."

"What plants?" Lettsome asked, as Jerry and Alicia came in from the back yard.

John put a finger to his lips and motioned them into the living room.

"You have a mixture of nearly equal parts of agave nectar, and juices from litchis, mango, and passion fruit. There are also traces of refined wheat and oats."

"Is dere anything unnatural in it?" Lettsome asked, scribbling in his note pad. "Any kind of drug dat would make a person angry?"

"Yes, but let's address the fruit cocktail first. That much sugar, even from fruits, could easily alter a person's behavior. Blood sugar would spike dramatically. The after-effects of that, if a person hadn't had enough rest, or was hungry, would certainly cause them to be very irritable."

"And di drug put in it?"

"We found trace elements of alpha-PVP."

That was one I'd never heard of and I gave Lettsome a puzzled look.

"What is dat?" he asked, with an equally bewildered expression.

"The technical name is a-Pyrrolidinopentiophenone," the woman said. "I encountered it once during a week-long mentorship in America. The street name there is flakka. It's a whitish to tan powder, similar to cocaine in appearance, or it can come in the form of a rough rock, like crack. It is a stimulant that causes the user to reach an excited delirium state. They will often hallucinate, and exhibit aggressive, angry behavior. In higher doses, it elevates body temperature to the point that the organs break down, usually resulting in death. The amount in the sample was very low. But combined with the sugar spike from the juices, anyone drinking it will almost certainly experience a nearly instant rage. It's short-lived and the crash afterward can cause emotional outbursts of sadness and uncontrollable sobbing."

"Thank you, Karen," Lettsome said, then reached for the phone.

Alicia stopped him, then pointed to the last two entries he'd jotted down.

"One more thing," Lettsome said. "Di wheat and oats. Thinking along the lines of making a person irritable or angry, is dere a connection?"

"There could be," the woman on the phone said. "Refined grains, which is what you have here, remove a lot of the essential nutrients of the grain. Good for an energy boost, but mostly empty calories."

Alicia nodded emphatically.

"Thank you again, Karen," Lettsome said, then picked up the phone and ended the call.

"Can you reach your friend?" Alicia asked.

DJ had left an hour earlier and was probably near the compound by now. "Yeah," I said. "Why?"

"Ask him if it's possible to see what they're feeding those people. I have a hunch it isn't much and probably a lot of it is high in sugar and grains, like bagels, crackers, and margarine."

I got on the sat phone and texted DJ, asking if he could call in. A moment later, he did so. I gave him the information the lab woman and Alicia had provided.

"I'm a half mile away," he said. "And I've got enough supplies to lay out for a couple of days, if need be. Might take that long to get an idea of their eating habits. Is it important?"

Alicia and Jerry both nodded. "Yeah," I told DJ. "We think it might be."

He agreed to stay on as long as necessary and would move up into a tree when it got dark.

We ended the call, and I turned to Alicia. "You seem to know a good deal about this. What should we be looking for?"

She looked down at my coffee mug. "That's your third cup. Coffee is a stimulant, just like sugar. What happens when you don't have your coffee?"

"Point taken."

"Then there's hunger and sleep deprivation, both of which can make a person irritable. Throw in the high sugar drinks and foods, and the drug use, and you have a boiling cauldron of negativity when the sugar high wears off. And the sugars found in most fruit absorb quickly. If they do this for a period of days, the mere suggestion of "blowing off steam" could send a person into a raging tailspin, not directed at any one person or thing."

I remembered what the man had said, as he and Sunna passed out the drinks. "Just after they drank it, the guy in charge reminded them that they'd be lucid and in full control, and that they shouldn't hurt each other."

"Lucid, perhaps," Alicia said. "In full control? Not so much."

"But with a week's conditioning of love, peace, and harmony?"

"That's brainwashing," Jerry said. "The same thing happened in Jonestown. How else do you get a thousand people to commit mass suicide?"

"Okay, so why the dead girl?" I asked, addressing the elephant in the room.

Everyone looked to Lettsome. "We haven't disclosed dis to di public," he said. "But we are treating dis as a murder investigation. Di limbs were severed using a saw."

"Could you tell what kind of saw from the kerf marks?" I asked.

Lettsome looked at me, surprised. "You know about tool marks on bone?"

"I found an arm once while I was out swimming," I said. "The ME educated me on how they could match the marks made on bone to the tool that made them."

He nodded. "Meaning we would need di tool dat made di marks—in dis case, a small chain saw. What kind is unknown, but it was definitely a chain saw."

I texted DJ. *Keep eyes and ears peeled for chainsaw.*

"So, why did the woman have to die?" I asked. "And why go to that length to make her body unidentifiable?"

"The body can still be easily identified through DNA," Jerry said. "If they have a sample to compare it to. But to answer the first question, it could be anything; she broke some rule, made someone angry, tried to escape, might even be a cover up of a natural death…"

"Or it could be some sicko," I said. "Someone who likes to kill and who found a way to lure the right kind of prey to him."

"Kidnapping for murder?" Jerry asked. "You mean a serial killer?"

Detective Lettsome only sat back, listening. But I could tell that he was processing everything, comparing it to his own thoughts, intuition, and suspicion.

"It would explain the disturbance outside the bar last night," I said. "The look on the girl's face was one of fear. I got the impression she didn't want to be there."

Being laid up made me edgy. I found my boots and socks and put them on, lacing the right one as tight as I could.

"Where you going?" John asked.

"Outside," I replied. "I don't think well with a roof over me."

Standing, there was little pain, but there was absolutely no mobility. It was like I had a metal brace on my lower leg. I could walk easily enough, but all my weight was being transferred from my foot to my calf through the stiff tape and my boot. Being unable to move my foot meant I'd lost my natural agility, if only for a while.

"You should be in bed," Alicia said. "You'll never heal if you don't rest."

Ignoring her, I stepped out onto the front porch. I'd suffered much worse injuries and continued the fight. But I'd also been younger.

I looked out over Bight Bay and beyond. I could see the rugged eastern cliffs of Flanagan Island, two miles away, surrounded by a ring of turquoise in a sea of azure. Bordeaux Mountain on St. John rose up in the distance behind it, clouds shrouding the peak of the dormant volcano.

John stepped out onto the porch. "What's on your mind, Jesse?"

"Heard anything new on that storm you told me about?" I began. It was a delaying tactic and we both knew it.

"Moved off the coast yesterday and kicked up a few squalls in the Cape Verde Islands."

"Low pressure?"

"Loosely organized," he replied. "The Hurricane Center said if it shows any development at all, they'll upgrade it to a depression."

"Tell me about the east end of Norman Island."

"Not much to tell," he said, leaning against a post. "Like all of these rocks, the east side gets the worst weather and surf, so nobody lives out there. It's rocky, with cliffs as high as a hundred feet above the break-ing waves. Fissures open inland, caused by runoff and wave action. There're no beaches, no piers, and no place to land a boat."

"But you said your friend saw the Onayan boat heading straight there."

He nodded. "There's a little bay with a sand beach on the south side. It ain't much, but a small boat could land there. It's a good half mile hike across rough terrain to where the commune is located. And that's only after you get to the top of the hill."

"What's it like underwater?"

John shook his head. "Steep drop off, mostly rocks, hardly any coral. Divers rarely visit that part of the island. Seas are too rough. Sharkers go out there at night, but it's illegal. Hammerheads feed in the deep current between here and Peter Island. Another reason divers don't visit."

"Hammer—?" I suddenly had a gruesome thought. "Wait! That's it."

I turned and went back inside, John right behind me.

"Aside from the missing body parts," I said to Lettsome, "did your pathologist find anything else unusual?"

"What do you mean? Dat's not unusual enough?"

"Humor me," I said. "What else did they find?"

Lettsome looked at me, then around at the others, before he answered. "Di doctor said dere wasn't very much blood in di body."

"Wouldn't that be normal after a decapitation?" John asked.

"It depends," the detective said. "When a person dies, di heart stops. If shot and dey don't die right away, a person could bleed out. But once di brain stops, di heart stops. Cut off a person's head or shoot dem in di head, and most of di blood stays in the body."

I spun toward John. "Got a chart?"

He hurried to the back bedroom and returned with a nautical chart, rolling it out on the table.

"The compound is here," I said, putting a finger on the eastern shoreline of Norman Island. Then I traced my finger northwest, to where the body was found on Little Thatch.

Lettsome leaned forward, looking at the chart. "Di prevailing current is to di northwest."

"Almost a straight line," I said, standing. "With nothing to stop a body from floating right up on Little Thatch from here."

CHAPTER EIGHTEEN

"I'm going with you," Jerry Snyder said, as John and I packed some supplies we'd need.

"No, you're not," I replied, without looking at him.

"You're still limping," he said. "You can't go it alone."

"I once spent more than a month alone in the deserts of Kuwait, son. Surrounded by the enemy night and day." Then I straightened and put a hand on his shoulder. "Besides, you're on your honeymoon."

"Yeah, well, the first three days were great."

I could understand the dejection the turn of events had caused him. He'd hoped the beginning of their marriage would be a series of wonderful, fun-filled days in the sun. At least they'd had three days, and his wife was still alive. Having lost my second wife on our wedding night, I knew his honeymoon could have been worse.

"Wouldn't be a bad idea," John agreed. "You're not at a hundred percent."

"Can't take the risk," I said, turning to John. "He's a cop, yeah. But he's way out of his jurisdiction here."

"And you?" Jerry said.

"I spent twenty years in the Marine Corps, doing just what I'm about to do now, infiltrating an enemy stronghold alone. Then I spent several more years with Homeland Security, teaching their operatives to do the same thing."

"That doesn't give you the authority to do what you're planning to do," Jerry said. Then he turned to Lettsome. "And as a police officer, you're just going to let him?"

"We have a long-standing working relationship with his employer," the detective said.

"Then hire me," Jerry said to John.

John rubbed his chin. "I'm not the one that does the hiring."

I already knew John was planning to recruit the kid. He had the background Armstrong was looking for.

I was planning to go ashore at the eastern end of the island, just to look around and see if I could find anything. If the body floated all the way to Little Thatch, maybe something with five digits had washed up on the rocks here, and the sharks missed it.

I looked Jerry over again. "You dive?"

"I'm certified," he said. "Made a couple hundred dives."

Turning to John, I said, "Call Jack. If it's okay with him, I'll take him along. If nothing else, just to keep the sharks away from me."

John went to the back room to make the call.

"How will we get there?"

"My boat's right out there in the bay."

"I looked at the chart," Jerry said. "Impossible to anchor, unless you have like a thousand feet of anchor line."

"I do, but we're not anchoring. John will drop me in the water and hang out offshore, like he's fishing."

Jerry looked toward the back of the house, his face a mask of concern, and then he leaned in close. "Are you sure? I mean, a one-eyed man in an unfamiliar boat?"

"John used to own her," I said. "And as far as the eye, or his *age* for that matter, you'll look far and wide to find someone more capable. Never judge a book by its cover, kid."

John stepped back into the living room. Mitzi and Alicia were out in the backyard, working in her garden.

"Here's the deal," John said to the younger man. "As a precaution, the company does background checks on just about every person one of us encounters, so we already know a great deal about you."

I knew what lay in store for young Snyder. John wouldn't have told him that if both he and Jack Armstrong didn't think Jerry would be a good fit. Since accepting the offer from Armstrong, I'd learned that John had been responsible for recruiting a lot of the operators Armstrong employed or contracted with.

"We look for a certain kind of person," John continued. "We prefer our operatives to be military- or police-trained. They gotta be bright and have good morals, blah, blah, blah. But they also have to be independently wealthy and have a desire to help others."

"What are you talking about?" Jerry asked, looking from one of us to the other.

"It's a job offer," I said. "A chance to make a bigger difference than you'll ever make in Newport Beach, even if you were to one day become the chief of police."

"I'm not looking for a *job*," he said. "I was just offering to help."

"Why?" John asked bluntly.

"Huh?"

"Why do you want to help? Mitzi didn't offer, and she's one of us. Alicia didn't offer either. It's a simple question. Why do you want to help?"

I knew that it was anything *but* a simple question. I'd seen the answer in a picture once. A snapshot someone took as they were evacuating one of the World Trade Center buildings, just before they collapsed. It was a picture of a fireman, facing the camera, moving up the stairs with all his equipment on his back, heading up nearly 100 floors. All the other people in the stairwell were moving down.

What made one person rush into a burning building, when others were running out? The reason was written all over the face of that young firefighter.

"I don't know," Jerry stammered. "I just feel the need to help out."

"Dig deeper, son. Why do you want to help out?"

Jerry looked from John to me, searching for the answer to a test for a job he didn't think he wanted. I saw the same look of resolve and determination that I'd seen in the young firefighter's face.

"They killed that woman," he said. "Nobody deserves what they did to her. They tried to kill us, to hurt Alicia. I want to understand why, and I want them brought to justice."

John scoffed. "That's right out of the police training manual. Sometimes, it ain't about justice. Sometimes it's about fixing things right."

Jerry gulped and stared out the back window where Mitzi and Alicia were tending the garden. Then I noticed a change; a fire in his eyes that hadn't been there before. "People who hurt others have no place in a civilized society," he said. "They're a blight on humanity that should be surgically removed."

John grinned, putting a firm hand on the younger man's shoulder. "*We* are the scalpel, son."

He went on to tell Jerry a little of what Armstrong Research did, both in the public eye and behind the scenes, even divulging the source of some of our funding—the U.S. government.

When he finished, John reached into his back pocket and handed Jerry an envelope. "You're on the payroll as of right now, if you want. Which, by the way, ain't much. We don't want people who do it for the money."

When his wife returned, Jerry took her to Mitzi's room to explain what was going on. I could hear them talking but couldn't make out their words. At one point, Alicia cried.

"Don't forget this," John said, bringing the case with the dive mask from his room.

I stuffed it into the top of my backpack. "Think he'll be okay?"

"Don't know about his seaworthiness," John said. "But that can be learned. I think he's got the heart, though."

A few minutes later, they came out of the bedroom. Alicia went straight to the kitchen and just sat at the table, looking out over the yard.

"You ready?" I asked Jerry.

"Yeah."

The chair scraped as Alicia got up. She crossed the room and hugged her husband tightly. "You be careful," she told him. Then she turned to me. "And you bring my husband back in one piece."

"We're just going to have a look around," I told her. "DJ's already sent pictures and information about what's going on in the Onayan compound. But Detective Lettsome needs more than that."

CHAPTER NINETEEN

Twenty minutes later, with the sun dipping toward the western horizon, John drove past *Pirate's Bight* and onto the beach. He slowly made his way around the beach chairs and stopped the electric cart next to my dinghy.

My ankle felt good. Not being able to move it was a big help. I wondered how it would be with fins. If push came to shove, I could just cross my legs and dolphin kick.

We quickly transferred everything to the dinghy and pushed it into deeper water before I climbed in. I lowered the engine and started it, and then John and Jerry got in. It wasn't far to where *Floridablanca* was moored and I kept the dinghy at a slow speed, so as not to attract attention.

We were aboard quickly, and after disabling the alarm, I opened the main hatch to the salon. "Go ahead and get her started," I said, handing John the keys.

I opened the lazarette hatch and started down the ladder, telling Jerry to follow me.

"This is a lot of space," he said, once he'd joined me.

Neither of us could stand up straight, but the aisle from port to starboard had shelves fore and aft, loaded with all kinds of equipment, spare parts, tools, and even canned goods. My passengers were always amazed at *Floridablanca's* storage capacity. The lazarette was pretty much the same size as the cockpit, and that was large enough for a picnic table for eight, with room to walk all the way around it. Lined with dozens of shelves and drawers, some removable, with additional hidden space behind them, I could outfit the boat for a four-man dive team to live off the grid for months.

"Ever use a rebreather?" I asked, taking one of the Draegers from a shelf.

"Went through the Air Force's combat diver training in Panama City," he answered. "But they phased it out soon after. I've only made a handful of closed-circuit dives."

"Simple, really," I said.

The two of us sat down on a bench as I explained the basics of how the Draeger equipment worked. The engine started, and a few minutes later, I heard the transmission drop into gear.

While John took *Floridablanca* out to sea, I put together the equipment we'd need, explaining what everything was for, and how to use each. Then we carried it up to the cockpit, staging each set separately. We tested one of the earwigs with the new mask, and it worked perfectly.

"You'll have to bend the bone mic a little forward on yours," I told Jerry, "and wear your mask slightly askew for the seal to cover the mic. But with the antenna that'll float behind you on the surface, we can communicate."

Wearing black Lycra suits, the two of us went forward to the command bridge. A quick glance at the chart plotter told me we were already halfway to the eastern shore.

"Head straight on out a half mile or so," I said. "Then turn and come back toward the spot where the compound is located. The boat will shield us from anyone watching when we go in the water.

"How far out?"

"At least a quarter mile," I said. I gave him an earwig. "Just give us the word."

I went to the watch bunk and raised the cushions, exposing a storage locker. After moving a couple of items aside, I pushed on the bottom and a section of it lifted up.

"Here," I said, handing Jerry a loaded Glock 9mm handgun. "We're only looking for evidence. This is just in case."

"And if they come at us with more than eighteen people?" Jerry asked, checking the chamber and sliding the magazine out. "Er, make that seventeen."

I figured he'd be at least familiar with the weapon. A lot of police forces issue Glocks.

"Don't worry about that," John said. "This old boat has more firepower than anything they have there."

"Really?" Jerry said, flatly.

I nodded. "Yeah, really."

Floridablanca was a lot more lethal than *Gaspar's Revenge* and *she* could deploy a .50 caliber machine gun or even an electric mini-gun. With all the extra room below *Floridablanca's* decks, I could hide and quickly deploy an arsenal. Rusty had once told me to never go out to sea unarmed. I might have taken his advice to the extreme. I'm a gun guy.

The eastern end of the island slowly passed by, as the sun fell behind distant clouds to the west. A little more than half a mile beyond the island, John started a slow turn to starboard.

When we were more than halfway through the turn, Jerry and I went aft and quickly suited up, keeping low behind the waist-high steel gunwale.

The sun, hidden behind the clouds, was disappearing over the horizon. Full darkness would be upon us when we went into the water.

"Nervous?" I asked, looking around the cabin at the approaching shoreline, now blocking the sun entirely.

"A little," he replied.

"Use that. Call it a sixth sense, nervousness, or apprehension—whatever. It heightens your awareness."

"We're 500 yards from shore, Jesse," John's voice said over the tiny speaker in my mask. "I don't see any movement on the cliffs."

I opened the transom door and stepped down onto the swim platform, fins in hand, and my mask dangling under my chin. It was bulky and heavy, but underwater, the mask would be nearly weightless with the air trapped inside.

Jerry stepped out behind me and we both leaned against the rail to put our fins on. My ankle ached a little, but the tape was doing its job. It would have to give a little, for my fins to extend and be of any use. I hoped it wouldn't present a problem, since it was a tendon on the side that was injured.

"Going to neutral," John said.

I pulled my mask up over my face, then turned and checked Jerry's full-face mask, making sure the bone mic was secure under the mask's seal. Outside, it could pick up vibrations through the mask, but his voice would be extremely muffled. When I heard the clunk of the transmission disengaging, I tapped him on the shoulder and stepped off into the water.

Turning, I saw Jerry right beside me, and together we kicked away from the boat, trailing our antenna tethers behind us.

"Clear," I said, once we were far enough away.

"Roger that," John said, at the same time I heard the transmission reengage, sounding much louder below the surface. "How's the ankle?"

"No problem," I said. "We're going to go deep. You won't hear from us for about five or six minutes."

"Roger that. Be careful."

Taking a bearing on the lowest part of the cliffs, I checked my wrist-mounted compass and we submerged

Descending, Jerry and I started toward the island. He swam next to me as I counted my kicks. I checked on him often, having never dived with the man. He seemed capable and confident, though diving with unfamiliar equipment.

We leveled off at thirty feet. The tape on my ankle wouldn't allow me to straighten my foot fully, but there was no more pain than before we went in. It was probably diminishing my speed per kick, but we were swimming right toward an island from 400 yards away. There was no chance we'd miss it. But old habits die hard, so I counted.

Switching on the topography generator, an opaque map of the ocean floor appeared in front of my left eye. It was like looking at the bottom with all the water sucked away. Though it was dark, I could "see" the bottom, all the way up to the shore. But the image didn't change as we moved through the water because the antenna was below the surface and out of contact with the GPS satellites.

The underwater terrain depicted on the heads-up display looked just as John had described, steep with deep fissures, the result of a long-ago volcanic eruption and eons of erosion.

Soon, the real bottom started to become visible in my right eye, lit in gray and black shadows by the filtered light of the half-moon. The bottom was totally out of sync with the chart. It was odd seeing the static topographic display laid over the real, but I quickly figured out where we were on the chart by identifying ridges and fissures on the bottom.

At fifteen feet, our floats broke the surface and the image in my left eye changed to one that was almost the same as the real thing. The GPS had updated on the float's new position, trailing behind me. It looked as if my left eye was looking at the bottom behind me, and my right eye, directly below. Still, I could see a lot of benefit in using the thing. Total black-out underwater ops would be one. It would eliminate the need to count kicks.

When we neared the shoreline, I could see and hear waves crashing on the rocks. I studied the terrain image in my left eye. There was an area a few yards to our left where the rise wasn't so abrupt.

"This way," I said.

Jerry's head jerked at the sound of my voice, probably unaware that we could communicate again.

I motioned with my hand and started swimming south, far enough from shore that the wave surge was barely noticeable.

Some fifty feet south, I turned and headed back toward shore. A small, sandy patch of bottom rose up toward us, littered with rocks and boulders; probably a recent mud slide from Hurricane Earl, which had passed just north of the islands only seven years ago. NOAA charts had been updated since then, but not to this accuracy. I silently thanked whatever boater had come by here with his sonar and GPS on.

The surge was strong as we settled to the sandy bottom in ten feet of water to remove our fins. The seafloor rose steeply, probably close to thirty degrees, and was littered with rocks of all sizes.

"Put your hands through your fin straps," I said, tapping Jerry on the shoulder. "One on each. Keep everything else on. Stay on the bottom until a receding wave touches your head, then scramble as high and fast as you can, letting the next wave push you up. Then look for something above you to hold onto when the wave breaks and leaves you high and dry."

Six-foot waves smashed against the rocks to either side of us as the low rollers met the relative shallows around the island and were pushed up higher. Just two miles to the southeast, where it was 1000 feet deep and still dropping, these man-sized waves might be mere ripples.

I went first. The sand was loose and shifting, and I had no way of knowing if the underlying jagged volcanic rock was an inch below it or a yard. Fortunately, we both had worn long booties under our fins that zipped up and had hard soles with treads.

Using rock outcrops and grabbing at an occasional loose boulder that tumbled downward, I pulled my way toward shore as the sandy bottom rose quickly. The surge got stronger with each wave, and I used it to move forward and upward. My head broke the surface and then my shoulders, as a previous wave receded. The next wave would be in a few seconds. Even before I felt the water rising, I scrambled hard, ignoring the flair of pain in my right ankle.

The wave lifted me, and I went with it, grabbing and pushing against anything for purchase on the loose sand. Then my head went under and I flattened myself against the rocks and sand as the wave broke against my back and washed me up the steep beach.

When the wave receded, I pushed off hard with my left leg. I spotted a ledge above and to my right, half covered in sand. I stumbled and dropped to my knees, then quickly came back up, reaching the ledge just as the next wave broke against the shore, crashing around me.

I rose again, adrenaline coursing through my entire body. I moved higher. The sand-covered ledge led upward at a sharp angle, giving way to rock, which had been cut away in places, creating a steep path with occasional steps.

"Look to your right when you surface," I said. "There's a ledge with a path leading up."

Looking back, I waited. Finally, Jerry's head and shoulders appeared as the water fell away below him. He moved quickly, climbing up the beach ahead of the next wave. When it came, it pushed him higher, from which point he continued to claw his way upward until he was on the ledge behind me.

"What a rush!" he exclaimed, though not too loudly. "You get to do this a lot?"

I motioned him upward and we climbed higher. "Not every day, but yeah, it's a rush."

Some of the old timers in the Corps had called it the *jazz*—that feeling of domination when you conquer something, or the sensation that comes from the high-intensity adrenaline boost of combat.

Finding a wide spot in the steep trail, I shed my shoulder bag, then pulled off my rebreather and mask, laying them to the side along with my fins and weight belt.

Jerry dropped his equipment next to mine, taking care to put the rebreather on top of the fins to keep the sand out. "Those steps in the rock aren't natural."

"No," I agreed, taking an earwig from a web pouch around my waist, and putting it in my ear. "You hear me okay, John?"

Jerry was still wearing the earwig I'd given him and nodded that he could hear me. Then he adjusted the web pouch around his waist, holding the Glock I'd given him.

"Five by five," John replied. "And I can see you, too."

"See anyone else?" I asked, knowing he had my night-vision scope.

"No, and no lights from higher up either."

Opening the water-tight shoulder pouch, I removed two pairs of night-vision goggles, turning one on and handing it to Jerry.

He pulled the goggles on and adjusted them to his head. He'd either used them before or was quick-witted. Probably both.

We reached the top, or at least a spot where the ground leveled out for a ways. We were on the edge of the cliff, a good eighty feet above the water. The terrain before us was grass-covered, with a few low bushes and an occasional small cactus here and there. It rose slightly toward the tree line about 100 yards away. Beyond that, the ground rose more steeply—to about 300 feet, and it was covered with denser vegetation. Up there was where the road and the compound were located. I didn't see any lights.

Turning slowly, the only thing I saw that was not a part of the natural landscape was *Floridablanca* chugging slowly into the current. I couldn't hear her, but through the night-vision optics, I could see the churning water at her stern.

There was nothing moving on the escarpment, aside from the leaves and fronds of the trees. We were alone.

"You go north," I told Jerry. "I'll go the other way. Look for any sign of recent activity."

I followed the cliff face, staying about twenty feet inland. I hadn't gone far when I came to the first fissure and had to work my way inland to get around it.

At the top, the ground was wet and muddy, barren of grass. Water dripped down into the shallow source of the crevice. Over time, storms, waves, and the constant drip, drip, drip, had weakened the volcanic rock, deepening and widening the chasm. The sandy shore where we'd made landfall, precipitous as it was, was probably created by the soil constantly raining down from here.

Working my way through the grassy field beyond the first mini-canyon, I came across a fire pit set back from the sheer drop-off by only ten or fifteen feet. The grass around it was trampled and worn. Pulling a glove off, I held my hand above the charred remnants of a campfire and felt nothing. I touched the end of a log that was at the center: cold.

"I found something," Jerry's voice whispered through my earwig.

"Me too," I said. "An old campfire, long dead. Whatta you got?"

"I don't know," he replied. "But I think you want to see this."

Rising, I turned and looked back to the north. I could see Jerry looking down at something before him. I angled toward the top of the fissure and hurried back, as fast as my ankle and the terrain would allow.

When I approached, I noted that there was a lot of disturbed grass. A large mat was arranged inside a partial ring of boulders, right next to a deep fissure. Next to it was a platform of sorts, cantilevered a few feet out over the deep crack in the rocks.

"What do you think it means?" Jerry asked, looking from the mat to the platform.

There was another campfire beyond the mat. I went over and felt it too. It was cold, as well.

"I don't know," I replied, turning and looking out toward the boat. "John, can you see any of this?"

"All I see is the two of you from about the waist up. You're too far inland."

"Move around so you can look up through this fissure."

Floridablanca turned and moved north for a few minutes. "I can see up into it a ways, but it looks like there's a dogleg. I can't see where you are now."

I made another slow turn. The slope we were on, though devoid of forest, save a handful of bushes and cacti, had no stumps or remnants of the tropical foliage that covered the rest of the island. It wasn't cleared intentionally but provided a great natural view.

I don't claim to be a geologist, but it was easy to see that a landslide had created this mostly flat area; a sudden huge shift of earth from higher on the steep hill. Perhaps it had broken loose in some long-ago storm.

Eventually, maybe in another fifty or 100 years, this area would be covered too. But I didn't think this change had occurred in my lifetime. Just long enough ago for vegetation to take a foothold.

Jerry moved over toward the platform. It had beams that extended across and then under the ground, where a massive boulder rested. There was underpinning bracing the platform out over the crevice.

"There's something below here," Jerry said, stepping out onto the wooden deck.

Moving around the top of the fissure, I had a better view, though farther away. He was right—some sort of structure was attached to the rock wall of the fissure, starting at the platform and angling steeply down. It ended abruptly over seawater churning at the base. But on this side of the dogleg it was invisible from the sea.

Jerry knelt and removed one of his gloves. He reached down and touched the wood at the edge of the platform, then rubbed his thumb and fingertip together. Then he rubbed his fingers on the edge of the platform and put his fingers to his nose. "Oh, no."

"What is it?" I asked, even though I already knew what the answer would be.

"Blood," he said. "Dried, but it's blood."

I hurried around to the other side, approaching the rickety-looking framework carefully. At the edge, I looked down, to see what the angled assembly looked like.

"What is it?" John asked over my earbud.

"Some sort of slide," Jerry said. "Maybe for discarding fish guts, but bigger."

I looked up to see a sturdy framework built above the slide. It made sense now. A big fish could be hoisted to the yardarm to drain the blood after severing the head. Once slick with blood, the head, guts, and everything else would slide right down to where the hammerheads would converge, drawn by the blood in the water. It was a chum sluice.

But it wasn't for disposing of fish heads and guts.

CHAPTER TWENTY

The inner circle sat around what looked like a normal conference table, with three pitchers of water down the center and glasses on silver trays. However, the table was only two feet tall, and everyone around it sat on plush mats and pillows. Another oddity was that the meeting was being held in the middle of the night. But not everyone worked dawn to dusk. Some worked dusk to dawn.

"The search continues," a young bearded man said, addressing the head of the table. "But we have little to go on. We found a place on the trail where the man slipped or stumbled. He dropped a battery of some kind when he fell. His tracks disappeared after that. Like a ghost."

"Keep looking, Ronald," Sunna said. "There can't be that many tall white strangers on the island."

The man nodded. Ronald Olafson had just moved up to head of security on Norman Island after his friend and predecessor had suffered a debilitating injury at the hands of the intruder.

Sunna turned a sheet from the stack in front of her over onto another stack off to her side. "Moving on," she said, looking toward the far end of the table. "Dante, the last shipment of 2000 kilos went out last week on time and actually arrived an hour early."

"Favorable conditions that night," a dark-haired man at the far end of the table replied. "We can't count on that happening all the time."

"But the customer said it was light again."

"We've isolated who is skimming," Dante replied, unfazed. "It is one of two people: the owner of the transport vessel out of the Abaco Islands, or the captain of one of the fast boats that comes out to meet the freighter off Miami. Both had fingerprints on this latest shipment. I'll talk to some people and try to isolate one or the other."

"It's a small amount," Sunna said. "Three kilos?"

"Three-point-two, Sunna," Dante replied. "About 10,000 pills. A street value of $250,000 in Florida."

"But it's more about the principle for you?"

At the far end of the table, the man's dark eyes smoldered. He nodded soberly. "Yes. If other outsiders in the network learn of this weakness, they may start stealing product as well. We can't have that."

Sunna turned the last page of the agenda over. "Bring them both to me on Norman Island tomorrow. I will learn which is the thief."

"The owner of the ship is a woman," Dante said, his eyes practically glowing with evil intent.

"Then you will stay after delivering them to me." Sunna turned to the others. "I can't stress enough the enormous importance of this endeavor. The capital this brings in will allow us to expand, to bring the word of Onay to more people. Already we are looking at property in the U.S. Virgin Islands for a new introduction facility, while work continues at our new headquarters in the mountains above the Sonoran Desert. The cash flow new followers bring us pales in comparison to what you people are doing. Thank you."

With that, most of the others, all trusted members of the upper tier of Onayan society, rose from their cushions and exited the room. Sunna turned her laptop toward her, checking numbers on a printed page against those on the screen.

Ronald Olafson and Dante Buccho stayed back and approached Sunna after the others had left the room. The tiny woman looked up at the two men standing over her, smiled and motioned them to sit.

"Thank you for taking the time to come down here tonight," Sunna said to Dante, as she leaned back on a lush pillow. "Dante, I want you to help Ronald get up to speed on security protocol *outside* the Norman Island facility."

"Yes, Sunna."

"Do you have something else?"

"A body was found last week," Dante said. "Up on Little Thatch island."

"Oh?" Sunna said, her ice blue eyes showing no concern.

"It is part of my job to listen and report," he said. "I asked Ronald to stay because I think it may concern him."

"In what way?"

Just then, something jingled in Ronald's pocket. He took his phone out and looked at it nervously. "It's one of our security people out by the cliffs."

"Take it," Sunna said.

Ronald touched the screen and held the phone to his ear. "Olafson."

He listened for a moment. "Hold on, I'm putting you on speaker." Then to Sunna he said, "There are intruders at the east end of the island."

"Who is it?" Sunna asked.

"I'm not sure," a woman's voice said, obviously a bit shaken. "I've called two others to my position. There are two men out by the cliffs."

"Anything unusual about them?"

"They're both tall," the woman said. "Dressed in black from head to toe, with some kind of mask thing over their faces."

Sunna looked up at Ronald. "Call out every person you can. I want them captured."

Ronald snatched up the phone. "Thanks, Erin." He ended the call and immediately made another, telling someone to get everyone up and go quickly to the cliffs.

When he ended the call, he turned to Sunna. "They will catch them."

"Back to the matter of the body that was found."

"We think it was that woman from last week," Ronald replied, nervous eyes averted.

Sunna put a finger to his chin, turning his face toward hers. "The couple that wouldn't succumb?"

"Yes," he replied, looking directly into her eyes.

"I thought they were disposed of in the usual manner."

Ronald swallowed hard, obviously hiding something from her. "They were."

"Then how did a body get discovered?"

"I'm sorry," Ronald said, Sunna's fingertip still on his chin. "We were rushed. I figured the sharks would still take care of her...after the boyfriend."

"How much time elapsed between the man and the woman?"

"About an hour," he admitted.

With a flick of her wrist, the fingernail of Sunna's index finger left an inch-long cut in Ronald's cheek, just above his meager beard. He flinched, but didn't put a hand to it, even as the blood trickled through his facial hair. Ronald's eyes showed terror as Sunna put a finger to his cheek again.

She delicately wiped a smear of blood onto her finger, then licked it clean. "Why did you wait an hour after disposing of the man?"

"It... it just seemed like... such a waste."

Sunna's eyes flashed. "I want to get this straight, Ronald," she said in a slow, measured tone. "Are you telling me that you killed the boyfriend in front of her, then had your way with the girl before disposing of her?"

Ronald hesitantly nodded, dread in his eyes at what she might do.

Sunna rose quickly. "I'm going to the cliffs. Dante, you come too, and send word to have the two suspected thieves brought down. I want them kneeling on the mat before me by dawn, as well as this tall man. We'll take care of him, his partner, and whoever is stealing our product all at the same time."

Ronald rose slowly. "Am I to come with you?"

At the door, Sunna turned, looking up at the two men, both nearly a foot taller. "Yes." Then she took a step closer to Ronald. "Forcing her to watch as you killed her boyfriend, knowing what her fate would be, was wrong. Next time, Ronald, do it in the right order. Let *him* watch."

CHAPTER TWENTY-ONE

After discovering what we'd guessed was some sort of an execution spot, Jerry and I spent nearly an hour searching both sides of the deep fissure with no luck. If any body parts got past the hungry sharks, they'd drifted out to sea. The shore was just too steep for anything to remain there.

So, with the moon setting off to the west, we swam back out for the pickup. That was where the new mask really made a difference. John was able to bring the boat straight toward our location, though we were ten feet underwater. He made his approach from the east, following the GPS signal until he could see the float right in front of *Floridablanca*.

When he stopped, Jerry and I clambered up onto the swim platform and into the cockpit, with the boat blocking anyone who might see us. Once aboard, we started to shed our gear.

"Keep your heads down," John said over the comm. "I'm seeing movement up on the cliff."

I quickly dug one of the night-vision goggles from my shoulder pouch and put it on. Three figures stood on the edge of the cliff. After a moment, several more joined them.

"I count eight," John said.

"Me too," I replied, as the boat motored slowly to the north.

One of the people on the cliff was much smaller than the others and wore a flowing robe of sorts, which caught the wind and outlined the trim figure of a petite woman. In the gray-green of the night-vision optics, her hair was nearly white. I'd seen her before. The woman who led the craziness at the compound, Sunna Johannsdottir.

We rounded the tip of the island and the people on the cliff disappeared as John turned the boat west.

"Just leave the gear on the deck for now," I told Jerry, as I kicked my Lycra suit off my feet.

Staying low, I entered the salon, continuing forward to the command bridge. Jerry was right behind me.

"That was close," John called back from the bridge deck. "A couple of those guys had rifles."

"Too close," I said. "But the boat was never in range of those hunting rifles."

"What do you think that spot they don't want anyone seeing is used for?" John asked, as we joined him at the helm.

I looked back somberly toward the high east end of Norman Island. "Executions."

"You really think that's what it's for?" Jerry asked.

"I can only guess," I said. "But it's very doubtful it's used for cleaning fish; the drain sluice is huge. Who wants to carry a giant grouper all the way up there to clean it? You're the one who said it was blood on the wood."

"I should have gotten a sample."

"Any word from DJ?" I asked John.

"He climbed up to hibernate for the night about an hour ago. Said he found a spot about halfway up the hill from the gate, where he can see the compound and the guard shack. He texted me a half hour ago that several people arrived at the guard shack and were quickly ushered up to the commune on the hill. Two were bound."

"Let's get back to your house. Is Lettsome still there?"

"He left just before midnight."

"You told him what we'd found?"

"Yeah, he went back to get a warrant. They're going to raid the place tomorrow."

"What time? We need to get DJ out of there."

"As soon as Bryce can get the warrant and get back here with more troops."

I sent a message to DJ telling him to leave the property as soon as it was prudent to do so and return to John's house. He had the coordinates.

When we reached the mooring field in Bight Bay, there was a boat at the small dock that I hadn't noticed before. A center-console with twin outboards.

"Keep your eyes and ears open," I said, bringing my dinghy to the stern.

I'd only slept a few hours the night before and was running on adrenaline for a second night. I felt like a horse that'd been ridden hard and put up wet.

When we reached the beach, we unloaded some food and drinks from *Floridablanca's* vast stores into John's cart to take up to his house.

"You go ahead," I told them. "I'm going to clean the gear and catch a few zees on the boat."

"Ankle okay?" John asked.

"Yeah," I said. "Call me when Lettsome is on his way here."

In minutes, John had the little electric cart headed back up the trail toward his house. I pushed the dinghy back out into deeper water and climbed in.

Once aboard *Floridablanca*, I rinsed the dive gear and took everything down to the lazarette storage, where I hung it up to drip dry.

The wooden platform and the long slide that ended over the water kept coming to my mind. Lettsome had said the body had been dismembered using a chainsaw. The gruesome part was that it wasn't the first time I'd encountered such abhorrent behavior in people.

As I sat at the laptop in the pilothouse, my sat phone buzzed an incoming message. It was from DJ: *Near the house. Something not right.*

I typed out the single word, *What?* And hit send.

Moving quickly, I pulled on pants and boots, again tightening the laces to try to immobilize my right ankle as best I could. It would be an arduous hike.

DJ didn't strike me as the kind of man who raised an alarm unnecessarily.

My phone buzzed again: *4 men, 1 woman, 2 carts.*

Sunna, I thought, as I quickly typed, *Armed?*

His response came immediately, as if he were already writing before I asked: *2 rifles, at least 1 handgun. too far away to engage.*

"Dammit," I mumbled as I went down to my stateroom below the pilothouse. I quickly pulled the bottom drawer out of the dresser and set it aside. It wasn't a deep drawer and looking behind it, you could see the hull curving toward the keel. At least, a casual observer would think it was the hull.

Reaching in, I pressed a small button on the inside face of the dresser and the "hull" rose up, revealing a space behind it.

I pulled the case out of its hiding spot and undid the clasps. It only took a few seconds to assemble the rifle and optics. I slung it over my shoulder and went to the galley, where I'd left the Glock and holster I'd given to Jerry. I grabbed my phone again, typing hastily, *On my way.*

In seconds, I was racing across the bay toward the beach, landing the dinghy hard at a spot nearest the path up to John's house.

I couldn't run and had to force myself to remain at a fast, limping walk. Halfway up the hill, my phone vibrated in my pocket. I took it out and quickly read DJ's message. *They left, took friends.*

Pushing harder, I tried to type on the little screen, asking DJ if they'd left John's cart. He replied that they had.

I was wearing night-vision, and the memory of the spill I'd taken was fresh in my mind as I hurried up the trail.

The pain was returning, too. I could feel the tape slipping. Having been submerged and stretched by my finning action, it was no wonder. I pushed the pain down, ignoring it, as I increased my pace to a slow trot.

This part of the trail was well-worn compared to the path that led up to the Onayan compound. I moved faster.

When I reached level ground near John's house, a figure emerged from the shadows. My handgun was up and leveled at him in an instant.

It was DJ. I holstered the Glock and moved toward him, limping. "The Onayans?"

"Bunch of hipsters in blue? Yeah. They took John and the others."

"Nine people on two carts?"

"Eight," DJ replied. "They left one man behind as a lookout." DJ lifted a scoped Winchester. "Can I keep his gun?"

Fortunately, John had left the keys in his cart. I turned it on and checked the battery level. Not fully charged, but close enough.

"Here," I said, handing DJ my phone. "Call *Ambrosia* and have them connect you to Detective Lettsome, wherever he is."

DJ made the call while I drove the cart up into the hills with the lights extinguished.

"He's coming," DJ said, handing the phone back. "But he's still on Tortola. Said he'd be here before dawn."

The cart kicked up stones and dust behind us as I raced eastward on the rutted trail. Soon, a glow became visible ahead; the headlights from the Onayan's carts.

I knew the compound was up the hill to our left, but the lights were moving off to the right.

"They're heading to the execution site," I said, trying to will the cart to go faster.

"We can't just go riding in there," DJ said, hanging on to the handle in front of his seat. "There's at least four, and they probably have reinforcements now."

"That should even out the odds," I said, through gritted teeth.

I visualized the gently sloping meadow where the platform was rigged out over the fissure in the cliff. I remembered seeing a large boulder near the tree line on the south side of the clearing. I didn't know if there was a path the cart could take, but that bit of high ground was the position I wanted.

The lights disappeared ahead and I braked to a stop, listening. I heard voices, but they were too far away to make out. I moved the cart slowly forward, the silent electric motor and soft all-terrain tires barely making a sound.

When we came around a slight bend, I spotted the carts ahead, stopped, nobody around them. Not two carts, as DJ had said, but three.

"This way," I whispered, getting out and grabbing my rifle.

I moved off the trail, picking my way carefully. I could hear the Onayans talking, giving orders. I could also hear the crash of the surf against the rocks below the cliff.

DJ and I moved stealthily just a little south of due east, and soon reached the edge of the clearing. The boulder I'd remembered was slightly to our right, so we moved that way.

Working our way up onto the large, flat rock, I took up a prone position, flipped up the front and rear sight covers, and turned on the optics.

The scene before me looked like something out of a movie. John, Mitzi, and the Snyders were being marched out to the area where the platform was. Two men with rifles walked behind and to either side, with the woman and another man leading the way. It was the same woman I'd seen leading the crazy rage-fest orgy, but a different man.

Beyond them, I could see four other people standing around a small fire; a black woman and three white men. One of the men looked vaguely familiar, but through the gray-green of the night optics I couldn't tell who he was. He was average height and build, a little flabby around the middle, with longish hair and a weeks' stubble on his chin. Both he and the black woman had their hands behind their backs.

DJ squirmed up next to me, an NV monocular at his eye. "Range is roughly 440 meters," he whispered. "Declination three degrees. A light wind on the nose, no value, maybe three miles per hour."

I made a slight elevation adjustment, taking into account the distance beyond what the rifle was zeroed at and the downhill angle.

"What's your plan?" DJ whispered.

"To keep any of our people from getting hurt."

DJ moved slightly as I continued watching. "It's an hour before dawn," he whispered.

"An hour before the cavalry gets here. Send a message to Lettsome and give him this location. Tell him there's a small, protected beach just to the south, where he can land his boats. Tell him this is going to be over before the sun comes up."

With the wind blowing directly at us, I could pick up an occasional word or phrase, as the two groups became one. The riflemen forced the four prisoners to kneel on the mat.

Then Sunna turned and faced the four who had arrived earlier. "One of you is a thief," I heard her say very clearly.

The black woman and the man I thought looked familiar both began protesting loudly, drowning each other out.

From their body language, I gathered that they weren't there voluntarily. That and the fact that the two men standing with them were both armed.

"Silence!" Sunna shrieked.

There was a change in the posture of the men who'd apparently brought the man and woman out there using the third cart. They both stepped away from their charges and drew handguns. *Five guns.*

"This doesn't look good," DJ whispered.

"Keep an eye on John and Jerry," I said. "If John sees an opening, he'll make a move."

"I wish there was some way we could signal them that we're here."

"There is. Tell me when John is looking at the woman wearing the robe."

With the rifle nestled in the crook of my left arm, and the reticles centered on Sunna's back, I moved my right hand from the grip to the scope.

"He's looking up in her direction."

Quickly, I switched the laser sight on and off, followed by three longer pulses; the letter J in Morse code.

When I moved the scope to our friends, kneeling on the mat, I saw John nod his head, then shrug his shoulders. He was asking me what I was going to do.

I knew that when I fired the first shot, the remaining Onayans would dive for cover. But they'd have no way of knowing where the shot came from. I could probably get one or two more before they zeroed in on my and DJ's location.

The dark-haired man Sunna had walked into the field with moved toward the black woman. Sunna said something and pointed at the man beside her.

The two guards with handguns pushed the man and woman toward the cliff. The woman went willingly, but the man seemed to be pleading, though I couldn't hear him at all.

"Who are those two?" DJ asked.

"Not my circus, not my monkeys," I replied. "My concern is to protect John and the others. Range me again. The two men with rifles."

DJ moved slightly. "Range to the nearest man is 437 meters, declination three-point-two-one degrees. Zero wind value."

I made the adjustment in my head. If I had to fire, the riflemen were top on my list. I moved the scope to Sunna and the others, now standing at the edge of the cliff.

My ears picked up the high-pitched sound of outboard engines, far away and moving fast.

The man was no longer pleading but now had more of an arrogant attitude. I heard him shout, "Do you know who—?" The rest was cut off by a crashing wave. As it receded, I caught the words South Carolina and attorney.

Couldn't be, I thought.

An old girlfriend and the mother of my youngest daughter, Florence, had an ex-husband who was an attorney and she was from Beaufort, South Carolina. I'd only met the man once, years ago, but the guy I was staring at looked similar. Except for his shabby clothes and unkempt appearance.

To her credit, the black woman stood with her back to the sea, head up, looking defiantly at Sunna.

Tactically speaking, they'd made a mistake in leaving the two long guns to guard our friends. I didn't see any sign of a handgun on either rifleman. In close quarters, a rifle is unwieldy and difficult to bring to bear, and the bolt action of the Winchesters required quite a bit more time to fire a second round, compared to the semi-automatic handguns the other three men had. The handguns were now too far from John and the others to be effective.

Sunna took the gun from the dark-haired man's hand, pointed it at the woman and fired. Before she went over the cliff, Sunna turned the gun on the man and fired again, sending him sprawling.

Moving my scope back to our people, I saw one of the riflemen shoulder his weapon, aiming it at Jerry. With only two rifles covering them, I made my decision. The M40 roared, splitting the quiet night air.

When the scope settled back to the group, I saw a mist explode from the nearest rifleman's back. I quickly racked the bolt, ejecting the spent casing, and putting another 7.62mm cartridge in the chamber.

The second rifleman hesitated, having heard the heavy report of my rifle. He looked toward the hillside far to our left as he raised his rifle in that direction. I fired again. When my scope settled back on him, the rifleman spun, dropping his Winchester. Apparently, he'd moved just as I'd fired or my aim hadn't been true, and my bullet had hit him in the left shoulder.

"John has the first man's gun!" DJ said, as the sound of the racing outboards grew louder.

I moved the scope to the others, out on the cliff. Even though my two shots had rung out in a matter of seconds, all of them seemed frozen, staring back at the fire pit. So much for situational awareness.

When I moved the scope back to our people, I saw Mitzi on top of Alicia, covering her, as Jerry jumped on the injured man who was reaching for his rifle.

In seconds, Jerry had clobbered the guy and was now pointing the rifle toward those on the cliff. "Police! Don't move!"

CHAPTER TWENTY-TWO

I t took several minutes for Lettsome and his police force to land the boats and climb up to the hilltop clearing. By then, Jerry and John had disarmed Sunna and the remaining two men.

The cops arrived at the clearing none too soon, as several people from the compound came rushing out into the clearing, shooting.

Lettsome's men fired back. So did we. Most of DJ's shots were merely for effect, as we were more than 100 yards from the group coming out of the woods. But he emptied the handgun's magazine and quickly inserted another. Lettsome was at least twice as far away as we were, but he had three men with rifles with him, plus John and Jerry.

The Onayans quickly realized they were not just outnumbered, but outgunned, and flanked between two forces. They were sitting ducks, and they knew it.

DJ and I moved quickly to cut off any retreat as the Onayans began to lay down their weapons. In minutes, it was over, and the cops began taking people into custody.

"Detective Lettsome," I called out, as DJ and I approached the group.

The police force numbered ten men, not all in uniform. One of the cops started to raise a rifle, but the detective put a hand on it.

"Ah, Cap'n McDermitt," he said, grinning. Then he nodded toward Jerry. "Your policeman friend told me you were out dere. I see dat he had things in hand before we got here."

"Well, before those others came out of the woods," Jerry offered. "I'm glad you got here when you did. I've never discharged my weapon in the line of duty."

Off to the north, another—much larger—boat was approaching the tip of Norman Island. Lettsome tapped one of his men on the shoulder. "Contact di boat and have dem anchor in dat little bay we found. Den start transporting dese people out to it."

Amazingly, none of the Onayans had been hit by the massive barrage they'd stumbled into. I know I was shooting at the ground in front of them, not wanting to hurt anyone who might just be an innocent person, brainwashed by the Onayans. As it turned out, Lettsome had given the same orders to his men.

"Four shot," Lettsome said, as he and I walked over to the edge of the cliff, where the man's body lay

The eastern sky was lightening, and the night vision was no longer necessary. I put the goggles away and looked down. The woman had gone over the cliff. Her body lay broken and twisted on the rocks below.

Detective Lettsome knelt beside the man and rolled him over. His lifeless eyes stared up at the stars as they winked out, one by one.

"Three dead," Lettsome said. "Dis one and di woman down dere were shot by di short blond woman over dere." He pointed toward his prisoners, Sunna standing at the front. "My men must have shot dose other two. Di ones with di rifles."

"That what the report's gonna say?" I asked.

"I know dis man," he said, standing and ignoring my question. "He is wanted in di Bahamas and in di States."

"Derrick Coleman," I said, hardly believing it was him.

Lettsome looked at me curiously. "You know him?"

"Not really," I replied. "Only met him once, many years ago. He was a slick, Southern lawyer then."

"I see," Lettsome said, as he looked over the edge again. "Dat woman down dere is probably Chandra Knowles. Di two were arrested here for running drugs, along with dis man's wife, Annabelle Coleman. From what I heard, she claimed innocent spouse status in di States, testified against her 'usband, and divorced him. Coleman was disgraced and disowned by his family. He escaped bail and dese two have been on di run since."

Savannah's ex-husband, I thought. *I should contact her and tell her. Everything.*

Savannah Richmond was the name I'd known her by. We'd had an affair many years ago, and she'd never mentioned a husband until the day she took off and went back to him, leaving me a note. I'd only met the guy once, briefly, outside a federal courthouse, where she and I had both been called to testify in a kidnapping trial. Many years later, I learned Savannah was also the mother of my youngest daughter, Florence. I'd debated for some time whether to tell Savannah that I knew the child was mine. Then about two years ago, the dead man at my feet had kidnapped Florence, thinking she was his. Fortunately, Charity Styles had been with Savannah that day and they'd gotten her back, exposing Derrick Coleman as a low-life smug druggler.

Lettsome and I returned to the group. The sun was beginning to peek over the eastern horizon and I suddenly felt immensely old and very tired.

The blond woman, Sunna Johannsdottir, stood with several others, all of them dressed in blue and hands cuffed behind their backs. She watched as we walked toward them, her eyes assessing me. They fell to my right forearm, adorned by the masked skull tattoo of my previous life as a recon Marine.

"You," she said. I turned to face her. "You were the one who was watching us. I recognize that tattoo."

She was shorter than most women and her robe did little to hide her abundant curves. A beautifully sculpted example of womanhood. Fair skin and hair, with pale blue eyes, the color of the tropical shallows. But her beauty stopped at the outside.

"And you're the one who grows pot," I said. "And makes MDMA for high school kids."

"I hope you got your enjoyment watching us."

"Not really," I said, as John and the others approached. "I just thought you were a bunch of really weird people."

"Can we go now?" John asked the detective.

Lettsome motioned us to follow him. I turned my back on the Icelandic beauty and walked away. She began to spew words so vile and disgusting, it would make a sailor blush.

In a blur, Alicia wheeled around, her arm extending outward, back-fisting Sunna and knocking her to the ground, while unleashing her own torrent of expletives.

Jerry grabbed his wife and pulled her away before she decided to kill the woman.

"Please," Lettsome said, "come dis way."

Jerry wrapped an arm around Alicia, leading her away. "I'm sorry," she said to the detective. "My kid sister died of an overdose. I... I just lost it."

"Do not worry about it," Mitzi said. "We have lost people to dat evil, as well."

When we were far enough from the Onayans, all now sitting on their mats and being guarded by nearly a dozen armed men, Lettsome stopped and turned toward us. "Thank you," he said to John. "But you know what has to happen now."

John nodded and turned to Mitzi. "You'll take care of my things? I'll let you know where you can ship them."

"What's going on?" I asked.

Mitzi hugged John and whispered something to him, then John motioned the rest of us to follow him.

"What's going on here?" I again asked Lettsome.

"You must go now," he replied. "Take one of der carts and never return to Norman Island. Nobody here knows who you are and it must remain dat way."

"C'mon, Jesse," John said. "This ain't the first time and it probably won't be the last. You need a first mate?"

Half an hour later, we arrived at John's house in two carts, where John grabbed a few things. Once outside, he hugged Mitzi again. "Why don't you stay at your little shack down on the beach for a few days," he said, nodding toward the Snyders.

She released the older man and he turned to Jerry, handing him the keys. "Stay here and enjoy the rest of your honeymoon, son. You can plug the cart into an outlet under the steps there."

"I don't know," Jerry said. "This doesn't seem right."

John shook the younger man's hand. "Sometimes it don't, son. Learn to embrace the suck. I own this house, free and clear. You and your new wife stay here for as long as you want. It might grow on ya." He gave Jerry a satellite phone. "I'm going to call you one week from today, okay? We'll talk about your future then."

Mitzi, John, and I took the Onayans' cart and drove to *Pirate's Bight*, where Mitzi hopped off the back without a word. Minutes later, John and I were climbing aboard *Floridablanca*.

"I don't get it," I said. Things were happening too fast for my exhausted mind to keep up with. "They're kicking us out of the BVI?"

"Not the whole country," John said. "Just Norman Island. It's an agreement we try to negotiate with host countries where we 'do business.' Bryce has asked me to leave Virgin Gorda, too. No big deal, Mitzi will handle the sale of my house."

I started the engine as John activated the windlass to retrieve the anchor. "So, where are we going?"

"Don't matter to me," John said, as he turned on the weather radio. The monotone voice recited local weather conditions for the Virgin Islands, then began the extended forecast.

At 0600 UTC, the National Weather Service upgraded the depression to Tropical Storm Irma.

"Ever been to Grenada?" John asked.

CHAPTER TWENTY-THREE

M other nature made our plans for us. John and I headed south, moving *Floridablanca* out of Irma's path, should she head for the northern Caribbean.

Situated only twelve degrees above the equator, Grenada and the southernmost islands of the West Indies are considered to be outside of Hurricane Alley, the path across the ocean from the coast of Africa that most Atlantic hurricanes follow. The southern islands rarely experience tropical storms.

At over 400 nautical miles, I thought it was a bit of an extreme move, but John said he had a nose for trouble and thought it might be a good place to stage the boat. It was about as far from the Florida Keys as you could get in the Caribbean Basin.

As we motored south, John listened to the forward-scanning passive sonar, as he usually did. Remembering the explosion of the sub and how the sound seemed to pulse, I asked him about it.

"It's all about differing ambient pressures and distance," he explained. "When something explodes underwater, it doesn't just blast outward against the water pressure. It pulses. If you slowed the explosion way down and could watch it, the gases would expand beyond ambient water pressure, then the water would push back against the still- expanding gases, shrinking them until that ambient pressure is passed and the gases push back out again. Slow it enough and you might see hundreds of micro-pulses within ten or so big ones. The pulse is far too fast to see or hear, but distance separates the different wavelengths of the sound the pulse makes, so passive sonar from a distance will register an explosion as a pulse. A good sonar operator can estimate the distance to the explosion based on the pulse rate."

John had spent a lot of time underwater at great depth, so I had to take his word for it. I filed the pulsing sound I'd heard in my memory as an underwater explosion, in case I ever heard it again.

By running the twin auxiliary engines, we made the crossing in a little over two days. On Guadeloupe, we stopped to refuel and stay the night, and had a surprise visit from Sara. John got a room in town.

Sara was gone when I woke up. But that's the way our relationship was. We made time whenever and wherever we could to just enjoy one another's company.

I called Jimmy and told him I'd be home in a few days, at least by Sunday. He was happy, since the dive trip with Peter and his photography crew and models had grown to include six divers, and Mac Travis wasn't available to help out.

Once we had *Floridablanca* secured at Port Louis Marina on the southeast side of Grenada, John left immediately for the airport. I knew he owned at least two other homes; I'd been to his little house in Coconut Groves. Or he'd said he owned others. For all I knew, Armstrong Research might own them. I didn't think it was the last time I'd see John. Nor Jerry Snyder, for that matter.

When I finally got to the airport, I'd already missed the last flight that would get me to Miami in time to connect to Marathon, so I got a one-way ticket to Key West through Orlando.

You could probably fill volumes with the names of people who'd bought similar tickets to that destination, but most were flying out of a far less hospitable location than the West Indies. Many of those same names could be found in other volumes of those who hitchhiked out of Key West, broken in wallet and dreams.

When I finally reached the *Rock*, as everyone calls the last island on US-1, it was nearly midnight. At the very least, you could say I was a bit cranky and my nerves were on edge.

It being a Saturday night, there was no shortage of people on the island, and since it was close to midnight, most would be highly inebriated and stumbling along Duval Street.

Leaving the airport terminal, I had several options. I could walk a few blocks to one of the resorts on the east side of the island, take a cab to a hotel near the docks on the west side and wait for Jimmy, or I could take a cab all the way up to Marathon, where I'd left the Grady at the *Rusty Anchor*, and sleep in my own bed. In about two hours.

I hadn't slept much in the last four days and my ankle was still sore, so I chose the fourth option and took a cab to the nearest bed.

The first hotel was full up, as was the second. At the Doubletree, they had two rooms left.

"How many nights?" the desk clerk asked.

Jimmy wasn't picking up the divers until Monday morning, so I told the man two nights. Why complicate things by going up there, when we were picking the divers up here?

"The only room available for two nights is a king suite." He looked disparagingly at my unkempt appearance and single backpack. "Will that do?"

"Yeah," I replied, sliding my AmEx Black Card across the counter. His attitude changed instantly.

I intended to sleep through the next day if possible. When I got into my room, I dumped my backpack on the bed and turned the TV on while I got ready for a shower.

The default guide channel on the TV had a small corner screen showing a satellite loop of what looked like a very big storm.

I found the Weather Channel and turned up the volume. The same loop was playing there and the reporter said Category-3 Hurricane Irma was still traveling west-southwest and was centered 689 miles due east of the island of Antigua.

Stripped of my shirt, and with one shoe still on, I sat down on the bed and watched. If Irma continued on its course, it would pass within a few hundred miles of Grenada and *Floridablanca*.

Hurricanes rarely move south of a westerly course for very long, and eventually they all turn north. So, I wasn't overly concerned; it was still hundreds of miles from making landfall.

The current conditions report changed abruptly to the projected path, or the cone of uncertainty, as the forecasters liked to call it. The cone spread out, curving more westerly, then turned toward the west-northwest. The Virgin Islands was in the middle of the cone, but the storm was still at least three days from making land-fall there.

There was no doubt that Irma was going to strike land, and it would do so somewhere in a 400-mile stretch of the island chain I'd just left. As at least a Cat-4 storm, with sustained winds exceeding 130 mph.

In dramatic fashion, the illustration zoomed out, with the twirling red dot representing Hurricane Irma moving to the bottom right of the screen. The forecaster drew a straight line from the end of the cone to Key West, then faced the camera. "After that, it's anyone's guess, but as you can see, south Florida may feel the effects of Hurricane Irma before this is all over."

Irma. It had that kind of name. The bad ones always did. A name that's heavy on the tongue; Hugo, Camille, Andrew, Katrina. Ominous-sounding names. Or did the names become ominous in the collective consciousness of those who live by the sea because of the devastation brought by the storms that bore those names?

I continued to watch as I absently kicked my other shoe off. The forecast predicted favorable conditions for further intensification, and the Hurricane Center had already sent out reconnaissance aircraft, recording a barometric pressure lower than any storm in the last ten years.

My whole body slumped and my eyes grew heavy as I watched the satellite loop again. I didn't need anyone to tell me this was going to be a bad blow. Wherever Irma ended up, death and destruction would be left in her wake.

After fifteen minutes of watching the reports, I turned off the TV, showered, and went to bed. I turned on the radio, knowing the background noise outside would be a distraction come morning. I moved the knob around until it landed on a song I recognized; Eric Stone singing the classic Crosby, Stills, and Nash song, *Southern Cross.* Good to hear that Eric was getting airtime. As I fell asleep, the station identified itself as *Pyrate Radio.*

When I awoke, I was still tired. And starving..I looked at my watch, and even though it was close to noon, the room was dark, thanks to the heavy drapes over the sliding glass door to the balcony. I called room service for breakfast and turned on the TV.

The storm forecast hadn't changed much, except the turn to the west had begun, and the cone now turned more northerly. The forecaster last night hadn't been far off the mark; if Irma followed the course they were now predicting, it would definitely bring bad weather to South Florida.

After a noon breakfast, I opened the drapes and looked out on the courtyard and pool far below. There were a few people in the water, and several more lying on chaise lounges around it, all enjoying the late summer sun.

My phone rang and I dug around in my backpack until I found it. The ID said it was Jimmy, so I answered.

"Where are you, *mi capitan*?"

"I'm in Key West," I replied. "Couldn't catch the shuttle to Marathon yesterday."

"Heard about this storm?"

"Yeah, it doesn't look good for the Leewards."

"You made a plan for if it heads this way, man?"

I sat down hard on the bed. "I was just thinking about that," I replied. "It's still way too far away to implement any plans—you know that."

"Yeah, man. Probably a week or so."

"You won't have any trouble getting the *Revenge* here on your own?"

"*No problemo*, dude. I'll be at Key West Bight Marina to fuel up at five o'clock. Peter said they'd be there no later than six."

"Good. We'll enjoy the dives and make plans when we're done."

"*Hasta mañana,*" Jimmy said, and I ended the call.

Staring down at the phone, I figured I'd delayed long enough. I scrolled through my short contact list and found the number Chyrel had given me a long time ago; the number I'd never once called.

"Hello?" The voice was hesitant, but it was Savannah.

"It's Jesse McDermitt."

There was silence for a moment. "I'd ask how you have my number, but knowing who you are, it goes without saying."

"I have news about your husband."

"Ex-husband," she said, her voice faltering slightly. "And I really don't care, whatever it is."

"He's dead."

Again, there was a moment of silence. "Did you—?

"He was involved in a dispute with illegal drug manufacturers and was shot."

Once more, there was only silence. The pause was so long, I checked to see if the signal was lost.

"And you didn't have anything to do with it?"

"No," I replied honestly. "But I was there. I just couldn't stop it in time."

She sighed. "It was bound to happen sooner or later, Jesse."

"I'd like to—"

"Was there anything else?" she interrupted curtly.

"I know he wasn't Florence's father, Savannah."

There was another sigh, then a squeaking sound, as if her breath had caught in her throat.

"No," she finally said. "He wasn't."

"She's my daughter."

"Yes," Savannah said, as if a great weight had been lifted. "Charity told me some time ago that you somehow got Flo's DNA. I really didn't know for sure, until then."

"I should have told you immediately."

"I didn't want to know," she said. "Then time went by..."

"I'd like to meet her," I said. "I mean, with everything laid out on the table. The one time I met her, she seemed like a great kid."

"She's not really a kid anymore," Savannah said. "She's wanted to meet her real father for years. I kept telling her the time wasn't right."

"Can I?" I asked.

She paused again. "Yes," she finally said, resolution in her voice. "Soon. But not real soon. Can I reach you at this number?"

"Yeah," I replied, sitting forward on the edge of the bunk. "Any time, day or night."

"I'll call you," she said, then ended the call.

Placing the phone on the desk, I thought about what kind of relationship I could have with Florence. My two daughters from my first failed marriage had been estranged until they were nearly grown. Now we had a good relationship and they were close; Kim lived right there on my island, when she and Marty were in. They spent a lot of time on assignment for Fish and Wildlife, though.

Before Kim found me, I'd resigned myself to not having contact with her or her sister, Eve. But Kim had quickly learned that what her mother Sandy had told them about me was mostly lies. Eve had been a more difficult sell.

Physically rested, but still mentally drained, particularly after the call with Savannah, I decided to wear my body down to match my brain. I put on a pair of trunks and a faded *Rusty Anchor* T-shirt and headed down to the lobby.

Passing through the expansive area, I overheard several conversations about the storm. I didn't want to push my ankle too much, so I walked out to the highway, crossed it, and turned right, following the seawall along Cow Key Channel toward the Atlantic.

There, I picked up the pace to a slow jog. It was a little over a mile to Smather's Beach, and as I ran, I thought about Savannah and Florence. Our affair had been brief, only a couple of weeks, but it was good. Or at least I thought it had been. I guess if she decided to go back to an abusive husband it couldn't have been all that great for her. But I knew that women often went back; the abusers had that kind of control.

My feet pounded the concrete, but the pain in my ankle was very minimal. I was convinced it had just been a sprain, as a torn ligament would still have had me hobbling along. A tall, dark-haired woman jogged past me in the opposite direction and smiled, her eyes making contact a bit longer than usual for two strangers passing. I smiled back.

When I reached Smather's Beach, I used the dune crossover and leaned against a palm to take off my shoes.

Then I removed my shirt, stashed the castoffs beside a trash can and waded into the warm, almost hot, water.

Setting out at a slow pace, swimming toward the sun and the end of the pier at White Street, about a mile away, I tried to turn my mind off and let my body set its own pace. I knifed through the water with practiced ease. I'd always considered swimming to be the ultimate exercise, bringing nearly every muscle in the body into play.

The little girl I'd met near the hospital just across the bridge on Stock Island kept creeping into my mind. She'd been eight or nine years old then, but tall for her age. She'd seemed shy, but in her eyes, I'd seen a quick mind. They flitted about, taking in everything around her. I hadn't known she was my kid then. She'd be a teenager now. Almost the same age that Kim had been when she'd snuck away from her sister's house in Miami with a friend and driven down to Marathon to find me.

Raising my head for a moment, I saw that I was nearly halfway to the pier. There was a powerful storm coming, and if it hit here, it would change the landscape. I wondered what I might have to do, should Irma come this way.

My house was solid, but against a Cat-5 storm, I wasn't sure how it would hold up. A direct hit would have a high storm surge. On the highest high tide, there was fourteen feet of clearance below the house, where I kept the boats, and the *Revenge* had an air draft of thirteen.

I had no doubt that a direct hit from a storm such as this would mean a surge at least as high as my house.

The boats would have to be taken out—all of them. The *Revenge* wasn't trailerable and I didn't have a trailer big enough for *El Cazador*. They'd both have to be moved to my hurricane hole in Tarpon Bay on Shark River, miles inland from the coast. I just didn't trust putting my boat up on the hard at a marina. Boats and parts of boats could get loose and damage others. Better off on the water, properly tied in a deep-water creek with a windbreak all around. The smaller boats could be trailered and staked down at the *Rusty Anchor*. Storm surge was less of a problem there, because it was slightly more elevated than other places in the Keys.

When I reached the pier, I turned around and started swimming back the way I'd come. I didn't need to look where I was going. My shadow, just ahead of me, would be my compass.

I wondered how Savannah would tell Florence. Would she prepare her, telling the girl that they were going to meet her father? Or would she wait and simply introduce me as *daddy*?

Finally, as I reached shallow water, I stood and looked around. I was roughly in the middle of Smather's Beach when I waded ashore; almost a two-mile swim. I walked back to the east end of the beach, passing a few sunburned tourists along the way. Again, conversations I heard were about the hurricane, nearly 2000 miles away.

"We should leave, Morris," I overheard a woman say to her pink, beer-bellied husband. "You call this a vacation? This is a swamp, Morris. Are you listening to me?"

Morris merely grumbled in return.

When I reached the spot where I'd stashed my shirt and shoes, I put them on and ran back to the hotel, still undecided on the best plan, should the storm arrive. My ankle felt fine after the workout, just a little stiff.

Back in my room, I showered, closed the curtains, and fell onto the bed, exhausted again. I left the TV off, knowing there would have been little change during the past two hours.

The next time I woke up, I felt a lot more refreshed than I had in days. It was dark outside, but there was still a faint glow to the southwest. I ordered a ribeye and baked potato from room service and turned on the TV.

Irma was still a Cat-3 storm with sustained winds of 115 miles per hour. The forecast track predicted a northeasterly turn taking it right through the Virgin Islands, then continuing past Puerto Rico. A straight line from there would be along the north Cuban coast and into the Gulf of Mexico. It didn't take a meteorologist to see that.

Even if I had a crystal ball and could predict exactly where it would go, it was still far too early to implement any sort of plan. If you moved a boat too early, you ran the risk of mooring it right in the path of the storm when it changed course.

But the time to implement a hurricane plan was fast approaching. I decided my go or blow time would be Tuesday afternoon, two days from now. There was a chance we might have to make the planned two-day dive trip just a single day.

I set my alarm for 0400 and got back into bed. I wanted to be fully rested before the dive tomorrow. Again, my thoughts drifted to Florence and her mother. Savannah had lied to me. Okay, it was a lie of omission, not telling me she wasn't exactly single. But it was a deception. Years later, I'd seen them get on a boat with a man to go out to his yacht. I hadn't seen him clearly enough to be sure, but it could have been her husband. At any rate, she'd moved on with her life, and I'd moved on with mine.

Some life, I thought, as I drifted off to sleep. A hermit's existence filled with occasional dangerous assignments.

CHAPTER TWENTY-FOUR

Waiting at the fuel dock the next morning, I watched *Gaspar's Revenge* idle into the marina and turn toward me. Jimmy skillfully brought her to the dock, where the gas monkey and I quickly made her fast. I handed the man my card and he went to turn on the pump.

"You don't look none the worse for wear," Jimmy said, as he came down from the bridge and pumped my hand vigorously. "I'm glad you're back, man."

"Glad to be back," I said, opening the fuel access hatch and removing the cap.

I heard a commotion at the foot of the dock and looked back. Peter and his entourage, consisting of one man and four women, were walking toward us. Even though it wasn't yet light, there was a handful of people around, getting boats ready for a day of fishing or diving. Everyone stopped to watch the four women walk past. Sidney's niece, Naomi, was among them.

They were all young, beautiful, and walked with the confidant stride of runway models. Hell, throw in a smoke machine and wailing guitars and it would have been a rock video.

"Whoa," Jimmy breathed.

"Down boy," I said. "Try to act professional."

"Hiya, Jesse," Peter called out. "Hey, Jimmy. Long time no see."

Neither Peter nor the girls following him paid any attention to the gaping mouths they were leaving in their wake. Peter's assistant, a young man I only knew as Claude, appeared overly self-conscious about all the attention, though.

"Good to see you, too, Peter," I said, noticing that they were all wearing sneakers. I smiled at the peculiar, Bohemian underwater photographer. "You're early; we're just fueling up. If the fumes are too much, you're welcome to go right on inside. The AC's on in there."

"What do you think about that hurricane?" Peter asked, as he stepped over, then offered a hand to one of the women.

"Hurricane?" the young blonde asked.

"Not to worry," I said. "It's still days from the Leeward Islands, and they're more than a thousand miles from here. We'll have blue skies and calm seas here for at least a week."

"That's good news," a second blond woman said, as she followed the first into the boat's interior. An unassuming, dark-haired woman was right on her heels.

Naomi stepped down into the cockpit and offered a hand to Claude, who was standing beside the boarding ladder with his arms full of camera gear.

Peter followed the girls inside as Jimmy hung up the fuel hose. The assistant followed Peter in, but Naomi remained in the cockpit.

"You're Rusty's friend," she said. "We met at the airport week before last."

"Yes, I remember. Sid's niece, right? Long vacation?"

"No," she replied. "I decided to stay. Mind if I ride up top for a while?"

Jimmy gave me a glance and shrugged. While we were underway, another pair of eyes on the bridge would free him up to talk shop with the two photographers.

"Sure. Why not?" I turned and signed for the fuel, pocketed my card, then followed her up the ladder.

I started the engines as Jimmy cast off the lines. Then I nudged the *Revenge* away from the dock.

"This is quite a dive boat," Naomi said, sitting on the edge of the port bench seat. "Looks fast."

"Thanks," I replied. "It's really a fishing boat, though. But I make an exception for Peter and his groups. What made you decide to stay?"

"Oh, where do I start? I love the people I've met, and everyone's attitude is so cool. The water's beautiful and the sand hot. I'm not real crazy about the rowdiness here in Key West so much, though. How far away is this place we're going?"

I grinned at her. "I know just what you mean. I came to the Keys a long time ago and just never left." I flipped on the roof-mounted spotlight and trained it toward the channel markers. "We'll reach Fort Jefferson in about two hours. Nervous about going that far on the ocean?"

"Oh no," she replied. "I've done some sailing."

"Good. It's always a bonus to have another pair of eyes."

"You need anything, Skip?" Jimmy called up.

"Yeah, could you bring me up some—?"

"Coffee, yeah," he said. "Anything else?"

"That's it for now," I said, pointing the bow toward the southwest. I turned to Naomi. "You care for a cup?"

"Sure."

"Bring an extra mug, Jimmy," I called down, as I slowly eased the throttles forward, bringing the speed up to eight knots.

"Why's he call you Skip?"

"I'm the captain. Skip's short for skipper."

"Aunt Sid said you used to be some kind of spy or something."

"Spy?" I replied, wondering where she'd gotten that idea. "Not hardly. I was in the Marines and after that, I used to move some of Homeland Security's people around sometimes. Definitely not a spy."

"So, this is your job now? A boat captain? Sounds exciting. Do you live here in Key West?"

So, Rusty's wife had told her I was a *spy*, but not that I lived on an island just a few miles from them and chartered for a living? I was going to have to talk to Rusty.

"It's not really a job," I replied. "I own *Gaspar's Revenge* and enjoy being out on the water. Chartering lets me do that while someone else pays for the fuel. I live a little north of Rusty's place."

Jimmy called up from below, and Naomi moved over and knelt by the ladder to take the Thermos and mugs from him.

"Thanks, Jimmy," she said with a smile.

I waited until she'd poured us each a cup, then pressed the intercom button and spoke into it. "We're clear of the outer markers, Jimmy."

His voice came back over the speaker. "*Si, Capitan*. Everyone is seated."

I pushed the throttles up to halfway and the *Revenge* came up out of the water, heading toward Southwest Channel. I moved the spotlight around to illuminate the water ahead of us and then switched the overhead lights to red.

"So, how long have you been doing this?" Naomi asked, straining her neck to look forward.

"You can sit over here," I offered. "The seat's higher. I started chartering soon after I arrived here in the Keys, in '99."

She moved carefully behind me and then lifted herself into the second seat by the helm. "Oh, this is a lot better. I was only ten years old then. I guess you were in college before you came here? I went to Oklahoma State."

I laughed. "No, I didn't go to college. Before I came to the Keys, I was a Marine for twenty years."

Out of the corner of my eye, I saw her turn toward me, studying my face. "You can't be that old. What's Jimmy's story?"

"Jimmy?"

"Yeah, I've seen him around the *Rusty Anchor*. Rusty's letting me work there, waiting tables and stuff."

"He was born and raised here," I said. "A true Conch like Rusty. Spent a few years in the Navy, then came home and worked as a shrimper until I hired him. One of the best flats guides in the back country."

Naomi talked almost non-stop for the two hours it took us to reach the Tortugas. Mostly chit-chat requiring little input on my part. But she asked a few more questions about Jimmy. Was there something there? She seemed intelligent, and our conversation covered quite a few subjects. Jimmy was very intelligent, though he tried to hide it behind a surfer façade.

"Was that where you met Rusty?" she asked, as I started to slow the boat. "In the Marines?"

"No, I met him on the bus that was taking us both up to Parris Island for boot camp."

She gave me a curious look. "How old was he then?"

"Rusty? He's a year older than me, so... eighteen."

Her face showed doubt. "Huh."

"What?"

"I just assumed he was older than you; about Aunt Sid's age."

"He is," I said. "A year older."

"I meant more than a year," Naomi said. "You look a lot younger than him."

I'd never really considered it. Rusty and I had known each other a long time and I just saw him the same as always. I guess we're all like that with people we've known a long time and see regularly. We don't see the lines in the face deepening, or the graying of hair, or in Rusty's case, the losing of it. He'd always been bald. He'd shaved his head before boot camp.

Jimmy climbed up to the bridge. "Peter wants to do some shots onshore first, save the afternoon sun for the reef."

There was already a sailboat in the anchorage, but the tour boats hadn't arrived. So, I continued past the shoals to the south and turned into the channel.

While I stayed on the boat, Jimmy went ashore with Peter and his group to explore the old fort and shoot some pictures.

Using my satellite phone, I pulled up the latest storm update on the NOAA site. Unlike the Weather Channel and local news stations, NOAA provided maps, charts, and raw data that were easy enough to understand with a little practice. Best of all, there wasn't any hype and fluff from reporters trying to sell ad space for the network.

The latest satellite image showed that Irma was a storm of massive proportions. The image ran in a five-second loop, depicting a six-hour span, and showing dawn arriving far to the east, as well as a huge pinwheel, spinning around out in the middle of the Atlantic. If the eye of the storm crossed the northern Leewards, there would be some weather associated with it halfway through the Windward chain, 400 miles to the south, and on Bermuda, several hundred miles to the north. It was that big.

If you lived on the coast it was hard *not* to keep up with a storm. Living on a sub-tropical island, I always tried to keep a weather eye out for storms. When one was looming, it just nagged at my brain.

Late tomorrow night and into Wednesday morning was when they were predicting the first landfall, somewhere in the Leeward Islands or the British Virgin Islands. And it would strike with wind speeds upwards of 130 miles per hour.

Having experienced a few smaller hurricanes, the most powerful being a close brush with a Cat-3, I couldn't imagine the terror of one of these monster storms.

When the group returned at 1100, the first thing Peter wanted to know was the status of the storm, which brought on a slew of questions from his models.

I did my best to calm everyone's concerns, explaining that it was still well over 1000 miles away and would take days before it arrived in South Florida, if it came here at all.

Still, the nervousness was palpable as we pulled away from the dock and headed to our first dive site. For the rest of the day, we anchored near Loggerhead Key and the wreck of the *Windjammer*, a couple miles west of Fort Jefferson. Again, I remained on the boat as Peter photographed the women, who were wearing what I assumed was the latest swimwear. The models were basically free-diving, though they had extra tanks and regulators for when they weren't posing in front of a reef.

While the divers were down on their last dive of the day, John called and patched me into a conference call with Jack Armstrong.

"Great work in the BVI," Jack said. "Right person in the right place at the right time."

"Thanks, Jack. DJ and that young California cop did most everything. What's happened there since John and I left?"

"The authorities raided facilities on both islands, as well as a new one being built on St. Thomas, and another location in northwestern Mexico."

"Mexico?"

"They'd bought several thousand acres in the Sonoran Desert," Jack said. "Outside of Puerto Lobos. They were already past groundbreaking to develop a huge commune and farm there. The Bahamas Defence Force recovered thousands of pounds of marijuana and get this: an estimated twelve-million tablets of MDMA with a street value of nearly a quarter billion dollars."

"Whoa!"

"My sentiments exactly, Jesse. You did good."

"Heard anything from Lettsome?" I asked. "What they're doing about the storm?"

"I just got off the phone with him," John replied. "They're already getting the outer bands and are evacuating the low-lying areas along the coasts. Hopefully it'll turn out to sea before it gets there."

I didn't really see that as a possibility. And more to the point, John shouldn't either. He knew the islands and knew about hurricanes. This one was headed straight toward his house on Norman Island.

"Why'd you really call me, John?"

There was a momentary silence before John answered, "The woman escaped custody. Sunna Johannsdottir."

"How'd that happen?"

"They were moving the prisoners," Jack replied. "Nearly fifty of them. They didn't have the facilities to process so many, and with the storm coming, they put them all on a flight to the Cayman Islands."

"Makes sense," I said. "Another British territory and out of the path of the storm. And they probably have adequate housing for that many prisoners there."

"That was the idea," Jack said.

"And Sunna escaped from Cayman custody?"

Again, there was silence for a moment.

"A flight attendant was found dead in the plane's lavatory after landing. She was a small, blond woman, new on that flight, and the rest of the crew didn't really know her that well. She'd been strangled and her uniform was missing."

CHAPTER TWENTY-FIVE

With the boat safely anchored off the lee side of the fort, I busied myself in the engine room while I thought about Sunna's escape. I cleaned the raw water strainers, though both were empty, checked the oil and hydraulic levels in both engines and transmissions. Everything was clean, bright, and full.

With the dead flight attendant looking similar to Sunna, and not well-known by the crew, Sunna might have been able to pose as her and get off the plane quickly after landing.

But what then? Sure, Grand Cayman was a lot bigger and more populated than Tortola, but it was still an island. The Brits would have people looking for her at the airport and every dock. I felt certain that John would be calling me tomorrow to tell me that she'd been recaptured.

After closing up the engine room hatch, I turned and opened the small cockpit fridge to grab a Red Stripe.

"Got another one of those?" Naomi asked, startling me. She was standing on the side deck in khaki shorts and the lime green bikini top she'd worn for the photoshoot.

I reached in, took out another of the stubby brown bottles, opening both using a bottle opener attached to the inside of the trash can cabinet, then handed her one.

"Thanks. I was up on the front, watching the moon come up."

The moon was nearly full and already several degrees above the horizon, blotting out the stars to the east.

"Come on up to the bridge," I said, leading the way.

She followed and I turned the helm seats around to face aft, allowing her to move over to the second seat.

"Okay," I said, "put your feet up and close your eyes."

"What are you going to do?" she asked nervously, as she stretched her long, tanned legs out, crossing them on the aft railing.

"Nothing," I replied. "I just want you to see something. Close your eyes." She complied. "Now keep them closed for about a minute."

I reached back and turned off all the lights, then stared down at the dark water for a moment, trying to see the bottom. When I looked up, my eyes had adjusted and a billion stars sparkled in the heavens.

"Okay, look up at the sky behind the boat."

I watched her face. She opened her eyes and gasped.

"Wow," she said, with a slow exhalation, dropping her feet to the deck and leaning forward.

"People rely too much on artificial light. On a clear night, away from all the light pollution of civilized society, you can see more stars than grains of sand on the beach. And the human eye adjusts, allowing all that starlight to guide our way, literally, astronomically, and metaphorically."

"Metaphorically? You're a philosopher?"

I chuckled. "No, Jimmy's more the philosophical type."

She looked out over the water again. "I've never seen so many stars."

"Most people today haven't. You never went out on the Oklahoma plains?"

"I grew up in Tulsa with half a million people." she said, smiling. "I didn't get away from the campus very often. I've never seen anything like this. They're even different colors. Do you know any of them? What they're called?"

As I pointed out some of the planets, stars, and constellations, the dark-haired girl came out of the salon.

"Up here, Trish," Naomi called down.

"What are you doing up there in the dark?" Trish asked. "How can you even see me?"

"Look down at the water for a minute," I replied. "Your eyes will adjust faster. Then climb up and join us."

A moment later, Trish sat down on the bench, facing aft. "I'm worried about the hurricane. That guy, Jimmy? He said you'd know more."

"I checked about an hour ago," I said. "It's been upgraded to a Category-4 hurricane."

"What's that mean?" Trish asked.

"It's how they categorize hurricanes, based on wind speed," I said. "A Cat-4 has sustained winds over 130 miles per hour, but less than 156."

"And you said earlier it was a little over a thousand miles away? That's ten hours!"

"I'm sorry," I offered. "A hurricane's a cyclone. The winds rotating around the center are going 130, but the storm itself is moving forward at about thirteen miles per hour."

"Ah, I get it." That seemed to calm her. "So, that's like more than four days away?"

"Probably closer to six or seven," I replied. "But don't be surprised if they order an evacuation of the Keys before that. Probably Wednesday or Thursday."

"Will you be evacuating?" Naomi asked.

I shrugged. "Depends on the track of the storm. I have to think of my boats. If I think it's going to hit the Keys, I'll take this boat north to my hurricane hole up in the Everglades."

"This boat?" Trish asked. "You have two?"

"I have a few other smaller boats at my house," I replied. "Jimmy and I will put them on trailers and take them to Rusty's place in Marathon. If the storm is still headed this way later this week, Jimmy will follow me in another boat that also can't be trailered."

"I thought the Everglades was a big swamp," Trish said. "Can this boat go into a swamp?"

"That's a common misconception," I said. "The Glades are more of a wide river than a swamp. And there are some deep-water rivers and creeks that flow out of it. There's one called Shark River, up on the wild south-west coast. It flows from a large lake called Tarpon Bay, deep in the Glades. There are a number of deep creeks that flow into that lake. That's my hurricane hole. I get up into one of those creeks and tie off to the mangroves to ride out the storm."

With a bright moon rising, Peter wanted to get the women back in the water for some night shots. "Right here's fine," he said. "There won't be any backdrop except the blackness of the water. Should make for some dramatic full-body shots."

The models would again free dive. Peter and Claude, using Jimmy as a target, set up bright lights on the sandy bottom, each light pointing up slightly, illuminating nothing but Jimmy, who hung motionless a few feet above the bottom.

Once Jimmy swam out of the light, I heard the distinctive clang of a tank ball—a hard, plastic ball with a bungee strapped to a scuba tank. Pull it away and release it, and the tank made a loud ringing sound; Peter's signal that he was ready to start.

I couldn't see much of anything, except a couple of patches of light on the bottom, and the three divers' glow sticks. Jimmy's was green, while Peter and Claude had red ones. The sticks would make it easy for anyone in trouble to identify Jimmy, a trained divemaster. The glow sticks were flexible plastic tubes filled with a chemical and a small glass vial. When you bent the tube, the glass broke, releasing a different chemical that reacted to the first and created a phosphorescent glow that lasted for

hours. Jimmy hovered above and behind the two photographers, ready in case one of the girls needed help.

There was a splash at the stern and when I looked
down, only three of the women were still hanging onto
the swim platform. One of the blondes, whose names
were Kate and Vickie, appeared in front of the lights. It
was impossible to tell who was who; they wore white
and yellow bikinis, which looked the same underwater. She floated there, as if in slow motion, turning and
posing, for about ten seconds before starting back up.

We were in fifteen feet of water. For the models to
stay neutrally buoyant in front of the lights, they had
to arrive there with their lungs about half empty. It was
kind of a balance, depending on the person's body fat,
and these girls had very little. Taking a full breath at
the surface and slowly exhaling while swimming downward for fifteen or twenty seconds was about all a person
could manage.

One by one they each dove into the area where Peter
had his lights trained. Each would pause and pose for a
few seconds before surfacing. As one came up, another
started down, so Peter had a beautiful woman in front
of his lens nearly all the time.

After about twenty minutes of solo shots, two of the
girls went down together, leaving two at the surface.
When Trish and Naomi came up, Kate and Vickie went
down, and they alternated several more dives, two at
a time. It didn't take long before I could hear labored
breathing from the girls at the swim platform.

All four rested together for a while, then they all dove in unison, moving around in front of the lights. My view wasn't great, what with the rippling of the surface and the fact that I was mostly looking down at the tops of their heads.

They did two more dives where they all posed together, each taking a longer surface break. Finally, the women climbed up onto the swim platform. I went down and got towels out of the locker for them.

I helped the divers get their equipment aboard as the women headed for the warmth of the showers. Jimmy and Peter stripped off their gear, dried off, and went inside to look at the pictures. I helped Claude rinse all the gear and put it away.

With everyone back aboard and exhausted, I assigned bunks, giving the private staterooms to the women, and pulling the convertible out of the sofa for Peter and Claude. Jimmy took the dinette and I rolled a mat out on the foredeck.

I've slept under the stars nearly as much as I have with a roof over my head. The sea was calm, the moon and stars were bright, and I could see the water's surface all the way to the horizon. I felt very secure, and quickly fell asleep.

Early the next morning, I went into the salon to find Jimmy on the laptop. "Cat-5," he whispered, holding up a hand, fingers spread wide. "It's about 125 miles from Antigua. Isn't that where Sara is?"

I poured a cup of coffee and took a sip. "No, it's where we met a couple weeks ago. She's aboard *Ambrosia*, down in the Grenadines. What's the new projected path?"

Jimmy clicked a few keys and turned the laptop toward me. The cone reached all the way into the Gulf of Mexico, with a dot just south of Marathon, labeled *2am Sunday*. But the cone itself engulfed all of Cuba and southern Florida, all the way up to Orlando, plus a huge swath of the southeastern Gulf.

"I think we oughta bug out, man."

I ran the numbers in my head.

Leaving now, it'd be early afternoon before we got back to my island. It'd take us two days to fully secure everything there, move the smaller boats to Rusty's place, put them on trailers—one of which I didn't have—and park them in Rusty's yard. I only had trailers for three of the four smaller boats. His house was the highest ground in the Middle Keys; eighteen feet above sea level, built on an exposed limestone ridge. Add a day for finding a trailer for *Knot L-8*, and another day to get the *Revenge* and *Cazador* up to Tarpon Bay, and we'd be well into Saturday. That left us with a full day's buffer. What could go wrong?

"Yeah," I think you're right. I turned toward the stern, where Peter and Claude slept back-to-back on the sofa bed. "Peter, wake up."

CHAPTER TWENTY-SIX

By the time we got the *Revenge* back to my island, Irma was clocking sustained winds of 185 miles per hour, with gusts over 200. Since our first stop after my home was going to be the *Rusty Anchor*, Naomi decided to come with us. She'd ridden with Peter to Key West in his big nine-passenger van and it was cramped with all the gear.

"If Category-5 starts at 157 miles per hour, and *this* one's already up to 185…" Naomi shook her head. "What's after that?"

"The crushing hand of the Almighty," Jimmy said, stepping down into my little Maverick and offering Naomi a hand.

She accepted it and smiled at him, but she still looked a bit skeptical. "Seriously."

"Might as well be," I said, starting the engine, then stepping over to Kim's Maverick and starting it. "There really aren't too many things that can withstand a constant 150-mile-per-hour wind. Some block walls and a few bushes might remain, stripped of roof and leaf. A high storm surge will decimate low-lying areas and alter coastlines. 'Head for high ground' isn't just a saying."

"Rusty's place is eighteen feet above sea level," Jimmy said. "It's never flooded."

He might need all that and the pilings his house sat on, I thought, as I tossed off the lines and pulled away from them.

We ran fast through the narrow cuts to the southwest, Jimmy right behind me. Once in deeper water, we spread out and headed south toward the bridge, only the arch visible on the horizon.

I hadn't seen Finn in nearly two weeks. Jimmy had left him at the *Anchor* before going down to Key West. As I slowed and entered the canal to Rusty's place, Finn came bounding down the dock and leaped over the stern of the end boat. He belly-flopped into the water, creating a massive splash, and began swimming toward my boat.

After shifting to neutral, I headed to the stern to help him aboard. Once in the boat, he was thoughtful enough to shower me before having a meltdown at my feet.

A person has never experienced true exuberance unless they've owned a Labrador Retriever and left their dog alone for a while. Black, yellow, chocolate, it didn't matter. If you leave them for an hour or a month, it's the same. They're thrilled that you're back with them, and they show it.

Finn barked as the other boat came alongside, and Naomi stepped back slightly.

"He won't hurt you none," Jimmy said. "Unless he steps on your toes." He snickered as Finn continued jumping around me. "That usually happens if you try to move them. He knows where they are and will dance around 'em."

I patted Finn on the flank a few times, then put the boat into gear. He rolled over onto my feet, tail thumping against the deck, for the short ride to the skiff dock at the end of Rusty's canal.

There wasn't much room, but we lashed the two boats together and tied off to the last ten feet of Rusty's barge, our bows only a couple of feet from the concrete seawall on the side away from the bar. My Grady-White was tied off to the other end of the barge, and another boat was lashed to it.

After tying up, we walked up the dock and across the yard. The parking lot was nearly full, too. Mostly pickups, many with boat trailers attached. I wasn't the only one pulling a boat out today.

The door opened as we approached, and Dink stumbled out. There wasn't anything to trip over and Dink rarely drank before Happy Hour, so unless you knew him, you couldn't guess what had caused him to stumble. Dink was a local flats fishing guide who people said had perpetual sea legs. He was clumsy on land, but fine on a boat out on the water.

"Well, hey, Jesse," Dink said, extending a big, calloused hand. "Where ya been, man?"

"Off island for a couple of weeks. Where you headed?"

"Pulling the skiff out. Did ya hear there's a storm coming?"

"Yeah, that's why I'm here, to start getting my boats out."

"Take a number," Dink said, heading toward his pickup and trailer. "They's a good half-dozen ahead of you."

We walked inside and found about a dozen people sitting and standing around the long wooden bar, eyes glued to the TV mounted high in the corner.

"When'd you get back in?" Rusty asked.

"About an hour ago," I replied. "Had to cancel the second day of diving."

"Was Peter pissed?" Rusty asked.

That's just how things were, living on an island. You could be gone for two weeks, with little more than a wave goodbye, but while you were gone, everyone knew what was going on in your life and would pick up a conversation like you'd just returned from the head.

"No," Naomi replied, sitting at one of two remaining stools at the end of the bar. "He was thrilled with the shots. Especially the night shots."

"You saw 'em?" Rusty asked. "He don't ever let anyone see his pictures till they're in the magazines."

"We all did," Jimmy said. "Well, except Jesse. He was messing around in the engine room. Naomi's right— the night shots were eerily beautiful, man."

Naomi nudged Jimmy with an elbow and nodded toward the empty stool next to her. After a moment's hesitation, he sat down.

"What's the latest on the storm?" I asked.

"Winds are really kicking up on Antigua and Barbuda," Rusty replied, as he reached into the cooler and pulled out a Red Stripe. I shook my head and he slid the beer down the bar to Al Fader, a shrimper out of Key West.

Rusty gave Jimmy a bottle of locally-bottled mango juice and looked at Naomi questioningly.

"I'll have what Jimmy's having."

Rusty pulled another bottle from the freezer, set it on the bar in front of her, and turned toward the coffee pot, and continued his summation of what I'm sure took two hours to report on the local news. "The outer bands came ashore a few hours ago, and they're getting tropical storm gusts already. Just under a hundred miles due east of Antigua."

The TV wasn't on a news channel. Rusty had it connected to the computer in his office behind the bar. Every minute or so, the picture changed to a different chart or report from NOAA. The current offering was a color-enhanced satellite loop lasting ten seconds. The date and time were displayed on a bar across the top. It was a twelve-hour loop.

The middle part of the storm was colored dark purple, representing hurricane-force winds, with a red ring around that for tropical storm winds. Hurricane winds extended more than fifty miles from the eye wall, and tropical storm winds another hundred. The storm was massive.

"You pulling your boats?" Rusty asked, spreading his beefy hands on the bar. His posture was unmistakable. It was time to get to work.

"Yeah," I replied. "Got the two Mavericks here now. I don't have a trailer for *Knot L-8*."

"I got a spare out back," a familiar, Aussie-accented voice said. Looking down the bar, I saw Sherman Crawford lean forward and tip his beer my way. "It's a might bigger than your little wooden boat, but just to get 'er outa the water so you can lash 'er down, I think it'll do."

"Thanks, Sherm," I said. "Beer's on me for the duration."

"Oy," he grunted as he stood. "No worries, cobber. I reckon Dink's had long enough, and I'm up next. See you fellas."

The other fishermen around the bar offered their best wishes to the old black man and Sherm went out the back door.

"What are you gonna do about *Island Hopper*?" Jimmy asked. "And where's your sailboat?"

"*Salty Dog's* on the hard in Bimini," I replied accepting a coffee mug from Rusty.

"She'll be safe there," Rusty said. "They'll get some weather, but no chance of a direct hit. From what you told me about that yard, they'll be prepared."

"I called Billy while we were bringing the boats down," I said to Jimmy. "He and a friend of his will fly down tomorrow and fly the Beaver up to LaBelle."

"You takin' the *Revenge* up to Tarpon Bay?" Rusty asked, again placing his hands wide apart on the bar.

"And *Cazador*, too."

Rusty frowned. "Use Sherm's trailer to get the little boat out and we can pull her off onto a coupla 8x8s I got out there and strap her down. Then you can put that big-ass Winter on Sherm's trailer to haul it out. His trailer's big enough for *Cazador* and *The Beast* won't have no trouble pulling her up the ramp. It's not like you're gonna drive in traffic."

"Good idea," I said.

"Tarpon Bay," Rusty muttered, shaking his head. "Might not be safe there, bro. If it's still a Cat-5, there ain't no place in Florida safe. They're saying it's gonna rip right up through the whole state."

"There," I said, pointing at the TV as it changed back to a newer version of the ten-second satellite loop. "Watch the Bermuda High."

"Well, I'll be," Rusty said, watching the swirling mass of clouds far to the north of the rotating Hurricane Irma. "It ain't moving much, and you can just barely see it, but it looks like the high just ticked a little to the west."

Hurricane Alley gets its name because most of the late summer storms originate as low-pressure areas off the coast of Africa. Steering currents move them westward across the Atlantic and the Bermuda High, a semi-stationary high-pressure system in the North Atlantic, rotates clockwise, further moving the counterclockwise rotating storms westward and preventing them from turning north. Where the high was located would determine where in the Americas a hurricane would hit, if at all. If the high was off to the east, a storm would loop around it and might not affect the U.S. coast in the slightest—what we called a fish storm. If it moved a little west of there, storms would loop into the Carolinas. Farther west, Florida. An even greater westerly shift, like I thought I was seeing, would push a storm across Cuba, or through the Florida Straits and out into the Gulf of Mexico.

Rusty had the intuition of several generations of Conch blood, while I liked raw data.

"I don't know," Rusty finally said, turning back around. "It don't look like it's far enough west to push Irma into the Gulf. She might turn right up the west coast, instead of running the length of the state all the way from Key Largo, like they're predicting. But turn north, it's gonna do."

"I'm less concerned about where than I am about how strong. Think that shift will be enough to shove her down closer to Cuba before turning north?"

"I see what you're thinking, Skip," Jimmy said. "Eastern Cuba is pretty mountainous, man. Hurricanes are bad-asses against trees and anything man-made, but mountains are a different story. They could weaken it."

"We'll just have to keep an eye on it," I said. "Right now, let's get the light work done."

When it came my turn, I went out back and started *The Beast*, while Jimmy went to the dock to bring the first skiff around. *The Beast* is my 1973 International Travelall, which I keep at the *Anchor*, along with the trailers for the two Mavericks and the Grady.

As I sat there letting the diesel engine warm up, I couldn't help but remember back to the preparations for another storm. Hurricane Wilma had passed just

north of here in '05, making landfall not far from Shark
River. I'd ridden that one out right here in Rusty's little
marina aboard the first *Gaspar's Revenge*, with Alex in
my cabin.

Alexis Dubois McDermitt. She'd been the one to name
this old truck. A couple of years later she was murdered
on our wedding night. In two months, it would have
been a dozen years ago.

I pulled the truck around to the back and hitched up
one of the Maverick's aluminum trailers. Several other
guides had already dropped their boats and trailers in
Rusty's five-acre backyard. There was a concrete pad
that ran the length of the eastern edge of the property,
with big eye bolts that were anchored deep in the concrete when it was poured. The boats were strapped down
and would likely be fine for the wind, with everything
stripped. The pad's elevation was only twelve feet above
sea level, so there was still a danger of a high surge. But
that'd only be if there was a direct landfall, and if that
happened, Marathon could look just like Jimmy had described it; wiped clean by the hand of God. Like Islamorada was in 1935. Living in paradise had its costs.

It took two hours, but we finally had the skiffs and
the Grady secure. Rusty offered to run us back out to my
island after dinner and help us secure everything there
and bring the other two boats back. Buttoning up his
house, the bar, and Rufus's little shack out back never
took him more than a couple of hours, and he didn't
plan to do that until Friday at the earliest.

Later that night, well past midnight, the three of us sat around the fire pit, having worked straight through the evening and into the night before stopping to eat our fill of lobster tails cooked over the open fire. Finn snored beside my chair.

"You don't ever get tired of living out here?" Rusty asked.

Jimmy shrugged. "Nope."

"Angie still up in Louisiana?"

"Been a year since I talked to her," Jimmy said. "Probably."

Jimmy and Angie had lived together on their houseboat for a long time before moving to my island. But she'd gone home to take care of an ailing mother, and then chosen to stay.

"We have plenty to keep us busy," I said. "Had our best crayfish haul ever just last month."

"What'd that bring in?"

"Almost five grand, dude," Jimmy replied.

Rusty glanced over at him. "You know he earns that much in interest in a week, right?"

"That money's not mine," I said. "I just found it. What Mam and Pap left me is right here; this island, my house, and the boats. I don't need much, nor does Jimmy. With the solar array we put up last year on the little island, we hardly ever have to run the generator. We're basically living free here. So, I use the money I found to help other people."

"I know that," Rusty said, letting me off the hook for snapping at him. We were all tired. "But don't it get lonely way out here?"

"It's not like we're on Gilligan's Island," I said, aware it would rekindle an old argument. "Town's only a half hour away. Though I wonder why old Gilligan never hooked up with Mary Ann."

"Ginger," Jimmy said.

"Mary Ann," I shot back with a half grin. We'd had this debate quite a few times over the years. Sometimes we even switched allegiances, depending on the subject of the debate. "Ginger'd be too high-maintenance on an island, and Mary Ann would take over the farming. Speaking of lonely," I said, turning back to Rusty. "Where's Sid?"

Our little group's dynamic had changed. Rusty and I had known each other for all of our adult lives, and I'd known Jimmy for nearly two decades now. He'd been with Angie for a long time. I'd found and lost love several times over. During all that time, Rusty had remained a steadfast bachelor. Until he met Sid, he hadn't dated anyone since his wife died giving birth to Julie. But his daughter was married now, with a son of her own.

"Oh, she had to run up to the mainland," Rusty replied, poking at the fire. "She'll be back in the morning."

The phone in my pocket vibrated and I pulled it out. It was Chyrel.

"Hey, Chyrel."

"Hey, Jesse. I got the latest update on the storm."

"Hang on, I'll put you on speaker." I touched the screen and set the phone on my knee. "Go ahead. I'm on the island with Jimmy and Rusty."

"Hey, y'all," she said, in her folksy Southern accent. "Irma just made landfall. The eye crossed over the north side of Barbuda at 0545 UTC."

I looked at my watch. It was nearly 0200. We were four hours different than Universal Time. "Just a few minutes ago," I said, absently. "Any report of damage?"

"It made landfall at peak intensity, Jesse. Winds of 185 plus."

"Hand of God, man," Jimmy mumbled, shaking his head sadly.

"Thanks, Chyrel," I said. "Anything else?"

"Yeah," she replied but didn't elaborate.

I picked up the phone, turned off the speaker, and held it to my ear. "Go ahead."

"A message from Jack Armstrong," Chyrel said. "Sunna Johannsdottir was picked up by a private plane flown into the Caymans from Mexico."

"Any idea where the plane was going?" I asked, rising and walking into the darkness away from the fire.

"It originally headed back toward Mexico. But when it passed the western tip of Cuba, it descended suddenly and disappeared from radar."

CHAPTER TWENTY-SEVEN

The next morning, we got started early, removing anything that wasn't physically attached to the island and storing it in my house, the highest of the four. Finn thought this was great fun and began dragging driftwood up from the water's edge. I thanked him and added each piece to our ever-growing pile of color-enhanced firewood. The fire ring was cast iron and half an inch thick. Where it was at now was where I'd found it after buying the island. So, I didn't think it would be going anywhere.

In times past, it didn't take much to prepare my island for a storm. But now there were four structures on it, each with windows that needed to be covered by corrugated steel panels. Then there was the problem of the garden and fish farm.

The aquaponics system was only five feet above sea level. It wouldn't take much of a surge to put the pumps underwater. Eight feet of water would breach the tank walls. If that happened, everything would die from saltwater intrusion. We picked all the vegetables and fruit we could, knowing the winds would likely take the rest if Irma came this way. And it was looking more and more like it with every hour. We took all the food aboard the *Revenge*, to hold us over through the storm, and possibly for some time after.

I don't put a lot of stock in material things, but there were a few pictures and mementos of my past life that I moved onto the boat, as well. If Irma came through here as a Cat-5, I was under no illusion about what I'd find when I came back. Nothing.

Jimmy had a small combination radio and lamp. It had a hand crank to charge its battery. We'd shut down the generator and transferred all the fuel into the *Revenge*, turning off all the breakers at the battery shack. Jimmy turned his radio on every hour to get the NOAA update.

As hot as it was, we had to work smart, taking breaks often. While we prepared, we listened to the updates and learned the fate of island after island as Irma made her way straight toward us. She'd made landfall on Sint Maarten before we'd awakened. By lunch time, Virgin Gorda and Tortola had received direct hits, as the storm passed through the Virgin Islands. No part of the long Antilles chain escaped the devastation, as Irma continued toward Puerto Rico.

At 1100, we got the word that a mandatory evacuation had been issued for the Keys. That meant different things for different people. The authorities wanted everyone out. Absolutely, all tourists had to leave; it wasn't their home and they'd just be in the way. But many locals never evacuated. Rusty was one of them. Some people just couldn't evacuate.

A few hours later, we learned that Irma had maintained a Cat-5 status all the way through the islands.

Having located a trailer faster than I'd figured, we were a day ahead of schedule when we finally closed up my house and installed the storm shutters. We split up and made one more pass around the whole island, making sure nothing was left that might be picked up by the wind and sent crashing through a wall.

We anchored *El Cazador* out in the channel, with Rusty's skiff tied off to the stern. I'd tow her with the *Revenge*. It took some shuttling of lines to get the two boats lashed together with a fifty-foot tow rope on a bridle. As I held the *Revenge* into the current, my canoe strapped to the foredeck, Rusty raised the anchor on *Cazador*. I felt it break free and had to keep both transmissions engaged against the extra drag.

Once Rusty had the anchor seated in the pulpit, he got into his skiff, tossed off the line, and came alongside me, Finn looking up from the stern of his boat. "You sure you won't need any help?"

"Nah," I called back. "Y'all go on ahead. I'll be there in a couple of hours."

As Rusty and Finn roared away across the flats, Jimmy following in *Knot L-8*, I bumped the throttles up and steered toward the light at the mouth of the channel. I wanted deep water all around me before turning south with the current. There weren't any boats tied up at Mac's place and from my vantage point on the bridge, I could just see the roof and upper parts of the windows. He was boarded up and gone.

It was late afternoon when I reached the markers at Rusty's channel. I slowed carefully as I made a wide turn—I didn't want *Cazador* ramming me. Once I anchored the *Revenge*, I swam back to *Cazador*. Her engine started immediately, and I tossed off the tow line. Jimmy was waiting at the ramp with Sherm's big three-axle trailer already in the water.

An hour later, with the sun nearing the western horizon, Jimmy and I had *El Cazador* secure on the concrete pad and the Revenge nestled snugly against the dock. We ate fish sandwiches on the deck behind the bar and turned in early.

Jimmy's younger than me by more than a decade, and no stranger to hard work, but I could tell even he was exhausted.

Through the next morning, Jimmy and I pitched in and helped anyone who needed anything done. There was no shortage of fishermen, lobstermen, divers, and boaters who wanted to use Rusty's ramp and tie-down area. By afternoon the concrete pad was full. Then, as if it'd been scheduled to the minute, a truck from the mainland arrived. On a trailer behind it was a skid steer loader with an auger attachment and a portable concrete mixer. In the back of the truck were four pallets of quick-set concrete mix and a gross of the same big eye bolts that were imbedded in Rusty's pad.

"Move it right around back," Rusty called out to the driver, as he came out the back door of the bar. "Jesse, can you run that thing?"

"We should be able to figure it out," I replied, as the truck crunched past us on the crushed shell.

"There's still a dozen boats what'll need to be secured. Maybe more."

"About three feet deep?"

Rusty nodded. "Yeah, that should get you far enough into the limestone for a good anchor."

As Jimmy and I started for the back of the property, a Cessna 185 passed over, flying low and slow. The plane had pontoons very similar to the ones on my plane. It turned southwest, then circled back to the left, lining up for an upwind approach in the bight. Billy had said he and his friend would arrive at noon.

Boat retrieval stopped for a few minutes as the float plane moved toward the ramp, then exited the water with a roar. The pilot turned it around next to my plane and shut the engine down.

A couple of years ago, Billy had bought his own plane; a Beaver like mine, but ten years newer. The Cessna's doors opened and Billy climbed out of the co-pilot's seat, stepping lightly to the ground.

As usual, Billy had his long hair pulled back in a ponytail at the back of his neck. I noted a few streaks of gray at his temples as he strode toward me in jeans, boots, and a Western-style shirt. Though we hadn't seen each other in over a year, I knew that I could count on my childhood friend.

"Thanks for doing this," I said, extending my hand.

Billy took it, locking our wrists together in the Indian way. "No problem," he said. "It'll be safe in the hangar. We just had a new one built last month, rated to withstand a 150-mile-per-hour wind."

He introduced me to his friend, a guy he only called Clark, without indicating if it was his first name or last. The three of us walked over to the *Island Hopper* and I handed Billy the keys.

"Flew her two weeks ago," I said, "and started her this morning. No issues."

Together, Billy and I did a complete walk-around and checked the tires, floats, control surfaces, and fluid levels. Satisfied, Billy climbed in and started the big radial engine.

Within half an hour of arriving, the two planes taxied down the ramp and out into the bight. One by one, they throttled up and were soon airborne. They circled out over the water and flew back over us, just above the treetops. Billy waggled the wings of my bird as they went over.

By mid-afternoon, Jimmy and I were ahead of the boaters, drilling three feet into the limestone bedrock and pouring concrete in, leaving anchor bolts sticking out of the top. The boats were parked between the concrete pilings with tie-down straps draped across them to be secured after the concrete had cured for a day.

Irma continued to spin like a saw blade along the northern spine of the Caribbean, passing close to the high mountains on Puerto Rico and Hispaniola. The updates reported sustained winds of 185 all day. The close brush with the mountains hadn't weakened the storm, and I was starting to rethink my plan. The only other option would be to head due west and try to make the Texas coast. But again, the storm could follow me the whole way and beat me up when I ran out of fuel. No, plan the mission, and execute the plan.

"Tomorrow morning," I told Jimmy during dinner at the *Anchor.* "You coming with me?"

Jimmy knew exactly what I was asking him. Hurricane Irma had us dead in her sights. Whether it passed by into the Gulf as a Cat-5 or made landfall as a Cat-3, we were going to be hammered.

"Yep," Rusty agreed. "If you're gonna go, tomorrow morning's the best time for it."

You know I'm in, Skip," Jimmy replied, raising his juice drink. "Another adventure, man."

As night fell, the trucks pulling empty trailers stopped coming. But the small parking lot was full. Locals, all of them. A storm was coming and the *Rusty Anchor* was where people tended to congregate in times of stress. Everyone had a computer or Smartphone these days, and the information was right there. But people still came. It'd been that way since Rusty's grandfather had the place, and probably before then.

We continued to watch the updates, alternating between the NOAA website forecasts and the national news outlets for damage assessment.

Irma was just south of the Turks and Caicos, battering the exposed shoreline on the south and east sides with 165 mph winds and twenty-foot waves. The storm center was nearly fifty miles from them.

Finally, the report came that I'd been hoping for. The interaction with mountainous land masses was taking its toll on the storm and she was downgraded to Cat-4. There was a collective sigh of relief in the bar. The monster could be tamed. But would she continue to weaken over the next two days?

Every hurricane model showed it turning north at some point. But most were focused right toward the Florida Straits between the Keys and Cuba, then turning north through the Upper Keys and Everglades, then right up the middle of the state toward Orlando. If that track held, the Middle and Lower Keys, as well as my hurricane hole in Tarpon Bay, would be on the west side of the storm, the weaker side, and would be spared the devastating effects that Key Largo or Miami might get on the northeast side of Irma.

"Weakening's good," Jimmy said, as we made our way down to the docks and *Gaspar's Revenge*, Finn trotting ahead of us.

"Good," I agreed. "But not great."

We both knew what might be coming, so we didn't need to talk much about it. Weathering a big hurricane in a relatively small boat was dangerous. Tucked into a deep mangrove-lined creek was the only place to do it. We'd have a wind break on three sides and the root systems were massive, intertwining with other mangroves for hundreds of feet along the marsh bank.

The island and the *Revenge* were as prepared as they were going to be. Rusty and Sidney were staying at the house and would board up after closing at noon on Saturday. Rufus decided to stay as well, though he had to be in his late seventies. So, Rusty had moved him into the guest room of his little house. Rufus's shack was sturdy, but it was down near the water, and only five or six feet above sea level. Rusty's house and bar were both built from sturdy Dade County pine. They'd weathered many storms, including the Labor Day Hurricane of 1935, which had killed thousands in the Keys, most by drowning.

CHAPTER TWENTY-EIGHT

Friday morning dawned gray and foreboding. Irma was still a Cat-4, and still barreling toward us. The location shown on the computer in the salon had it almost on top of Inagua Island, just fifty miles or so northeast of the eastern tip of Cuba. Less than 500 miles from Marathon.

Rusty brought down some fish sandwiches wrapped in foil. "So you don't have to stop working to cook," he said. "You'll have a lot to do when you get up there. You sure you got enough dock line?"

Rusty could worry more than a hen sometimes. "You know I do. We'll be fine. I'll call you when we finish tying up."

Several minutes later, we idled slowly out of Rusty's canal and into Vaca Key Bight. I brought the *Revenge* up to thirty knots, turning wide around East Sister Rock, and its single multi-million-dollar home. It sat exposed, a good quarter-mile off the accessible mainland at Tingler Island.

As I continued the wide turn and lined up for the high arch of the Seven Mile Bridge, I found myself wondering if the house would still be there when we returned.

The crossing was uneventful, seas were calm, and the sun finally broke through the gray clouds. If you didn't know there was a massive hurricane bearing down, you'd think we were just a couple guys heading out for a relaxing day of fishing.

At 0900, we were approaching the turn into Ponce De Leon Bay and the many mouths of Shark River. Jimmy got to his feet with the binoculars. "Somebody ahead of us. A small sloop."

"Hail him," I said, watching the chart plotter.

There were shallow banks to the north and south of Shark River, with several false channels that led to a sandbar or just dead-ended. The main channel itself is only deep in a winding path through shallow water. Not much of a problem for the *Revenge*. She only drew about four feet at idle, but a sailboat's keel could be much greater.

"Sailing vessel entering Shark River," Jimmy said into the mic, "this is *M/V Gaspar's Revenge*."

The reply was almost immediate. "*Gaspar's Revenge*, this is the sailing vessel *Whole Nine Yards*. Is that you in the fishing machine approaching from the south?"

"Switch to one-seven, Captain."

The other boat acknowledged and Jimmy changed channels, reestablishing contact. "Affirmative, *Whole Nine Yards*. We're about two miles behind you, going up to Tarpon Bay for the duration of the storm. You?"

"Same thing," the man replied. "Name's Griffin, Stan Griffin." The name didn't ring a bell, but the voice, though garbled slightly by the distance, seemed familiar.

"Jimmy Saunders here, with Captain Jesse McDermitt at the helm."

The man didn't say anything for a moment. I could see that he'd taken the correct inlet through the shoal water. Finally, he responded. "Feel free to take the lead if you like."

"We're good," I told Jimmy.

"We'll follow you in, Stan," Jimmy said into the mic.

"Roger that."

By the time we reached shallower water and I had to slow, we were less than half a mile behind the sloop, which I was guessing was exactly twenty-seven feet long, based on its name.

We followed the sailboat up the river at idle speed. The narrow confines of the deep river made it difficult to pass, and we still had plenty of time, so I hung back a few hundred feet, in case he ran aground.

Mangroves and an occasional bald cypress tree closed in around us on both sides as we continued upriver, their branches rising higher than the roof over our heads. Reaching a long, wide part of the river, we could see out over the trees to the east and south. The vastness of the 'Glades stretched before us. Beyond it all, hanging in an arc that probably stretched a couple hundred miles, a curve of dark gray clouds was approaching—the first big outflow band from Irma.

"Looks pretty ominous," Jimmy said.

"And it's still 500 miles away," I replied, looking at the clouds that dominated the southeastern part of the horizon. "That's just a feeder band."

After an hour, we finally moved out into Tarpon Bay, and I nudged the throttles to catch up to the sailboat. The guy seemed to have a spot already picked out, though he hadn't said much of anything on the radio. When we came alongside, I looked over. He glanced up at me and grinned.

"Good morning, Jesse," DJ Martin called out.

"Well, I'll be," I said, throttling back. "What the hell is that you're riding in?"

He drifted closer and I slowed the engines to an idle. "Just bought it," he shouted up. "Moved *Reel Fun* to Armstrong's yard on Bimini and found this for sale there."

"I didn't know you sailed."

"Neither did I until I was halfway back. The storm kinda surprised me. The only electronics aboard are the radio and a chart plotter. Didn't hear about it until yesterday in Boot Key Harbor. I sailed through the night to get here."

"Wanna raft up?"

"Sure!" he replied. "Lead the way."

"Hang back and let me get a couple of anchors down." I pointed toward the creek mouth a little to port. "It'll take us about twenty minutes."

I punched the speed up and turned toward the creek I'd anchored in once before. With Jimmy on the bow, we moved slowly into the creek mouth as far as we could.

Depth wasn't a problem as much as width and over-hanging branches.

When we got as far as we could, I nudged the bow to starboard, getting as close to the side of the creek as possible. Jimmy released the safety chain and I toggled the windlass, dropping a seventy-pound Danforth anchor six feet below to the muck-covered bottom. Jimmy tied a float ball to the chain before we let more rode out, in case debris blocked us after the storm and we had to retrieve the anchor by hand. I reversed the engines and with the help of the light current flowing out of the creek, the *Revenge* backed to the mouth of the creek, paying out 100 feet of rode. I braked the windlass and backed down, pushing the flukes into the primordial ooze.

With the wind and current on the bow, Jimmy and I worked quickly, putting the canoe in the water and lowering another seventy-pound Danforth into it, along with an eighty-pound plow anchor.

In no time at all, we had the second Danforth down on the other side of the creek, also with a hundred feet of chain rode, and the plow 100 feet astern.

DJ maneuvered his little sailboat alongside. We both put several fenders over to protect the boats from banging into one another, and soon had them lashed together securely.

"How's the ankle?" DJ said, reaching over to shake my hand.

"Your ankle?" Jimmy asked.

"Hurt it a few days back," I said. "Jimmy, this is DJ Martin. DJ, my first mate, Jimmy Saunders."

The two shook hands. "Wait. Didn't you say your name was Stan Griffin?"

"We work together, Jimmy," I told him.

"Oh. Yeah, man. Makes perfect sense."

"Jimmy can be trusted," I told DJ. "Come on over. Let's check the storm and eat lunch before we get started."

"Get started on what?" DJ asked, stepping over onto the *Revenge's* gunwale and down into the cockpit. If Jimmy noticed the titanium rod between DJ's shoe and shorts, he didn't let on.

"There's a lot of work to do, man," Jimmy replied. "Gotta tie off to about a dozen of these bigger mangroves, then cut away any branches that are dead or diseased.

Inside, Jimmy went to the computer and I put some of Rufus's fish sandwiches into the small microwave.

"Whoa," Jimmy breathed and looked over at me. He spun the laptop around. "All the spaghetti lines are pretty much in agreement."

The image showed dozens of different forecast models, maybe hundreds. All of them based on different computer models. The lines were tight and compact until just south of Miami. Each one predicted Irma to turn north, some earlier than others. But all of them had it making landfall somewhere between Homestead and Key West. None were outside that 120-mile stretch.

The microwave beeped and I put the sandwiches on paper towels on the settee. "What's the current status?"

"Still a four," Jimmy replied, turning the computer back toward him. "Changed course slightly more westerly. It could make landfall on Cuba before hitting here."

We ate in silence as Jimmy paged through several screens on the NOAA site. "Looks like there's some kinda eye wall replacement going on right now. That could be bad."

"How so?" DJ asked.

"Usually an eye wall replacement happens when a 'cane encounters more favorable, warmer waters. A new eye will appear near the old one, where the more favorable spot is, and it just sucks up the old eye."

"So, that means it might intensify?"

"Possibly," Jimmy said. "We can check again in a couple of hours."

Finishing the sandwiches, we got to work. DJ had a single anchor, which Jimmy carried far up the creek in the canoe, until the low branches blocked him.

"Still four feet deep up here," he shouted back. "I can get out and carry it farther. It's pretty straight."

"I only have about twenty feet left of the 200-foot rode," DJ shouted back.

"Drop it there," I shouted through the mangroves. "DJ, tie it off to your strongest cleat with enough of a tail to tie the bitter end to your mast step."

There was a splash ahead and a few minutes later Jimmy shouted, "Got her set deep in the muck!"

Aboard the *Whole Nine Yards*, DJ and I hauled on his anchor rode together; it was set firmly. When Jimmy returned, I lowered four heavy dock lines to him and he paddled off toward the port side of DJ's boat. He glided among the mangroves, tying the lines off to low, thick trunks. The lines uncoiled as he paddled back.

When Jimmy passed the lines back up to DJ, I handed him four more, and he moved the canoe around to the other side of the *Revenge* to do the same thing there.

The air cooled and a gust of wind brought the rain smell to my nostrils. It had been blistering hot all morning, so the cooler air felt good against my sweaty skin.

Then the rain came. Not a misty summer rain, usual for this time of year, but a full-on torrent with gale-force winds.

We went inside and dried off, after reveling in the cool for a moment. Finn was sleeping soundly, lying on the deck at the corner of the couch. Jimmy went straight to the computer and let out a low whistle.

"What is it?" I asked.

"She's back up to a five."

"You're kidding."

"Wish I was, *hermano*."

DJ and I looked over Jimmy's shoulder. The storm was massive, bigger than anything I'd ever seen. Its trailing edge was still battering the Virgin Islands and Puerto Rico with heavy rain, and the leading edge was dumping rain on the western tip of Cuba, a distance I knew to be well over 1000 miles.

When the rain stopped and the sun came back out, the humidity ratcheted up. We spent the rest of the afternoon putting out more lines, strengthening our boat-holding nylon web of dock lines, then fell into our bunks with nightfall, exhausted. Just as I was drifting off to sleep, my sat phone buzzed. It was a text message from Chyrel.

Flying home to Alabama in the morning. Thought you'd want to know this. A boat with Cayman registry was found abandoned on the beach earlier this evening in Key West. One body aboard, a small man stripped to his shorts. They think it's the boat owner. Also found on the boat was a flight attendant's uniform.

I texted a thank-you reply and wished her luck.

Sunna, in Key West?

She'd stolen the uniform of the flight attendant she'd murdered. Allegedly, anyway. But my brain doesn't need a lot of proof to make the obvious connections. Why would she go to the Rock? And from where? She'd been spirited away from the Caymans by a private jet that originated out of Mexico and appeared to be headed back there when it disappeared off radar. She was probably somewhere in Mexico. Why would she come to the States? The question was still on my mind as I fell into a restless sleep.

CHAPTER TWENTY-NINE

Hiding out in Key West would be easy. Sunna left the dead man on his boat and went ashore wearing his clothes. She should have dumped the body before reaching shore, but the side of the boat was high and she couldn't lift him over it. He was small, but not as small as she, so the pant legs and sleeves were rolled up, and his clothes hung limp on her small frame. She didn't see anyone on the beach, and quickly faded into the darkness between a condo and a museum of some kind.

A block and a half away, she realized that she'd left the flight attendant's uniform on the boat. "*Modur ridill!*" she muttered as she turned to go back. Sirens could be heard as she neared the beach, and she saw several people standing around the boat. She turned and disappeared down a narrow street.

She'd been filled with rage since the tall man had ridiculed her and the Onayans on the cliff, insinuating she was nothing more than a common drug dealer. He'd been behind the multiple coups on the Onayan communes, she was sure of it.

She ran things, not Onay. He was simply a figurehead, nothing more. He was polished and people liked him, so Sunna provided him with a steady supply of young girls to satisfy his appetite. But where would he be without her wits?

They'd set up the new communes in the Virgin Islands after he'd started his original in Japan and branched into Europe. Sunna had taken over most of the planning. Onay brought in new people, with promises of enlightenment. The ritual the tall man had interrupted was but one of many, stripping away the resolve of the new recruits and turning them into obedient followers, who freely gave up their wealth and all their belongings. There were other such communes all over the globe, and Onay moved among them, teaching his spiritualism.

But it was Sunna who had organized the many far-flung outposts, which soon began to draw in more and more affluent people. She'd made Onay rich. It was also Sunna who had taken care of the troublemakers, bleeding them and feeding the corpses to the hungry sharks on Norman Island that the blood drew in. She used other means to dispose of the bodies in other locations. Her methods always ensured the bodies would never be discovered. And her security team did the dirty work. Most of the time.

Sunna had people outside the Onayan communes, as well—people who gave her information when she needed it. Others moved the merchandise the small labs on the islands created. Yes, it was drugs. But the people in the streets would get them from somewhere, so she might as well make money from their misery. Someone was going to.

One person on Norman Island had given her the name of the tall man's boat. From that, it had been a simple matter to find out his name and where he lived. Jesse McDermitt, of Marathon, Florida, now just forty-odd miles away.

She walked through residential streets, keeping to the shadows as she snuck away from the beach. The boat and the body of the man who'd brought her from Grand Cayman had been discovered sooner than she'd hoped. But there was nothing she could do about it now. Glancing down a side street, she noticed the next block over was better lit, so she went that way.

At the corner, tucked into the shadow of tall tropical vegetation, she looked both ways. The signpost said it was Duval Street, which she had heard of. There were no cars at this late hour, still an hour before dawn. She moved along Duval, looking for a clothing store of some kind.

Killing the flight attendant had been simple. Sunna had overheard that she was new. The woman worked in the back of the plane, where Sunna and the others from the communes had been sequestered. There were two lavatories, one forward and one at the tail of the plane. Before landing, a woman passenger in the front went to the forward lavatory and tripped, causing a commotion.

Sunna told the policeman sitting two rows in front of her that she needed to use the facilities and he'd obliged by removing her handcuffs. Sunna had waited in the restroom until the new flight attendant came to the aft compartment, where they stored drinks and snacks. Then she'd made her move, first closing the curtain, then strangling the woman from behind. In the confusion of the landing and the injured passenger, Sunna had put on the flight attendant's uniform and quietly slipped off the plane unnoticed.

The ruse the following day, of running out to the private plane, its boarding ladder on the side away from most prying eyes, had worked well. She made sure someone had seen a blonde flight attendant run out to it just before it took off. It was a plane she'd summoned just for that purpose. Sunna had continued around the plane to a building and had waited for the plane to leave before hiring a boat to take her to Key West. Hopefully, the pilot had done his part and flew low enough to not be seen on radar, so the authorities would have no idea where she went. Doing so would reinforce the idea that she was on the airplane.

She noticed a number of stores on the next block and checked the opening times. After locating one that opened at 8:00 am, she found a place nearby to hide out until morning.

When Sunna suddenly appeared next to the young man opening the store an hour early, she startled him.

"I need clothing," she said, matter-of-factly. Then she flashed the man a demure smile.

Her intent was to lure him into a backroom, offering sex if need be. Men were so very simple-minded in that regard. Then she would kill him with the small gun in her pocket, which she'd taken from the dead man on the boat after seducing him and getting him to disrobe.

The store owner looked down at her and smiled. "You sure do, girlfriend. What happened to you?"

Sunna immediately realized she wasn't going to be able to seduce the man. So, she lowered her head and began to sob. "My boyfriend left me here."

"There, now," the man said, turning the knob and pushing the door open before patting Sunna's back comfortingly. "Come on in, Sugar, and we'll get you fixed right up. That man must have been a jerk—you are just too cute."

She stepped inside and the man turned and locked the door. He stepped back and studied her a moment. "You're a size two, right?"

CHAPTER THIRTY

The rain started soon after Sunna left Key West. The store owner's early arrival had surprised her, but she'd gotten everything she needed and then some. Dressed in more suitable clothes, she'd re-locked the door and quickly located his car by pushing the lock button on the key fob and following the sound of the beep.

The car was a nondescript import and it had nearly a full tank of gas. Knowing she could probably get to where she was going before anyone else arrived at the store and found the man's body lying beside a pillow with two burn holes in it, she pressed on. The pillow had muffled the shots enough that she doubted anyone had heard.

It had taken her a while to find her way out of Key West. The visibility from the storm didn't make it any easier. Then, the closer she got to her destination, the more cars there were, all going the same way. Several times, she passed police cars on corners. The first one she'd seen nearly panicked her. But it seemed as if they were ignoring the speeders, as if waiting for something else.

Sunna finally arrived at a very long bridge at 10:00 am, after nearly three hours of stop-and-go driving to get forty miles. She was worried, because the storekeeper's body was bound to have been discovered by now. The rain had stopped, but there were more clouds approaching from farther ahead and it was still quite windy. She much preferred the weather of the Virgin Islands, especially Tortola.

Once she made it safely across the long bridge, Sunna slowed and watched the addresses of the places she passed, while other cars sped past her on the four-lane highway. Finally, she found the right number, painted on an old mailbox, leaning slightly to the side. Sunna turned off the highway, the tires of the stolen car crunching on the shell driveway. Her excitement level was peaking.

The wind diminished as the car was swallowed by a tropical jungle. She let the car creep forward slowly. This was the address she'd been given by a contact in London who was good with computers. The place she hoped to find McDermitt. She would dispose of the interloper and then disappear. The Onayan numbered accounts in Zurich held enough wealth for several lifetimes of opulence, and Onay wouldn't be able to access it. She could disappear forever.

The dense foliage opened up and the driveway widened into a parking area half-full of cars and trucks.

It wasn't the tall man's house at all, but what looked like a restaurant, though there was no sign saying that.

"Ah," she said, as she drove further into the parking area and a house behind the business became visible. "I've got you."

Parking the car, Sunna got out and looked around. The rain had started again, a fine mist, as if the low-hanging clouds were trying to hold it in. There was a marina also, though it was nearly empty—only one small boat was docked next to a rusty barge. Far out behind the buildings, dozens of boats were parked on the grass and a concrete pad.

Perhaps the cars and boats are only stored here, she thought. It might be a good idea to see if there was anyone in the business before proceeding to the house behind it.

With the little semi-automatic handgun tucked into her brand-new purse, she walked toward the door, pulled on the handle and was assailed by a blast of cold air. As she stepped inside the place, she removed her new sunglasses. It took a moment for her eyes to adjust, even though there was no bright sunshine outside. She wore the yellow-lensed "driving" glasses she'd found on the rack at the clothing store to conceal her, not to protect her from the sun.

There were about a dozen people inside, mostly men, and none seemed to notice her entrance, except a rather tall young woman with dark red hair. Everyone else was busy watching a television behind an expansive wooden bar.

The woman approached Sunna, carrying a menu. Her smile was bright and sincere. "Care for a table?" she asked.

When the scent of food wafted into her nostrils, Sunna suddenly realized she hadn't eaten anything in over a day. "Yes, please."

"I'm Naomi," the woman said, leading her to a table next to a window. "Are you on your way out of the Keys?"

"Um, yes," Sunna replied.

She took Sunna's drink order and left her with the menu, explaining that she didn't really work there, but was just helping her aunt.

Sunna looked at the menu while listening to the conversation among the men at the bar. A loud ring came from behind the counter, and the bartender, a short, fat, bald man with a mostly red beard, yelled for quiet. He took an old desk phone from under the bar, placed it in front of him, and lifted the receiver.

"Y'all hunkered down, Jesse?" the bearded man said, instantly getting Sunna's full attention. "Looks like we might get a direct hit here." He listened a moment, obviously talking to the tall man, Jesse McDermitt. "Anyone I know?" he asked.

The bearded man nodded at one of the patrons and put a beer bottle in front of him.

"Not exactly," the bald man said. "We're all boarded up and everything's secure, but I put a few folks up in the house. Me and some of the guides are gonna ride it out here at the bar."

Sunna didn't quite understand what he was talking about but suddenly realized that she couldn't see out the window she was seated next to. The storm shutters were pulled closed.

"Yeah," the fat man replied. "Heard about some looting already. It was down to Key West, though. A store owner was robbed and killed when he opened up this morning. The killer got away with his credit cards, a couple hundred in cash from the till, and his car."

While the man listened on the phone, he raised his chin in question toward another bar patron. The man shook his head, and stood to leave, pulling his wallet from his back pocket. The bartender waved him off.

"We'll likely lose telephone and power tonight," the man said into the phone. "Check in with me on my satellite phone first thing tomorrow, okay? I just turned it on."

He hung up the phone and put it away. One of the men at the bar said, "Is McDermitt riding it out at his little house up in the Content Keys?"

"Nah," the man behind the bar replied. "He took the boat up to Tarpon Bay."

"Gutsy call," the other man said, as Sunna slipped out the back door.

The man who'd left the bar was heading toward the docks, and she hurried after him.

CHAPTER THIRTY-ONE

Saturday morning was dark and gray, but it wasn't raining. The wind had started to kick up, whistling eerily through the branches all around us. By mid-morning, we'd cleared the mangrove canopy of any dead branches, and went to work on the boats.

Deciding to break for lunch as another squall bore down on us from the southeast, we headed inside. Finn was dancing around the door, and I realized he hadn't been able to relieve himself since last night. He didn't have a problem aboard *Salty Dog*. I'd converted the shower pan in the forward head to a place any dog would be proud of, even adding an overhead portlight.

I clipped his leash on and took him to the transom door. "Don't jump in," I cautioned him. "It might look like shore's just beyond the mangroves, but we're in the 'Glades. No land for miles."

He looked disappointed but did what he had to do on the swim platform, and then I hosed it off.

"What's the latest?" I asked, as Finn and I stepped back inside the salon.

"After making landfall on Cayo Romano late last night, it buzzed right up the Cuban coastline, bouncing ashore in several places." Jimmy looked at me and grinned. "You called it, man. Down to a Category-3 now and they expect further weakening. The storm center is 200 miles south-southeast of Miami."

"Tonight then?" DJ asked.

"No," Jimmy replied. "The interaction with land has slowed it down, too. They're still saying it's gonna turn north and are now predicting a landfall in the Keys tomorrow morning."

"But weaker," DJ said. "Maybe not even a hurricane as fast as it's weakening?"

"There's over eighty miles of warm water in the Straits," I said. "It'll likely strengthen some."

Using my sat phone, I pulled up Rusty's landline at the bar. "Y'all hunkered down, Jesse?" he said by way of hello. "Looks like we might get a direct hit here."

"Yeah, I think we're good," I replied. "We're rafted up with a friend we met along the way."

"Anyone I know?"

"No, you never met him. Sort of a co-worker. Have you closed up yet?"

"Not exactly," Rusty said. "We're all boarded up and everything's secure, but I put a few folks up in the house. Me and some of the guides are gonna ride it out here at the bar."

That was typical for Rusty. He'd give a stranger the shirt off his back. There was no doubt that they'd be without power at some point, so he was probably feeding everyone, too. And I also knew that once the storm passed, the men would fan out into the community, helping others before ever checking on their own homes.

"So, everything's okay there?"

"Yeah," he replied. "Heard about some looting already. It was down to Key West, though. A store owner was robbed and killed when he opened up this morning. The killer got away with his credit cards, a couple hundred in cash from the till, and his car."

"Yeah, well, we both know these things bring out the loonies."

"We'll likely lose telephone and power tonight," Rusty said. "Check in with me on my satellite phone first thing tomorrow, okay? I just turned it on."

I told him I would and ended the call.

"All that's left is your mast and rigging," I told DJ. "It's deck-stepped and I have plenty of tools. It'd probably be better to take it down."

"And do what with it?" DJ asked. "Even lashed to the deck, it could come loose and do all kinds of damage."

"Coil the rigging, and stow it and the wiring inside," I replied. "We can sink the mast and put a dinghy anchor on it, so it doesn't drift away."

The wind was out of the east and had built to a steady twenty or thirty knots. Jimmy shackled a dock line to the turnbuckle on the forestay, and once I had the clevis pin pulled from the front of the step, we carefully lowered the mast, hinged on the aft bolt of the step.

Fortunately, *Whole Nine Yards* being a small boat, its standing rigging consisted of only the forestay, a single aft stay and two shrouds. Once the mast was down, we removed them from the masthead and carefully coiled them, using cable ties to hold them together. DJ carried them into his boat and stored them in the salon.

Then we turned to the mast itself and removed the antenna, wind vane and cups, the masthead light, and all the wiring. I tied a string to the end of the antenna coax and we pulled all the wiring out at once, leaving the string in its place. That'd make it easier to reinstall everything later.

"Hey, DJ," I said, as he headed down into the cabin with the wind cups. "Rather than store that below, how about bringing it over here? You're gonna stay aboard the *Revenge*, right?"

"You gonna run the AC tonight?"

I grinned. "Yeah. And bring the wind gauge that connects to the other end. Might come in handy, if we can wire it up somehow."

An anemometer looks like four measuring cups joined together at the handles. The cups catch the wind and spin around, measuring wind speed.

"It has a battery backup," he said, handing the anemometer over. "Supposed to last for six hours of continuous use."

By midafternoon, the rain was constant, but not too heavy. Below the tops of the trees, we were shielded from the bulk of the wind. Jimmy took the small anchor, wedged it into the sand beside DJ's boat, and then we slowly lowered the aluminum mast into the water.

"I sure hope this works," DJ said. "A sailboat isn't much good without a mast."

"We'll do the same thing with the canoe, man," Jimmy said. "Best place for them to be is underwater."

Standing on the foredeck of the *Revenge*, I surveyed both boats and our surroundings. The sun would go down soon, even though we wouldn't see it, and the storm would build throughout the night. But the worst wouldn't come until late tomorrow morning.

Seeing nothing to worry about, we retired to my salon and again, Jimmy went straight to the computer. I'd have to remember to start the generator before we went to sleep. With no sun for most of the day, the solar panels on the roof hadn't been able to collect much energy.

"She's down to a Cat-2, man!" Jimmy was practically jubilant. "But it's headed north-northwest now, just moved back out over water near La Teja."

I looked at the screen and Jimmy changed to the forecast cone. It showed Irma's path prediction, strengthening to Cat-4, and moving right through the Middle Keys in the morning, before making another landfall between Cape Sable and Tampa Bay later tomorrow afternoon. In twenty-four hours, this would all be over. But first we had to get through those twenty-four hours.

"We'll be in the northeast quadrant of the storm," Jimmy said. "Dude, this could totally harsh my mellow."

"We've been through it before," I reminded him.

"You guys went through a hurricane on this boat before?" DJ asked.

"Right here in this very creek, man. Hurricane Irene, right, Jesse? We holed up here with that girl—what was her name?"

"Yeah, Irene," I said, ignoring the reference to Savannah. "That was a long time ago, and it was only a Category-1 when the eye passed over us. This will be worse, but then, varying levels of hell aren't all that different, really."

"You were in the eye of the storm?" DJ asked.

"Like I said, it wasn't much of a blow. This one's gonna be worse, but we're completely prepared."

We assigned a simple four-hour watch as we ate dinner, and DJ volunteered for the mid-watch. Since he was the youngest, I thought it a good idea. I used to be able to get by on just a few hours' sleep here and there for days on end, but the last two weeks had really taken a toll.

I took first watch and after dinner, DJ and Jimmy turned in.

Sitting in the salon, I read a book on lost treasure ships while the storm raged outside, building steadily. Finn lay beside me on the deck and I reached out a hand to give him an ear scratch. He didn't move, but his tail beat a fast tattoo on the deck.

My mind shifted to the Icelandic woman from Norman Island. How could people go so far off the deep end? Drugging innocent people without their knowledge, kidnapping them, using them for their own perverse games, and even killing some? I could never understand it.

The flight attendant had just been the wrong person in the wrong place at the wrong time. As had the poor sap who'd brought her to Key West from wherever the plane had landed. The dismembered and beheaded body that had washed up on Little Thatch was obviously one of their own; they all wore the same clothes.

Suddenly, something Rusty said earlier clicked in my mind. He'd told me that a Key West store owner had been murdered. Who kills a store owner? Especially for just a couple hundred bucks? I pulled my phone out of my pocket and texted Rusty.

A moment later, I got his reply. *Yeah, it was a clothing store.*

So, the man killed in Key West owned a clothing store, and the last thing Sunna had been seen wearing was a flight attendant's uniform, which kinda stuck out.

I texted Rusty back and told him to keep an eye out for a very short blonde with pale blue eyes, who might come looking for me. I doubted she'd be running around in a hurricane looking for anyone, but the *Anchor* was my address on record. Then again, the killing of the store owner might have been just a coincidence.

I checked the computer every hour and ran the generator constantly. The *Revenge* was completely closed up, so we'd stay dry, but the outside temperature was still in the 80s and the humidity was right at 100%, so the air inside was hot and saturated. I ran the AC so we could rest comfortably.

With the 2200 update, Irma had slowed her forward speed considerably, wobbling as if uncertain what she wanted to destroy next, after disrupting life throughout the northern and eastern Caribbean. She was whirling around in the Florida Straits, maybe sixty miles south of Marathon, moving in a zig-zag drift toward the Seven Mile Bridge and gaining strength.

A huge gust of wind passed over us and Finn looked up at me.

"You worried about the storm, boy?"

He cocked his head and his ears came up, as if saying, *Not as long as we're together.*

I leaned down and scratched the soft fur under his chin. His nose pointed upward and his ears lay back on his head in total bliss.

Suddenly, the boat jerked. Finn's ears came back up and he looked toward the starboard side. My eyes followed his gaze, but I could see nothing through the large, rain-swept porthole. All I could hear was the wind and the beating of the rain on the roof. But the boat had moved, and Finn had definitely heard something. Finn had been at my side for years, and I'd learned to trust his hearing. He often warned me of distant thunder while out on the water.

The wind was on our bow, so I went aft and opened the salon hatch to check the lines. I really had to tug on the knob; the vacuum created by the wind howling past had it sucked tight to the frame. Finally, I got it open and felt the pressure change in my ears.

"What happened?" Jimmy said, as he and DJ came up from the forward berthing area.

"Don't know," I replied, grabbing a flashlight and stepping out into the cockpit. The wind was whipping the treetops at what I'd guess would be close to tropical storm strength.

Jimmy and DJ stepped out behind me, but I told Finn to stay inside. I went to the starboard side and pointed my flashlight toward the mangroves. I saw the problem right off.

"One of the mangroves has snapped." I had to yell to be heard over the wind. "The line is hanging loose where the branch fell in the water."

Earlier, I'd used a clamp and attached DJ's wind vane to the more exposed starboard handrail on the side of the cabin, strapping the cable to the rail all the way to the cockpit. There, I'd brought the cable under the small overhang and stored the gauge in a mesh netting that held the boat's life vests, turned so that the gauge could be read from below. Jimmy had switched it on and was staring at it.

"Gusting over forty-five," he shouted. "It hasn't dropped below thirty yet."

I looked up at the treetops around us. "Probably higher than that above those trees."

"How far away is it?" DJ asked.

"Still a good hundred miles or so," I replied somberly.

Jimmy whistled; the sound being sucked away by the wind. "Man, there aren't many storms I've heard of with tropical storm-force winds a hundred miles from the center."

As I moved the flashlight from line to line, we studied each one. We had more than a dozen lines and four anchors out, though the aft one served little purpose until the storm passed. Later, the wind would come at us from the south, then southwest, but diminishing. The aft anchor would keep the wind from pushing us farther up the creek.

"I think the other lines will hold," I offered. "You guys get back to sleep."

"It's an hour till my watch," DJ said. "You go ahead, I'll take over."

Too tired to argue, I agreed. In my cabin, I toweled myself off and changed into dry clothes before lying down on the bunk. Sleep didn't come easy with the violent wind roaring over the foredeck just above my head, but finally, I drifted into a fitful rest.

CHAPTER THIRTY-TWO

I woke just as tired as I'd been when I went to bed. Light came in through the overhead portlight. Not sunlight—just a dim, gray, non-directional light. Rain was sheeting onto the roof and the starboard side of the hull. Irma had moved further north, and the winds were starting to come around to a slightly more south-westerly direction.

When I went to the galley, the rocking of the boat threw me into the bulkhead. I steadied myself and used both handrails to go up the three steps to the galley. Jimmy and DJ were both there. Jimmy lifted a Thermos from the seat between them.

I grabbed a plastic mug with a lid and handed it to him. The way the boat was rocking, he'd burn my hand if I held it. He got it half full and wedged the lid down. I accepted the hot, Costa Rican coffee with relish.

"I took Finn out a while ago," DJ said. "He didn't look real happy about having to squat to pee on the swim platform."

"Thanks," I said and turned to my first mate.

"The eye shifted west," Jimmy said. "The center is fifteen miles south of Summerland. It looks like a landfall somewhere between the Saddlebunch and Big Pine in an hour or so."

I drank down half the coffee in one big gulp, feeling the caffeine jolt almost instantly. "What are the winds?"

Jimmy's face told the story. "One-thirty, man."

"Any mention of storm surge?"

Coming off the coast of Cuba, I knew the surge wouldn't be as high as it could be, having only ninety miles for it to build.

"Nothing definitive," Jimmy said. "But seas beyond the reef in the Middle Keys are reported to be higher than ten feet and they're predicting a five-foot surge."

To keep from falling, I squeezed in beside Jimmy. "Any surge will grow higher in the shallows of the back country."

I looked at my watch. It was 0800, but I decided to call Rusty anyway. He answered on the second ring.

"How're the conditions down there?" I asked.

"Shitty and gettin' shittier. I think you had the right idea. How's things there?"

"We had a mangrove break last night," I replied. "Maybe the anchors dragged a few inches and the line to it was stretched too tight. But we have thirteen more, plus four anchors."

There was silence for a moment, and I thought I'd lost him. "We had an incident here yesterday," Rusty said.

My thoughts went back to the day after Hurricane Wilma had passed near the Keys, when two looters had tried to rob us at the *Anchor.* "What happened?"

"The Other Jack's dead."

"What? How?"

The Other Jack was one of the local flats guides. When he came to the Keys, many years ago, there was a guide by the name of Jack Gentles, so people took to calling Jack Clark "The Other Jack." Long after Gentles went back up north, the name still stuck.

"It was some time after I talked to you on the phone. Shot dead right down at my docks, bro."

"They catch who did it?"

Again, there was a pause.

"Before he was found, Naomi said she was serving a woman who got up and left before her drink even arrived. Left right after The Other Jack went down to move his boat onto a trailer. Naomi said the woman was smallish, with blond hair and pale blue eyes. With the windows boarded up, and thunder crashing, nobody saw or heard anything. Whoever it was, they took The Other Jack's boat."

"In a hurricane?" I asked, incredulously.

"What's this all about with the blonde?" Rusty asked.

Figuring that Jimmy ought to know as well, I told Rusty to hang on and put the phone on speaker. Then I had Rusty explain everything again, and then I told them who Sunna Johannsdottir was and how she'd escaped custody in the Caymans.

"Well, keep your powder dry," Rusty said. "Sounds like she's already killed a few people. If Irma doesn't swallow her up, I'm guessin' she's coming for you, for whatever reason."

I ended the call and, having emptied the Thermos, went to the coffeemaker to refill it. Remembering another time when I'd tried that in a storm, I dropped a damp towel onto the deck before pouring. This time, only a few drops slopped out, and I turned off the coffeemaker and secured the pot.

The update at 0900 showed Irma had made landfall on Cudjoe Key, about thirty miles down island from the *Rusty Anchor*. With its counterclockwise winds, Marathon to Ramrod Key would be getting the brunt of the storm, with winds up to 130 miles per hour and heavy surf.

I knew Rusty's place was sturdy; it'd survived quite a few lashings, and the combined surge and wave action wouldn't reach it. But I still worried.

Over the next hour, things started getting really nasty. The wind roared across the Everglades like a bullet-train, with barely anything to slow it down but sawgrass for a hundred miles. Its direction moved slowly from southeast to south as the storm began to pass us not far to the west.

Jimmy and I were both concerned about my island. The storm had been moving due north at fifteen miles per hour when it made landfall, putting my little island, at best, five miles east of the center. Irma's northeastern eye wall would have brushed very close to it. Most of the wave action would have spent itself on the reef, the other keys, and the shallows, but that dome of water called the surge would only rise, like a small ocean wave rises and crests before falling onto the beach. We'd done all we could to protect the houses and everything I'd built over the last thirteen years. It was out of our hands now.

I sat on the couch, looking out across DJ's boat. I could see the mangroves on the opposite side intermittently. The constant rocking and bumping of the boats made it difficult to get comfortable.

"You're worried about the house, huh," Jimmy stated.

I could read his own worry in his eyes.

"We did what we could," I said. "Everything's in Irma's hands now."

"There won't be much left, man."

"I know," I whispered. "I know."

By noon, the hurricane update on NOAA had Irma positioned about twenty-five miles west of our location, still headed almost due north. The wind was now out of the south, almost broadside to us. The *Revenge* rocked violently, tugging at her lines as if attempting to uproot the whole Everglades.

Jimmy went to the large porthole aft, protected slightly by the overhanging flybridge. "Gusts to a hundred," he said. "And not dropping below sixty."

"Wait," DJ said. "I thought high winds extended farther out. That's not even hurricane force, and it's no more than forty miles away."

"Twenty-five," I corrected him. "The wind vane isn't high enough to catch the windspeed aloft."

"Just above these mangroves," Jimmy said, pointing upward, "it's probably well over a hundred sustained."

Talking was difficult. Our voices were already becoming hoarse from trying to be heard over the maelstrom outside. We just tried to find a comfortable spot to sit without getting thrown around. Finn lay curled on the deck, his head on his paws. But his eyes were open and he was watching me, reading my attitude. I tried to relax.

At 1400, things had calmed enough that we could get outside for a damage assessment. We hadn't lost any more lines, but it looked like the boats had shifted in relation to one another. Not much, but the forward lines holding the two boats together were straining the cleats, while the aft ones hung loose. My two anchors had dragged a little. But DJ's, with another hundred feet of scope out and less windage on the hull, had held. We readjusted the lines and, with another squall quickly approaching from the southwest, hurried inside.

Less than two hours later, Irma made landfall again, roaring up through the Ten Thousand Islands into the heavily developed city of Marco Island. After making its final landfall, Irma weakened quickly over land, as hurricanes always do. They need warm ocean water for fuel.

On Tarpon Bay, the sun was shining, still an hour or so from setting, and winds had dropped to twenty knots. The scattered clouds were moving very fast, heading off to the northeast, trying to catch up to the now fast-moving storm.

Before darkness fell, we got to work rewiring and stepping DJ's mast. We had the stays retightened to the tape DJ had put on each turnbuckle before we took the mast down, and then we were able to start untying the boats from the mangroves.

After we ate, we pulled the canoe up from the bottom, where we'd sunk it with every diving weight I had aboard. After dumping the water out and stowing the weights, Jimmy got in to retrieve the anchors and untie the lines. DJ moved out into the bay a few hundred yards and I anchored nearby, then invited him over to enjoy the AC for another night.

Jimmy was able to use the laptop's satellite connection to get news reports from the Keys. Eight hours after landfall, it looked like a war zone down there, as people came out of nearly demolished homes to find their property destroyed beyond repair. Boats had been washed away, and the highway connecting the islands was impassable.

NOAA had put images up on the internet; recent satellite images. Jimmy zoomed in on Boot Key Harbor. When we'd left, I'd caught a glimpse through the old Boot Key bridge span and saw dozens of boats still swinging on mooring balls. The images showed the harbor was nearly empty, save for four or five boats, and there were a lot of vessels driven onto the northern shore and into the mangroves. He zoomed in on each one still moored, and we realized that most that weren't swept away were partially sunk.

We'd already decided that it would be far too dangerous to make the run back home in the dark. There would be debris in the water and broken limbs hanging over Shark River to contend with. Since there was nothing we could do, we retired in order to get an early start. By the time we were ready to turn in, Irma was passing to the east of Tampa as a weakening Cat-1 storm.

I tried Rusty's satellite phone, but he didn't answer. As I was putting the phone back on the charger, he called back.

"We're fine," I said without preamble. "How are things there? Jimmy picked up some news reports. Looks awful."

"We haven't been out any farther than Boot Key," he said. "Can't drive anywhere. Lines are down, sand's washed over the road, and parts of houses and boats are everywhere. Found a boat in a tree on the way over there."

"How'd your place hold up?" I asked, afraid to hear the answer.

"Nobody got hurt," he replied. "And no structural damage. Can't say the same for *Dockside*."

"What happened there?"

"It's still there, but the pilings shifted, and most of the roof tore off."

A couple of years ago, after *Dockside* had been closed up for a while. Eric Stone, who sometimes played at the *Anchor*, started a crowdfunding to buy and renovate the place, and then reopened it as *Dockside Tropical Café.*

He'd sold out just a few months ago and gone on the road, taking his trop-rock music all over the country.

"Guess Eric got out just in time," I said.

"Yeah," Rusty agreed. "We have a lot of trees down here on my property. Been working on cleaning up since about noon and hope to open on generator power tomorrow afternoon. Jesse, the eye passed right by your place."

"I know," I replied. "I'm not holding my breath in hopes of finding anything left."

"When ya comin' back?"

"We're anchored in the middle of Tarpon Bay right now, planning to leave in the morning. I want to run by my place first. Probably get to the *Anchor* about noon. Is your canal open?"

"No," he replied. "But it will be before you get here."

"We'll need space for the *Revenge* and a twenty-seven-foot sailboat."

"Consider it done. Y'all be careful."

We said our goodbyes, and as I lay in my bunk, I could hear Jimmy and DJ talking in low voices. I couldn't hear what they were saying, but Jimmy sounded dismal. My island had been his home for quite a while now.

CHAPTER THIRTY-THREE

The man had been in a hurry to get to his boat. With the restaurant's windows covered, Sunna knew that nobody could see her run after him and catch him at the dock. She'd asked if he knew where the Content Keys were and how to get there, and he'd told her the only way to get there was by boat, and then only if you had the GPS numbers. She'd asked him if he could show her.

He'd been reluctant, saying he had things to do, but when she'd pulled the gun from her purse, he'd become more compliant. She'd ordered him to show her exactly where it was on his boat's navigation equipment. He'd complied, muttering that she would be stupid to go there in the storm. When he'd finished, and sat back on the side of the boat, she'd shot him in the forehead. His body fell backward into the water.

It had taken nearly two hours to reach the group of islands where McDermitt lived. The conditions were much rougher in the Keys than in the tranquil waters of Tortola. And shallower. She'd run aground twice before realizing that although the navigation equipment showed a straight line, she had to work her way around many islands and follow the depth lines on the screen.

A torrential rain started falling as she got closer. Finally, she could see the metal roof of a house above windswept trees. There was a very low dock in front of it. The man at the bar had said that McDermitt had taken his boat to Tarpon Bay, wherever that was. But sooner or later, she knew he'd return.

She tied the stolen boat to the dock, close to the house, confident that nobody was inside. There were two large doors below the house, reaching all the way down to the water, but she saw no latch on the outside of either one.

With rain dripping from her hair and face, Sunna went up the steps cautiously, gun in hand, just in case her assumption that no one was at home was wrong. Her clothes were wet, but the air was very warm, so she didn't feel uncomfortable.

When she reached the top, she found a deck that wrapped around three sides of the house. The only thing on it was a wooden table, which seemed to be attached to the deck.

She tried the door and found it locked, and the windows were all covered with metal. Looking through the rain, out toward the middle of the island, she saw three more small houses.

The wind tore at her clothes as she stood on the back deck, flattening her soaked shirt to her back and snapping at it in front. Likewise, her wet hair stood almost straight out from her face.

At the bottom of a second set of stairs, she walked past several water tanks, two of which had plants growing in them. Though mostly bare, she recognized many of them as vegetable plants.

Continuing to the nearest house, she found that door also locked and the windows covered with metal panels, the same as the house on stilts. She found the third and fourth houses similarly closed up; no way to get inside any of them.

Sunna's anger rose inside her again. She stood in the middle of the small island and screamed up at the fast-moving clouds. The storm was getting worse and she needed to seek shelter.

She went back to the main house and looked for another way in. There was a smaller door on the first level, just below the stairs down to the pier. When she tried it, the door opened easily. There was no floor inside, just water, with a narrow walkway around three sides, and another in the middle. Other than that, it was empty.

A place to store boats, she thought, as she noticed some sort of locker at the end of the far walkway.

Another one behind the door had several shelves, with large canvas bags on each one. She unzipped one and found it full of scuba-diving equipment. When she opened the closet at the end of the far walkway, she found a blanket of sorts, along with tackle boxes and fishing gear. The blanket was camouflage-colored and quilted. She took it and went back to the entrance door.

Starting to get a chill, even in the warm summer air, Sunna looked outside at the slanting rain. The wind was whipping the treetops, making them sway back and forth.

At least I'm out of the wind, she thought, looking for a dry place to rest.

Water dripped down through the gaps in the deck planks above. But it looked like the closets were covered. At least the stuff inside had been dry. The blanket wouldn't be much use if she didn't find a dry place to get out of the rain.

Sunna went back to the door and looked out. The rain was pouring down and the wind whistled through the trees. The house covered part of the docking area below it, but the only part of the walkway it covered was along the far wall.

The closets, she realized, clutching the dry blanket.

It would be dark in a few hours. With no other option, she removed all the gear from the floor of the closet next to the entrance, as well as everything on the first shelf, then removed the shelf itself.

With her clothes soaked through and now cold against her skin, she removed her shoes and placed them on the shelf above, in the hope that they would dry out by morning. She wrapped the blanket around her, squeezed into the small space at the bottom of the closet, and pulled the door closed behind her. Even through the blanket, she could feel the rough wooden planks of the floor.

He'll return, she thought, as she pulled the blanket tighter around her. *He has to return. And when he does, I'll be waiting.*

The storm got wilder outside, and when she thought it had peaked it got even worse. The wind howled past the house and sheets of rain pounded on the side. Huddled in the blanket, her clothes slowly shed water, and her body heat helped dry them to dampness.

Suddenly she realized what was happening. She'd heard stories on Tortola about a devastating hurricane that had hit there nearly thirty years ago; Hugo it was called.

Was this a hurricane? she wondered.

The blanket she was nestled in smelled of dog. Outside, she could hear the tempest continuing to build, hour after hour, the screaming wind louder than a locomotive. The building itself seemed to move with each gust of wind. Or maybe it was just her imagination.

As the storm worsened, it became darker. Night was falling. Surely the storm would end soon. Even hurricanes didn't last forever. When it was over, McDermitt would return. Once she'd gotten revenge for his slanderous comments, she'd go someplace that didn't have storms.

Bunched in the bottom of the closet, Sunna was at least warm. Her clothes had soaked the section of the blanket she was sitting on, but her shirt felt a little dryer.

She lost all track of time, but it had to be all over soon. Inside the closet, in the dark confines beneath the house, she could see nothing, not even her hand waving in front of her face. She closed her eyes and dozed, but nothing could close her ears. Minutes turned into hours. She drifted into a sleep-like state, not really asleep, but not fully awake either. She was beyond exhausted, after two days on the boat and the ordeal to reach this island, and slumped against the wall, drifting in and out of a fitful slumber.

Suddenly, she felt something wet against her bottom. More wet than the blanket. Thinking her butt had become numb from sitting on the hard floor, she attempted to reposition herself. Her foot splashed into the water.

Panicked, Sunna first tried to stand, banging her head against the shelf above her. She calmed herself and noticed there was a faint light coming from under the door. It was nearly dawn. If anything, the storm was worse.

She felt around for the doorknob and turned it, pushing the door open slightly. What she saw sent a chill of fear down her spine. The water under the house had flooded over the walkway. Either it was rising or the house was sinking.

How high could it go? she wondered. Would she be trapped inside the closet by the rising water?

The big doors were bowing inward from the force of the wind. Outside, waves were splashing against them, straining the latch. In the blink of an eye, the far door burst off its hinges, exploding inward until it lodged itself at an angle, stopped by the center dock and something she hadn't noticed the night before.

But the wind didn't stop there. Almost instantly, the back wall flexed outward and blasted apart. Boards were sucked away into the growing daylight.

Sunna screamed and fell back into the water inside the closet. But not before what she'd seen registered in her mind. Perhaps due to the growing darkness the previous night, and her having entered the gloomy confines of the lower dock level of the house, her eyes had not adjusted quickly enough. She hadn't noticed the metal ladder that rose straight up to what looked like a trap door.

Peeking out again, she saw it. Yes, a ladder made of metal pipe. After pushing the door open further, she got to her feet. The wind was whistling through the opening it had created. Sunna doubted the other door would last long. She looked at the entrance door. It was actually vibrating in its frame. Going outside would be far too dangerous.

With the water continuing to rise, the trap door at the top of the ladder was her only hope now. She moved past the entrance door, her feet sloshing through water that had already topped her ankles. With one hand, she held onto the rough timbers supporting the house; with the other, she clutched the blanket around her neck as she moved cautiously along the walkway to the corner.

As Sunna reached the corner and turned toward the middle dock and the opening torn out of the wall, a tree branch was sucked right through the underside of the house, taking more of the siding with it as it exited through the gash. The door was deflecting some of the wind but was banging up and down at opposite corners. The other door creaked and groaned against its hinges and bolt.

Gusts of wind snatched at her and Sunna had to drop to her knees and crawl the last meter to the middle walkway.

With the wind tugging at the blanket, searching for her, bent on carrying her away to Valhalla, she held onto the edge of the walkway and looked up at the inviting hatch above the ladder. A massive gust blew through the opening, pushing the large door around. It nearly pulled her off the narrow walk. She had to release the blanket to grab the edges of the planks in both hands and the blanket was pulled immediately through the opening in the back wall. Sunna dropped to her belly.

Waves were washing into the dock space, lifting her from the walkway. Staying low, Sunna pushed against wind and wave with her legs, feeling the skin tear on her knees as she pulled with her hands. The saltwater stung the cuts and abrasions.

Finally, with one great push, she reached the bottom of the ladder and gripped it, looking up. The floor of the house was an impossible distance away, nearly five meters.

She pulled herself up, the wind tearing at her clothing and hair, trying to snatch her off the ladder. One step at a time, she moved higher. The round metal rungs hurt her bare feet.

Hugging the ladder tightly, she looked down. She'd left her shoes in the closet. Terror filled her eyes when she saw that the water had almost reached the closet's doorknob.

Pushing on, she climbed higher. The wind nearly dislodged her twice because her wet feet were sliding on the slick metal rungs. Finally, she reached the trapdoor and turned the handle. It gave and she pushed up on the hatch. It rose perhaps a dozen centimeters and stopped, banging into something above.

Sunna lowered the hatch, stepped up one more rung, and flung it upward with all her strength, pushing with her forearm. It slammed into the obstruction, failing to give way, and sending a jolt of pain through her arm.

Putting her back against the hatch, she tried to push with her legs. She could see inside the house. It was dark, but dry. The hatch wouldn't open enough to get her head through, much less her body.

There was a cracking sound from outside, louder than the roaring of the wind, and then a heavy thud shook the house violently. That was followed by a clamor that seemed straight out of hell; cracking timbers and the sound of metal being twisted and torn away.

It was suddenly light in the house above her. The roof had been torn away and now the wind and rain was coming at her from above and below, reaching for her, like the angry embrace of a jilted lover.

Sunna pulled the hatch closed and latched it. Then, getting as high as she could, she clung desperately to the ladder. The water continued to rise. Soon it reached her feet and once more she screamed. But the roar of the wind stole her cry right out of her mouth as large waves reached her hips, their force threatening to tear her from the ladder.

CHAPTER THIRTY-FOUR

We took our time navigating out of Tarpon Bay, leaving right after it was light enough to see the water's surface clearly. I took the lead in the *Revenge*, using the sonar on forward scan, and hoping we wouldn't find a fallen tree that had completely submerged. There were some cypresses down, but fortunately all were on the north side of the river and had fallen away from it. Jimmy stood on the bow and used the boat hook to move an occasional branch out of the way. The last thing we needed was to have one sucked into the props. DJ's little boat had a full keel and protected prop, so that was less of a danger for him.

After nearly an hour, we finally made it to open water. Once we cleared Shark River's mouth and entered the Gulf of Mexico, we turned south and maintained DJ's slow speed. He had a nice beam reach and was able to make seven knots, motor-sailing with a single reef in the main.

It took us five hours to reach my island. Even from a distance I could see that it wasn't going to be good.

None of the islands looked the same; the mangroves that fringed them were bent, broken, and mostly bare.

As we passed Mac Travis's place, I could see past it to where my floating dock should have been on the north side of my island. It was gone. Mac's house wasn't usually visible through the trees, since it was built back in the middle of the island, but many of his trees were now down, and the leaves were mostly stripped from them. There were no boats tied up or on shore.

We idled single file down Harbor Channel. I could see the south dock; it was still intact. I'd built it low to the water, barely above it at high tide. The slightest storm surge would have covered it and protected it from the wind.

"Holy hell," Jimmy breathed, as I slowed the engines and prepared to drop anchor.

"We'll anchor here and go in in the canoe," I said, surveying the damage. I could see that one of the big doors to the dock area had folded inward against its hinges, and my roof was completely gone. "The channel might be completely filled in with sand."

The gumbo limbo that stood next to the deck was now leaning against it, its branches mostly nude. The upper branches now occupied the space where my roof used to be.

"Doesn't look good," I said, as the anchor chain rattled across the rollers. "Have DJ tie off to us and then you two bring the canoe over. I'm gonna swim ashore."

"What about Finn?"

"Bring him. But put a leash on him. There's bound to be dangerous debris lying around."

Once I was sure the anchor was holding and we had enough scope out, I shut down the engines and stripped out of my T-shirt before climbing down to the cockpit and stepping out onto the swim platform.

Finn was anxious to get to shore, but I told him to stay put, then slid off the swim platform into the water. Diving in would have been foolhardy after such a storm. I might have dived right into my roof or something, though I felt pretty certain the roof was somewhere north of here.

I swam slowly—a modified breast-stroke—keeping my head above water. There was no telling what might be lurking just below the surface. When I reached the pier, I carefully climbed up, in case anything was loose.

A couple of planks were missing from the pier, but it looked solid. Those boards had been screwed down with ten three-inch-long brass screws, two into each beam. I couldn't imagine the force required to tear one up.

It was then that I noticed something wrong, besides the devastation. A dock line was tied off to one of the cleats and the bow rail of a boat was just sticking out of the water a few inches. Somebody had been here.

Somebody could still be here.

I moved cautiously to the cleat the sunken boat was tied to, and without looking down, I squatted and grabbed it. With my head on a swivel, I stood and pulled on the line until the boat rose a few feet off the bottom.

I glanced down and recognized the bright orange hull of The Other Jack's flats skiff.

Sunna.

I doubted there'd be much fight left in her if she was still alive. She'd obviously arrived before the storm. Surviving this carnage, and then another day and night on my island without a fire or shelter would be difficult. At best, she'd be injured or in shock. At worst, armed and dangerous.

Retracing my steps, I whistled loudly to get Jimmy's attention. He and DJ were about to launch the canoe. When he looked my way, I mimed a gun with my hand, and pointed toward the end of the pier.

Jimmy went to the gear locker and came up with the binoculars we kept there, training them on me. Again, I pretended to hold a gun, and pointed toward the house. He moved the binoculars and must have seen what I meant. He quickly disappeared into the salon.

A moment later, DJ and Jimmy were paddling toward me, with Finn in the middle of the canoe. Normally, Finn would be excited, his tail thumping the side of the boat. But he seemed to pick up on Jimmy and DJ's vibe, and was instead standing with his head and ears up, looking and listening intently.

I took my Sig from Jimmy, noticing that he had another one tucked into his shorts. I didn't have to ask if DJ was armed.

"That's The Other Jack's boat," I said. "It's sunk in the channel."

"The woman from Norman Island?" DJ asked, scanning the shoreline.

"I think so," I said, nodding at him and then turning to Jimmy. "You two go around to the east side and beach there. Jimmy, I want you to keep Finn with you, and watch that side of the island while I check the other side." Then I turned back to DJ. "Deej, see if the back steps of the house are intact and go up and check there."

They both nodded and paddled away. Jimmy wasn't trained for this, but I knew he'd be insulted if I didn't give him something to do.

When I reached the stairs, they were mostly gone. The runners were still intact, but the wind had ripped away nearly all of the treads. Below the stairs, the side door to the berthing area was open.

Cautiously, I poked my head inside. The back wall had been almost completely blown out by the wind coming through the large, mangled door.

I was now armed, and Rusty had told me that The Other Jack had been shot, so I had to assume my adversary was armed. But so were my friends. If she was here and still alive, we'd take her captive and I'd contact Lettsome and the sheriff's department.

I had to step down into the water where the pier normally ended. The shoreline had been washed away for a good four or five feet. I went along the edge of the house toward the back corner, my Sig leading the way. I paused there and surveyed the scene, taking it all in at a glance. The rear steps were still intact. Nothing moved.

My roof was leaning against the eastern bunkhouse—Kim and Marty's house—partially wrapped around the side of it. Jimmy's house was also missing most of its roof, and the western bunkhouse, where Chyrel sometimes stayed, was mostly gone. The floor remained, but the walls and roof were in shambles.

The aquaponics garden was in ruins, two tanks split open, probably by the impact of the roof or wall of my house. All the water had drained out. Not that it mattered. I could tell by the stain on the wall that the rising water had reached to within three feet of the floor of my house.

The storm surge hadn't been predicted to exceed seven feet. I looked back toward the pier. The water between the islands to the south of me stretched for miles. During the peak of the storm, the winds must have been channeled between them, creating a localized storm surge that was much higher.

All over my island, the grass that we'd spent the last two years trying to grow was gone. Or more likely covered up with sand.

The hand of God, I heard Jimmy's voice echo in my head.

Jimmy and DJ came through the trees to my right. I signaled for Jimmy to stay put while DJ checked my house.

I headed toward the west side, staying close to the toppled trees and circling toward Jimmy's house, as DJ moved cautiously up the steps.

Just before I started the turn along the west side, I heard a twig snap behind me, and the unmistakable sound of a hammer being cocked.

Where had she been hiding?

"Drop your gun and turn around," a woman's voice behind me said. I recognized the lightly-accented voice.

She must have been behind the door when I looked into the boat house. How could she have survived the water swirling across the whole island?

I tossed my Sig aside, and turned slowly, keeping my hands out and away from my body.

I wasn't prepared for what I saw when I turned around. Sunna Johannsdottir, all five-feet-nothing of her, stood at the corner of my house, pointing a semi-automatic handgun at me. Her clothes were in tatters, barely covering her body, and not covering parts of it at all. Her knees, elbows, and forearms were scraped raw, covered with crusted blood and dirt. She had a gash on the side of her head and her right eye was nearly swollen shut.

She took a couple of hesitant steps toward me, pointing her weapon at the center of my chest. "You said I was nothing more than a common drug dealer."

"No," I replied, loud enough for DJ to hear me. "I said you were nothing but a drug *maker*."

"Because of you, we have lost everything. Now it is time for you to pay us back. With your life."

I heard him before I saw him. The huffing, menacing snarl of my dog running flat out to protect me. Out of the corner of my eye, I saw Finn's paws churning up the sand between him and the woman. Finn was close to ten years old but could still outrun the wind. He probably outweighed the woman by ten pounds and was moving at full speed, teeth and claws ready to rip her to shreds for her transgression.

Sunna quickly turned and started to point her weapon at Finn.

That was strike three. Her first was simply that she was a lowlife turd fondler, and her second was that she was crazy enough to come out here during a hurricane.

Two shots were fired, nearly on top of one another, and Sunna fell on her back onto the littered ground, dropping her weapon.

Finn yelped, but not because he'd been hit. Sunna never got the chance. DJ stood on the deck above, his weapon pointing down at her, and Jimmy was standing on the other side of the clearing, pointing one of my Sigs at her, as well.

Finn turned and ran toward me, seeing that the woman was no longer a threat. Together we approached her, lying on the ground with blood pulsing from a wound in her side and another in her upper shoulder.

She wasn't dead, but she was knocking on death's door. She tried to get to her weapon, but I kicked it away from her.

She looked up at me, her breath coming in short rasps.

"*Rassgat*," she muttered, pink foam trickling from her lips, a sure sign that the shoulder wound had been from DJ firing downward, and his bullet had ripped through her lung.

Her head fell back and her eyes glazed over. I wasn't sure about Icelandic customs, but I was fairly certain Valkyries weren't carrying her off to meet with Odin in Valhalla.

"Are you okay?" DJ shouted from the deck.

I knelt and checked Finn out before calling back, "Yeah, we're fine."

As DJ moved to the steps, Jimmy shuffled toward me, nearly stumbling over a tree branch. His face was drained of color and there was dread in his eyes. I moved quickly to my friend.

"Is she...?"

"Yeah," I replied, taking my Sig from his hand.

"She was gonna shoot Finn, man. Why would she *do* that?"

I put my arm around his shoulder, turning him away from the grim scene. "There's a measure of desperation when you are fighting for your life, Jimmy. Or for the life of a friend. She gave you no option, man. The onus is completely on her. I know it's no consolation, but your shot didn't kill her."

Finn whined at Jimmy's side, nudging his hand with his muzzle. Jimmy absently passed his hand along Finn's head and neck, then dropped to his knees, hugging Finn tightly as he sobbed.

DJ came down the steps as quickly as his prosthetic leg would carry him. He took one look at the woman and slid his weapon into a holster behind his back. When he saw Jimmy, he stopped and looked at me.

"Is that the ice queen from Norman Island?"

"Yeah," I said, taking another look around my island. A single tear slowly fell down my cheek. It wasn't for the damage caused by the storm, and it damned sure wasn't for the dead woman. Though beautiful on the outside, she was as rotten as month-old garbage on the inside.

I felt bad for my friend and first mate. Though Jimmy was a Navy vet and had been part of the support during the First Gulf War, he was a machinist's mate and electronics tech. The closest he'd ever come to killing anything was fishing and lobstering, and he did that quickly and humanely.

"There's nothing to do here," I mumbled, wiping the back of my hand across my cheek. "Let's get the fuck down to Marathon, where we can help."

EPILOGUE

The first few days after the storm were surreal. The Middle Keys had been hit harder than any storm Rusty could remember, and he'd seen them all. When we'd arrived at the *Anchor* in the early evening the day after the storm, locals had already started to work. With the *Anchor* serving as a base of operations, much as it had for three generations, they used boats to get around.

I made two calls as soon as we arrived. I contacted Jack Armstrong, and told him I'd be unavailable for a while, and then I called Detective Lettsome to let him know that his escaped prisoner was dead. They'd been hit just as hard, or worse, on Tortola. But he'd promised to contact the Monroe County Sheriff's Office the next day to apprise them and let them know that Sunna was wanted for capital murder in the BVI.

Some people were dazed, lacking any sort of guidance or focus, as they stumbled out of their wrecked homes. It was strange; some houses had been leveled, or knocked completely off their foundations, while others just next door were relatively undamaged. One house on Big Pine had ended up in the middle of US-1, a twenty-four-foot center-console, standing on its transom, leaning against it.

The first thing I did was rent dock space from Rusty, paying in advance for six months. It'd take at least that long to rebuild my island. He knew there was more to it than a place to stay. The Middle and Lower Keys were cut off, and what was going to be sorely needed was a huge influx of cash.

I immediately hired anyone whose work had been interrupted by Irma, and there were many. Businesses didn't fare any better than homes; it would be months before many could reopen and quite a few never would. We put people to work, paying them with food, water, and cash. I always kept bundles of Benjamins stashed on the *Revenge*.

The worst damage was on Big Pine, Ramrod, and Saddlebunch. Irma had made landfall just beyond there on Cudjoe Key.

The sheriff himself called me the next day, said he was sending deputies out to my island, and asked me to join them. I'd agreed and then told Jimmy and DJ. Jimmy was still in a funk but agreed to go along. DJ had rented dock space behind the *Revenge* and planned to stay over for a few weeks to help out. He'd said that he had no problem going back up to my island.

When we got there the next morning, Sunna's body had been baking in the sun for two days. It was bloated and barely recognizable as human. Crabs had gotten to it.

The lead deputy took our statements, and the new doctor from the medical examiner's office took the body back with them. We spent the rest of the day salvaging what we could, which didn't amount to much.

Back at Rusty's, during the first week, we concentrated on our own immediate area, as other communities worked in theirs. I put *The Beast* into service, and, armed with chains and chainsaws, we drove out into the neighborhoods, cutting up anything in the way and dragging it to the side of the road—or where we guessed the side of the road should be. Sand had covered it over in many places.

I remembered again how I'd done the same thing with Pap all those years ago; using his powerful Dodge 4x4 to move trees in our neighborhood after a hurricane.

As I was pulling a fallen palm tree out of the way, Jimmy directing me, my cell phone vibrated in my pocket. I hadn't even known cell service had been restored.

Jimmy'd waved me to a stop and I'd pulled forward a little to take the tension off the chain so he could unhook it. I was about to get out of the truck and just ignore the call but instead, I'd pulled my phone out and saw that it was Savannah.

"Hi," I'd said, after pressing the *Accept* button.

"It's Savannah. Can you talk for a minute?"

"Yeah," I'd replied, waving Jimmy off as he approached *The Beast*.

"Is it bad there?"

"We're digging out." I don't know why, but I'd felt nervous.

"Then this week isn't a good time?"

"To meet? Yeah, sure. When and where?"

"How did your island take it?"

I'd paused a moment. Probably too long

"Jesse?"

"It's destroyed," I'd told her. "Total loss. But I got the boats out."

"Then we should wait," Savannah had said firmly, taking the wind from my sails. "At least until things start to open up again."

She'd been right. I had a ton of work to do, and it would be a while before I could even start cleaning up my own place.

"I really do want to meet her and acknowledge our relationship," I'd said. "Have you told her yet?"

"Yes, I did. We're coming to the Keys, but it's going to be a few weeks. Look, I'll call you next Saturday. Maybe you and Flo can talk a while."

I'd looked down at my phone then and saw that the call had ended. I'd just have to wait for that next call.

A few weeks? I'd thought. They must be a long way from the Keys.

The Corps of Engineers had surveyed the Seven Mile Bridge and deemed it safe for travel, but no traffic was coming. The road itself was washed out in some places up island, particularly at the foot of the many bridges connecting the islands. Wave action had undermined and washed out the transition from road to bridge in many places.

It didn't take long for help to arrive, though. Military vehicles at first; the National Guard out of Homestead. They followed right behind the road crews, who filled in and patched the road so the Guard could get across. They brought in the essential items first; food, water, and clothing.

We were cut off from the mainland for over a week. Unless you could show proof of residence, nobody was allowed to travel into Monroe County. But slowly, more help started pouring in. Rented trucks began to arrive by the hundreds, carrying donated plywood and shingles, along with all kinds of building materials, and more food and water. The outpouring of goodwill restored my faith in humanity.

The *Rusty Anchor* and Rusty's house sustained very little damage. They were built by strong hands and backs, in a time when early settlers in the Keys had to get by on their own all the time. He was open for business two days after the storm, just as quick as we could get the fallen trees out of the way. People ate and he tallied a single dollar per meal against their tab.

Rufus's grills and ovens ran on propane and Rusty had laid in a good supply. Local fishermen went out, ignored quotas and limits, and brought in lots of fish, lobster, and crab. Word spread quickly through the coconut telegraph, and people poured in at mealtimes.

Rusty could have raised his menu prices and made a killing. But that's not the way the man was put together. He, Sidney, Naomi, and Rufus served thousands of meals and the cash register never rang once.

Kim and Marty were temporarily assigned to Big Pine Key to help with the cleanup. I drove over there on the fifth day after the storm and found Kim at the school, handing out clothes with the National Guard. I took her aside and told her about her and Marty's little house.

She'd simply looked around at all the people who were coming in empty-handed and leaving with food and clothing, then looked up at me and smiled. "It's just stuff, Dad," she'd said. "We'll rebuild it, right?"

I'd taken her in my arms then and hugged her. She got it.

A week after the storm, when Jimmy and I came in, exhausted and tired, Naomi was standing at the dock. She saw us, came over, and without a word, took Jimmy by the hand and led him down the docks toward the wrecked boat ramp.

Rusty and Sidney approached and the three of us watched as they continued all the way out to the sea wall.

"He's a good and gentle soul," Sidney had said. "My niece likes him and she's worried."

Work continued through the rest of September and October. I talked to Savannah again, and she let me talk to Florence. The girl on the other end of the phone sounded a lot more grown up than her years. She told me that she and her mom would be in the Keys at the first of the year, and I should concentrate on just getting my life in order. Sage words from a teenager.

We became numb to the daily grind. Mounds of debris reaching twenty feet or more were piled on both sides of US-1. Fleets of dump trucks moved back and forth on the Overseas Highway, hauling parts of peoples' lives to the dumps far up on the mainland. Day by day, they had to go farther, as the amount of debris was overwhelming the landfills in South Florida.

Then one Thursday in early November, as we were sitting out behind the bar eating lunch, Rusty looked over my shoulder and said, "What the...?"

I turned and followed his gaze. Half a mile out, a large ship was coming into the bight. It was *Ambrosia*.

My sat phone rang on the table at my elbow. I picked it up and saw that it was Sara. "What are you doing here?" I asked. "I'm at the *Anchor* and can see *Ambrosia*. Are you aboard?"

"Yes," she replied. I could *hear* her smiling. "We have supplies."

I stood and started walking toward the water, my friends following behind me. "We're pretty much set on food and water," I said, as I watched the massive anchor splash into the sea. "But we could always use some extra hands."

She laughed. "Well, we have those, too. But we didn't bring much in the way of food and water. We're loaded with construction people and enough building materials to build four modern houses. See you in a few minutes."

As I watched, a launch was quickly lowered and began speeding toward us, Jack Armstrong at the helm. Beside him was John Wilson, and in the bow, her smile visible from a hundred yards, was Sara.

Jimmy stepped up beside me, Naomi holding his hand. Rusty and Sidney came up on my other side.

"We should have a party, bro," Rusty said. "Tomorrow's the tenth, ya know."

"Oohrah," I grunted softly.

"Semper Fi," Rusty acknowledged.

The End

If you'd like to receive my newsletter,
please sign up on my website:

WWW.WAYNESTINNETT.COM

Every two weeks, I'll bring you insights into my
private life and writing habits, with updates on
what I'm working on, special deals I hear about,
and new books by other authors that I'm reading.

The Charity Styles Caribbean Thriller Series

Merciless Charity
Ruthless Charity
Reckless Charity
Enduring Charity
Vigilant Charity

The Jesse McDermitt Caribbean Adventure Series

Fallen Out   *Fallen Angel*
Fallen Palm   *Fallen Hero*
Fallen Hunter   *Rising Storm*
Fallen Pride   *Rising Fury*
Fallen Mangrove   *Rising Force*
Fallen King   *Rising Charity*
Fallen Honor   *Rising Water*
Fallen Tide

THE GASPAR'S REVENGE SHIP'S STORE IS OPEN.

There, you can purchase all kinds of swag related to my books. You can find it at:

WWW.GASPARS-REVENGE.COM